RISE OF THE STRONGEST SOVEREIGN

BOOK 4

RISE OF THE STRONGEST SOVEREIGN

BOOK 4

KAZ HUNTER

Podium

Cover design by Xiaoraini

ISBN: 978-1-0394-5461-3

Published in 2025 by Podium Publishing
www.podiumentertainment.com

Podium

RISE OF THE STRONGEST SOVEREIGN

BOOK 4

CHAPTER ONE

Level: 35]

[Name: Jason Lee]

[Skills:]

[Monster Trainer: Tame a wild monster of an equal or lower power.]

[. . .]

[Weapons:]

[Photonic Dagger]

[Dagger of Damage]

[Seeking Dagger]

[Dagger of Kings]

[Dagger of Doom]

[Rainbow Dagger]

[Enlarged Dagger]

[. . .]

[Initializing Livestream . . .]

[Connected.]

I fall through the portal, dark energy flashing around me in a torrent of chaos. Suddenly, I find a great stone tunnel flashing past on all sides as I tumble down a long shaft.

Wham!

The bed slams into the floor, and I slam into the bed. As the mattress was little more than an old hotel mattress, it *hurts*, but I survive with only a small divot in my health, which heals quickly. As I bounce to my feet and land on the stone floor of a dark cave, the portal over my head flickers and closes, and I draw out my Photonic Dagger. Its pale light flickers around the area but doesn't tell me much.

[ChaosRider: Huh? This just came on? It's the middle of the night!]

[IceQueen: Jason? You okay? I thought you were sleeping, not out dungeon delving!]

[ShadowDancer: Give him some space! He looks like he just woke up!]

"I did. I did." I turn my dagger into a sword, giving myself a bit more light, and keep turning in circles. I really can't tell you how confused I am at this point. "Elrith? I could use you right now."

There's a flicker as my pocket dimension opens, and my new elven servant steps through. He's now wearing a tailored suit, something fit for a butler, and bows his head.

"Good morning, sire. Are you ready for your tea?"

"Uh . . ." I'm really not sure how to respond. "I was actually hoping you could tell me something about this place. Since you're a sentient being, and all." I'm honestly still a little confused that I have an elf as a creature at all, but . . . Meh. If he's helpful, he's helpful.

Elrith looks around, and he shrugs. "Honestly, sire, I haven't the faintest idea. I would hazard a guess that we're underground, but that's really all I can tell you."

[ChaosRider: He's a real Sherlock, isn't he?]

[IceQueen: Hey now, hey now! Let's not insult him! He *is* an elf, after all. He's most likely used to trees and things.]

"Thanks, anyway." I draw out the Dagger of Doom in my other hand, wondering when I'll see something else. "Are you good with a sword?"

"Oh, of course not!"

"A bow?" I guess.

"I wouldn't even know which side of it the arrow is shot from." The elf shakes his head.

"Knives?" I guess. "Can you kill someone with a teacup?"

"I'm afraid, sire, that I'm a strict pacifist." Elrith shrugs. "Not that I mind other people killing each other. You go out and do your business, but I've done my fair share of violence. My time is done! I live to serve, not to slay."

"Uh-huh." I rub my brow. Something is starting to growl off in the darkness of the cave. "Well, then, I suppose I'll call you when I'm ready for tea."

"Splendid! Cheerio!"

Elrith walks back through the portal to my pocket dimension, and I wave my hand.

"Alright, let's do this. Astrid, since we're underground, I'll need you to feel things out. Burnie, light me a path, but be careful. You don't have much room to maneuver."

My faithful animals come sweeping out, ready to do their business. Astrid growls, and the ground trembles. I imagine that she's doing something akin to echolocation. Burnie, meanwhile, takes a more direct approach and fires a great ball of flame down the tunnel ahead of us.

In the light of the flame, I see half a dozen long, snake-like things creeping along on the walls and ceiling of the cave. They each have a handful of legs, heads like a dragon's, and are probably thirty feet long apiece. In the light of the fire, their eyes flicker, and I can see a hungry glint upon each and every one of them. Wyverns.

To be clear, I don't have a clue why I'm here. Ali and John *should* have been with me, but they're gone. For some reason, I was brought here, and now there are things trying to kill me.

I suppose that just means that I have to kill them first.

I race forward, deciding not to wait for them to come to me. Astrid runs right alongside me and lets out a powerful growl. Cracks spread across the tunnel wall, and a great deal of rubble comes pouring down, pinning several of the wyverns. The others shriek and drop to the ground, and with that, we're into battle.

The closest one, a red-scaled beast, lifts up its head and launches a great blast of fire at me. I duck underneath it, then lash out with my sword of light. The weapon slams into its neck scales, biting deep and sending it reeling backward. Before it can recover, I follow up the strike with an attack from my Dagger of Doom.

[Dagger of Doom has discovered an [acid] weakness.]

The dagger turns green, and steam rises up in the air as it begins to melt through the scales. The wyvern snarls and draws back, but I follow it, stabbing it several times. Before I can finish the beast off, a second wyvern attacks, leaping forward to bite down on my shoulder.

I spin out of the way, and the teeth snap down only a millimeter from my skin. This brings me within range of a wyvern right behind me, and *it* bites me on the other shoulder from behind. My health drops slightly, and the wyvern twists sharply, trying to yank me down and batter me to the ground.

[DarkCynic: Oh no! What a thing to wake up to! Jason is in trouble!]

[GrendleH8tr: I certainly hope so.]

[ViperQueen: Quick, Jason! Behind you! Kill it!]

I grit my teeth against the pain, then stab backward with the Dagger of Doom. The monster yelps in pain, which is just enough. Quickly, I spin around and slash through the throat of the thing. Blood gushes down, and the monster opens its mouth. It's a green one, and I have a feeling that it's about to vomit acid all over me. Without anywhere to run, I brace myself for the pain.

Fssssssssssssssh!

The creature's head begins to smoke as the acid comes up, but it finds the gash in the wyvern's throat instead of its open mouth. Acid gushes down its skin, eating away at its body from the outside. I spin and cut cleanly through the neck with my sword of light, and the head falls to the ground.

Foooom!

Another of the creatures launches a fireball at me, which I take in the opposite shoulder. It spins me around into the wall, but Burnie comes to my aid before I'm taken down.

FOOOOOOOOM!

A great blast of blue-white fire hits the monster in the head, knocking it backward. I leap forward to finish the job, only for the wyvern to explode through the flame, shrugging it off with ease. I slam into the beast head-on, driving every last ounce of air from my lungs. It reacts instantly by blasting me in the chest with fire at point-blank range.

I react by stabbing it in the chin.

My blade turns white hot as it pierces up into its mouth. The wyvern shrieks and draws back, and I go right along with it. Another comes up from the side, but Astrid snarls and buries it under a torrent of stone and rock. I continued to follow the monster, then use my sword of light to stab it deeper in the neck. My blade comes clean out the back of the monster, and with all my might, I rip both blades free at once.

Blood gushes across the ground from so many wounds, and the creature sways and collapses. With that, I spin to the right, blades gleaming in the firelight. The next wyvern in line doesn't stand a chance as I cut his head clean off. The body remains standing as the head lands with a wet *splat,* and I slowly glance around.

The other wyverns are climbing out from under the rubble, snarling and spitting. I quickly jump forward to meet them. It isn't hard to take them down, not in the slightest, and within a moment, I'm standing alone in the tunnel. Blood drips down from my shoulder and my chest, but I'm alive, and I'm not going to complain about that. Slowly, I turn in the direction I need to be traveling and start in that direction.

[LunarEclipse: That's what I'm talking about! Good work, Jason!]

[ChaosRider: Yeah, that was super cool! Now, if you could only figure out where you were, that'd be great!]

[RazorEdge: Hey, give him some time. Do *you* know where he is?]

[ChaosRider: No, but if I was down there, I bet I could figure it out!]

I ignore the chat as I slowly advance forward. It's true, I don't know what's going on, but I would wager a guess that the dungeon boss knows a thing or two. One thing I've been learning is that the bosses usually have the ability to move around the portals leading to their dungeons as they desire. Now, if it were *me* running a dungeon, I'd keep it as far away from the action as possible so my monsters didn't get killed by warriors, but I *also* wouldn't be trying to kill humans, so . . .

In any case, the tunnel remains dark, lit only by my sword and Burnie's fire. Ahead, the tunnel seems to open up a bit, and I find myself walking along a bit quicker. I don't know what that means, but there's a good chance that it will bring answers.

However, as I arrive, I find just the opposite.

The tunnel opens into the bottom of a large pit, which rises upward sharply. A narrow path winds up the side, only a few feet wide, passing a great many dark holes and recesses. Inside, I can see a *great* many creatures moving about, and I grip my weapons a bit tighter.

"Alright. No answers. Just more wyverns." I draw myself upright, then slowly walk out into the middle of the pit bottom. Thankfully, a bit of light trickles down from the heights now, though I can't quite make out its source. "Attention, everyone! I will now be killing all of you unless you desire to make your escape. That is all."

[GoldenShield: WHOA! Now *that's* epic. Have any of the other livestreamers done anything like that???]

[IceQueen: Not that I know of, but then again, I only watch Jason.]

[ShadowDancer: I'll admit it's pretty cool, but I bet I could have come up with a better line. Something about bringing them something to eat. Something cold and sharp.]

[DarkCynic: That's really stupid.]

[ShadowDancer: Hey!]

If I'm being entirely honest, I don't really know what I was hoping to achieve with that statement, except maybe to look cool for the livestream. Overhead, a hundred wyvern heads suddenly poke out of their holes and dens and stare down at me, blinking. Suddenly, I remember that I technically have an Innocence skill that probably could have gotten me through the room without having to fight a single one of them. Oh well. The more kills, the more XP, the faster I level up.

A wyvern high up the wall lets out a shriek, and they all come charging down. Thankfully, there are so many of them that they wind up falling all over one another, slipping and tumbling down to the bottom. I step back into the tunnel as the mass of monsters comes crashing down, and with that, I throw myself into the heat of battle.

"*Ahhhhhhh!*"

I swing my sword of light with all my might, carving through several of the monsters in one blow. There are so many, and so close together, that I can't really pick out any individual creatures. All I can do is swing and swing and hack away. Blood flows freely as my dual weapons carve through the monsters, and, slowly, I force my way forward.

The wyverns soon begin to fight back. It takes them a few moments to recover their bearings, but as they do, they let me have it. Fireballs, acid bursts, ice attacks, darkness attacks—it all explodes across me in a great torrent of destruction and pain. I'm knocked backward toward the tunnel entrance, catch myself, and push forward once more. A massive wyvern lunges at me, and I duck out of the way before stabbing it in the throat. It hisses and staggers, and I follow with an uppercut that opens the thing from gullet to chin. I then step out of the way as blood and guts come down and spin on to the next beast.

[RazorEdge: Is anyone counting kills here? This is incredible!!!]

[FireStorm: Yeah! Those wyverns are incredible!]

[DarkCynic: Excuse me. I don't want to be picky, but those aren't wyverns. They have no wings, just legs, which makes them drakes.]

[FireStorm: The identification tag marks them as wyverns.]

[DarkCynic: I don't see any tag, and those are drakes.]

[FireStorm: You have to pay for the Premium subscription.]

[DarkCynic: I don't care about paying for the Premium subscription, especially if they're wrong.]

I roll my eyes at the chat, then brace myself as the last few of the monsters come forward. The ground is slick with blood and bodies. The first of them draws itself upright, only to be hit by a fireball from Burnie. It's knocked back into a wall, and collapses, senseless. The next one lunges forward, but the ground beneath it crumbles, and it's sucked down into an Astrid pit. The last two look at each other, then draw in deep breaths and roar.

I'm expecting a physical attack, so when I'm suddenly hit by a piercing noise that almost shatters my eardrums, I'm utterly unprepared. I stagger backward under the pain, grasping the side of my head, and the monsters advance. One of them jumps, then spins and whacks me with its tail. I'm lifted off the ground and slam back into the wall, and the second one pounces. Sharp teeth bite down on my torso, and it lifts me up to shake me around several times before slamming me to the ground. My health drops to the halfway mark, and I groan.

Suddenly, I realize something even more alarming than the health. My limbs aren't working!

[Condition: Paralyzed. You will be able to move once again in 00:03:00.]

The wyverns—or drakes; the argument is still continuing in the chat—come stalking toward me, and I know that I don't have three minutes left. Whatever I'm going to do, I have to do it fast . . . or this is the end of Jason Lee, dungeon warrior.

CHAPTER TWO

O*oooooooooooooooooooo!*

Bjorn's howl echoes through the cave, and both wyverns suddenly grow a thick coat of ice. They snarl and thrash about, breaking it away only for a new coat to grow in its place. The monsters continue to thrash about, breaking away each new layer of ice in turn. They're not being held in place quite as firmly as I might like, but they're also not attacking me, which, in my mind, is a key benefit figuring into all of this.

The monsters suddenly lunge forward, breaking through, only to be whacked by horse hooves. Lightfax, my noble steed, steps forward to stand over my body. She's mostly built for speed, not for combat, but I'm happy enough to see her. I smile, or at least try to, only to find that the show isn't over yet. Balder, the new puppy belonging to Bjorn and Astrid, leaps forward to stand over me. He's not yet ready for combat, but he's even larger than the night before, and he snarls softly. Suddenly, I glimpse a little green blob floating through the air, puffing its way along toward the two worms. The wyverns look down at the thing, confused.

And then it explodes.

Fire blazes through the room, slamming both of the wyverns back against the walls. Dead bodies are bounced all around, landing in mangled forms, and Blub, my Living Bomb—now quite shrunken—falls to the ground. He's about the size of a bouncy ball, and assuming that form, he quickly bounces back out of the way.

[Condition: Paralyzed. You will be able to move once again in 00:01:00.]

[00:00:59]

[00:00:58]

The clock ticks downward, and I watch it closely. The monsters aren't dead yet.

Burnie swoops down. He lets out a great gout of fire that drives them back, and all my faithful monsters charge into battle as best they can. They're able to keep the wyverns driven back away from me, and that's just what I need them to do. Finally, the paralysis wears off, and I slowly climb back to my feet.

"That's alright. Thanks, everyone! Back inside the portal."

My creatures respond instantly and flood back behind me. The wyverns, suitably confused, turn and look at me, and I stalk forward slowly and purposefully.

Shing! Shing!

Two blows from my sword of light and the monsters collapse, dead. I let out a long sigh. My health healed a bit while I was paralyzed, so that's one positive, and I turn to the winding pathway.

"Alright, everyone. Let's see where this goes!"

I quickly start to climb. It's far more difficult than I originally guessed. The path is too short to just walk up, so I have to turn sideways to keep from falling. That, of course, makes it harder to keep my balance, and as we wind up higher and higher, I find more and more that when a rock juts out into the way, I nearly stumble and fall. I don't, of course. I've taken down more than a few boss monsters; I'm not going to be taken down by a path. That said, it *is* annoying. The stone gets crumblier and crumblier until, finally, I reach the top.

There, I find a narrow tunnel so short that I have to crouch down. John might not be able to fit at all. Judging from the claw marks, this is a wyvern tunnel of some sort, and I quickly start crawling forward as fast as I can.

"Will this be a hard transition or a cutscene transition?" I wonder out loud.

[DarkCynic: What does that mean?]

[ViperQueen: Will the tunnel just open up into a room, or will the ground collapse underneath him? Or something like that.]

[DarkCynic: Ah, I see. My vote is on cutscene!]

Thankfully, this kills the debate over what race the dragonish monsters belong to. I rather hope that it's a hard transition, though I fear that it'll be the latter. This is confirmed when spiderweb cracks begin to flicker across the stone next to me. Quickly, I slide backward, and not a moment too soon.

Crash!

A massive green orcish fist smashes through the stone wall

and snatches at me. Thankfully, it grabs the air *ahead* of me instead of my actual body, and I lunge forward as hard as I can. My Dagger of Doom is in my hand, and it sinks into the wrist of the beast.

[Dagger of Doom has discovered a [piercing] weakness.]

"Great," I mutter as the hand is ripped back out of sight. I don't have a solid hold on the weapon, and it's pulled clean from my grasp. Knowing I'm going to have to face whatever's out there, I snatch out my Rainbow Dagger, then slide forward.

"Come out, come out, little one!" a deep and guttural voice calls out.

"Who are you calling little?" I glance around the corner, where I find two ogres standing there. They look like a cross between a troll and an orc, with green skin but the chubby, thick stature ordinary to trolls. The room they're standing in has been carved from the stone, forming something akin to a human room, albeit bigger. It seems to be a kitchen, judging from the pot bubbling over a fire. My dagger hangs in the wrist of one of them and doesn't seem to bother it in the slightest.

Great. That means I'm dealing with tanks.

Slowly, I climb out into view. For a long moment, the ogres don't move a muscle. I half-expect one of them to crack a joke and start talking about how hard it is to be an ogre instead of a person, but no such luck. Instead, the closest one grabs a frying pan off a nearby counter, the second one grabs a meat cleaver, and both of them leap at me at the same time.

The area is too small to call any of my creatures. I duck out of the way of the frying pan, but I'm too slow for the cleaver.

It slashes down my left arm, which *hurts*, but I bear the pain as best I can. Quickly, I dive forward at the one with the frying pan, and active the fire damage on the Rainbow Dagger. Long flames explode off the weapon as I swing it through the air and slam it into the belly of the beast, then slash sideways to carve a long line.

Wham!

The monster reacts instantly, smashing me in the shoulder with the frying pan. Yup, I'm dealing with tanks. I stagger and fall into the kitchen counter, and the second one attacks with the cleaver once more, coming down in an overhanded strike. I dive to the side, then activate the lightning damage on the weapon.

This time when I stab the beast in the arm, I get a result.

Lightning arcs up its arm and across the chest, making the great, fatty body tremble. It snarls and tries to step forward, only to collapse against the table. Quickly, I stab it with the sword of light, but the monster spins away. Both of my weapons are pulled from my grasp due to the rather solid nature of its skin. The one ogre now has three of my weapons protruding out of it, which is annoying to say the least.

[RazorEdge: Hey, that's cool! We can name him Pincushion! Jason, can you tame him?]

[IceQueen: Yeah, that'd be EPIC!!! Do it! Do it!]

[RazorEdge: Guys, just let him kill the thing and be done with it.]

I roll my eyes at the chat, then draw out the Dagger of Damage. If these things are going to be tanks, I'll just have to tough it out. I run forward quickly and stab the beast as many times as I can.

[Damage Dealt: 1]
[Damage Dealt: 2]
[Damage Dealt: 4]
[Damage Dealt: 8]
[Damage Dealt: 16]

The damage counter starts to climb, but before I can do much, the second ogre runs around the first and swings the frying pan once more. It catches me clean in the head, and I'm knocked flat to the ground.

Bong!

My head rings loudly, and my vision swirls in front of me. The two monsters laugh, and the one with the cleaver lifts its weapon to bring an end to me.

"Not so fast." I roll out of the way and leap back to my feet. A punch hits me in the chest—I can't really see which one did it—and I'm knocked backward. I quickly lash out with the dagger, hitting them both at least a few times, though my vision is swirling so badly I can't tell exactly how much damage was done or where I managed to hit. Another fist hits me, and I'm tossed back against the wall. The flickering heat of the fire crackles around by my legs, and I grit my teeth.

[DarkCynic: Oh no! Is this the end of Jason?]

[ViperQueen: Dude, someone asks that *every* single time he winds up in a pinch. Just sit back and watch, and he'll be alright.]

I gulp, then raise my hand as one of the ogres, blurry and shifting, raises a hand.

"Tame monster!"

A blast of energy explodes out of my palm and hits the beast square in the face. It comes to a halt, and the second ogre, frowning, comes to a stop as well. My vision clears as my health has a chance to stabilize, and I find the second ogre staring at the pulsing bit of energy. It slowly reaches out and waves its hand through the beam, but nothing happens. It taps the one I'm trying to tame—which *does* happen to be Pincushion, by mere coincidence—on the shoulder, but nothing happens.

"Hmm." It frowns at me. "What human doing?"

[Ogre Cook is resisting your efforts to tame it.]

[Ogre Cook is still resisting your efforts to tame it.]

I hold my breath. I'd really like to open up my inventory and grab out a Pumped! to really heal myself back up, but I know that would be too much.

[Ogre Cook has been tamed!]

My chat goes wild, and the beam of light fades. Pincushion shakes his head, then slowly drops to one knee.

"What are your orders, master?"

The second ogre, Frying Pan, glances back and forth between the two of us. His little ogreish brain can't process a lot, but he seems to get the gist of what's happening. Before Pincushion can do a thing, he swings his frying pan into his face.

Bong!

Pincushion's face appears on the bottom of the frying pan, and a great deal of blood drips down from behind it.

[Ogre Cook has been killed.]

[DarkCynic: No! Pincushion, you were the real MVP.]

[ChaosRider: You will be missed!!!]

[ShadowDancer: Guys . . . He tamed the thing for like 3 seconds!]

[IceQueen: And that was enough to make it into our hearts!]

Frying Pan chuckles and turns to me, but by that point, I've already gone into motion. Quickly, I reach over and slash my dagger through the ropes holding the large boiling pot in place. It tips over, and a great gout of boiling water explodes across the floor. Frying Pan howls in pain as the water washes over his feet, and he falls backward. I wait a moment for the water to cool, then charge forward.

"*Hi-ya!*"

I grab my sword of light out of Pincushion's body and stab it deep into the belly of Frying Pan. The ogre grunts, then slowly starts to stand up. Now, though, I have a much better idea of where the weak points on the creature happen to be. After all, I'm *not* a tank, and I took his frying pan to the face without permanent damage. Pincushion took a single blow and was downed.

Before he can do anything, I kick him in the face, knocking him backward to the ground. He groans as his head whacks the stone floor, and I quickly spin and slash my sword through his throat. A great deal of blood is added to the growing carnage on the floor, and he swings his frying pan. I step back as the ogre staggers slowly to his feet, though blood continues to leak down his chest. He lifts the frying pan . . . only for it to drop to the ground.

"And there we have it." I give a small nod.

[GoldenShield: You know, you could have just killed it outright if you had cut off its head. Just saying.]

[FireStorm: He could probably also do better without fans complaining about his every move.]

[RazorEdge: Hey, he's doing the best he can! Maybe he didn't think of that?]

This time, since I have a bit of time on my hands, I decide to respond to the chat. "No, I thought of it. My aim was just a bit off, so I only hit his throat instead of his spine. It'll have an effect, though. And here we go!"

With a loud *thump*, Frying Pan falls to his knees, sways, and then falls forward. He smashes into the floor with resounding force, and I give a nod.

"And there. He's dead. Good to go!"

[You have leveled up!]

[Congratulations! You are now Level 36!]

I slowly walk forward and pull the rest of my weapons out of Pincushion. I do have to admit a bit of pity for the ogre, but then again . . . if he hadn't tried to kill me in the first place . . .

In any case, he's dead, and I need my items back. Once they're retrieved, I quickly take a look around the place. It's quite a mess, but that doesn't necessarily mean that I can't use anything. Kitchens are good places to find things, and for whatever reason, it doesn't seem like I got a reward for hitting level thirty-six. I'm not exactly sure why that is, but I suppose I can figure that out later. Rifling through all the drawers and cabinets of the kitchen yields nothing but a few ogreish spices—bone meal, dried sweat powder, dog hair—and some rotten meat, as well as a single bottle of carrion-flavored Pumped! ("effect: lose one health per second for two minutes"). When I'm satisfied that there's nothing around that I can use, I turn toward the door of the kitchen.

And that's when I get a surprise.

Standing there is a knight in old armor. I'm talking straight out of the old castles of Europe, with a rising sun emblazoned on his chest and a cross on his shield. He stands at attention and slowly lifts the visor on his helmet. I tense myself, and, after a moment, he speaks.

"Sir Lancelot, at your service."

CHAPTER THREE

[ChaosRider: Sir Lancelot? Who's that? I don't recognize him in the list of approved slayers.]

[DarkCynic: How's *he* here?]

[ViperQueen: Wait, you know who he is?]

[GoldenShield: Is he some sort of newbie?]

[LunarEclipse: I bet he's no one compared to our Jason!]

Now, I have to admit that I'm a little confused by the appearance of the knight. He holds out his hand, which I walk forward and shake.

"You're . . . you're Sir Lancelot?" I ask.

"Yes, indeed! Perhaps it isn't the custom where you come from, but in *my* culture, it's polite to introduce oneself after someone else has given you their own name." He shoots a rather pointed look at me.

"Uh, yes. Jason Lee," I answer. "It's a pleasure to meet you."

"So, you've heard of my exploits?" Lancelot smiles.

"More than a few of them." I nod. "How's Arthur? Or Gawain?"

"Gawain is still recovering from that whole business with the green knight. Shook him up something terrible, I'm afraid." Lancelot shrugs. "As for Arthur, I'm afraid I simply don't know. There were rumors of a dragon in the hills around Camelot, so I went to investigate. Walked into a cave, and all of a sudden, I was here. That was some time ago. Ever since, I've just been making my way around through these tunnels, killing the infernal beasts."

Now, I'll admit that I haven't a clue if this guy is lying through his teeth, or if he's telling the truth. Maybe it's another warrior just trying to play a trick on me. Maybe he's the dungeon boss trying to earn my confidence. Maybe he's just insane and believes himself to be something he isn't. I don't have the faintest idea. What I *do* know is that, if he's legit, he'll be handy to have on my side.

"Well, Lancelot, do you happen to know the way out of here?" I ask. "I was fast asleep when I fell through a portal into this place, and I'd like to get back to my friends and to my world."

"I'm afraid I don't," Lancelot answers. "I know these tunnels like the back of my hand, and there's not a one of them that leads back to the surface, except for now and again one of them will pop up into a wasteland of a place."

"Great." I frown in thought. "Then . . . do you happen to know of a boss? A particularly powerful monster that seems to run the place?"

"Ah! Indeed, I do." Lancelot gives a nod. "That would be Grendel. He's *way* down below."

"Great." I slip past Lancelot and into the ogre-carved hallway. "Take me there."

"We can go, but you should know that I killed him ages ago," Lancelot calls after me.

I sigh and come to a stop. "You did? Did anything happen at that point?"

"A big swirling portal opened up, but one must never go through such places idly," Lancelot says, cautioning me. "I stayed put until I could have a chance to reconnoiter properly, but by the time I thought up a way to do that, the portal had closed. I've been here ever since."

"I see." My mind goes back to the crystal that I found in the rift. "If you could take me there anyway, I'd sure appreciate it. Maybe I can find something. I've gotten used to these dungeons and portals and things."

"But of course!" Lancelot strides off. "Only one thing to warn you about, my good sir. The path to that place has been overrun by ogres for some time now, and I haven't gotten around to clearing them out. Seemed a waste when I had other places to guard. Are you in for a bit of a scrap?"

"I always am." I give a confident nod.

"Wonderful! You'd get along well with Arthur, I think."

Lancelot quickly takes the lead, and we strike off through the tunnels. My chat is wild with speculation, but I ignore it and do a good bit of thinking by myself. Now, I've been in quite a few dungeons at this point, and this one just feels different than some of them. Lancelot quickly leads me out of the ogre-infested portions of the tunnels and into a connected cave system that feels a bit more natural, like where I first entered. From there, we make our way through a labyrinth of caves and pits, climbing up ladders and rappelling down ropes, until we come to a small wooden doorway.

"I made this myself out of the armor of some goblins I found in the lower sections of the tunnels," Lancelot announces. "They were pathetic creatures. I hardly had to bat an eye to take care of them all. Almost made me feel sorry for them. Almost."

He pulls open the door, where I find a cave, tight and narrow, that slopes sharply downward. No . . . It's not just a cave. It's a hand-cut staircase, one that plunges into the depths of the earth. Torches light the way below, and Lancelot starts downward at a trot.

Ahead, I can hear grunts and groans, and he begins to move along a bit faster. The staircase takes a sharp turn, and I brace myself for whatever we'll find next. As we come around the end, I find myself looking upon a large cavern with ogre homes spaced out all around the edge. A handful of the giant monsters stomp back and forth, some holding weapons, others just holding assorted tools. I can see hammers, pickaxes, and all sorts of things. At the far end of the cavern there are two enormous stone doors that have been cracked rather badly.

"And here we are." Lancelot steps out into the open. "Ah, this has gotten worse since the last time I took a look. Advance boldly, my good fellow, and we shall see victory today!"

Lancelot charges forward. The ogres slowly turn to look at us, their stupid eyes blinking a few times.

"Human! Came back!"

Two of them charge at Lancelot, both wielding great clubs. The first one swings at the warrior, and Lancelot draws his sword.

"Ascalon, protect me!"

The blade blazes with light, and he catches the club as if he were parrying a child's stick. The ogre staggers back under the attack, and Lancelot rather casually slashes the weapon through the belly of the creature. It falls to one knee, and with a backhanded stroke, Lancelot cuts off its head. The second ogre pauses, uncertain if it wants to join the fight.

That indecision costs it its life.

Lancelot simply steps forward and gives two quick slashes with the sword. The ogre slowly topples backward, separating into three pieces, which land with a loud *splat.* I draw out my own weapons, the Photonic Dagger in one hand, the Rainbow Dagger in the other. I set the Rainbow Dagger to deal fire damage, then charge forward.

Together, Lancelot and I throw ourselves into battle. An ogre grunts and swings a massive fist at me. I duck underneath it, then slash the Rainbow Dagger through its wrist. Flames explode across the skin of the monster, and I follow it up by stabbing the thing in the side with my Photonic Dagger. The monster grunts, and I stab it twice more before leaping to the side.

Another ogre approaches with malice in its eyes, snarling and grunting as it swings a log at me. *That* one hits, and I'm battered back into the wall of a nearby hut. I stagger, then duck as it swings it once more. The log explodes into splinters as it strikes with extraordinary force, and I leap forward to stab it several times in the belly. It responds by driving its knee into my chin, and I'm knocked backward once more.

"Leave him alone, foul beast!"

Lancelot's sword cuts the monster clean in two, and the halves fall to either side. Lancelot steps across the corpse to pull me back to my feet, and he turns to look at the area. More ogres are massing, preparing themselves, and he gives a nod.

"Just tell me what you want."

"To kill as many of these things as possible." I switch out my Photonic Dagger for the Enlarged Dagger. I don't really plan on using the sword function, and I'd sort of like to try the new weapon out.

[LunarEclipse: Yeah, Jason! That thing looks so cool! Just check out the hook. That's going to cause some *carnage!*]

[IceQueen: Or it might simply provide a tactical advantage.]

[GoldenShield: Who cares about tactics? BLOOD!]

I give a nod to the chat, then look down at the Enlarged Dagger. It's somewhere between a dagger and a short sword, with a nasty little hook on the end. IceQueen's suggestion of using it for a tactical advantage is a good one, and my mind spins with the possibilities. Unfortunately, I'm given no time to really process them, as the ogres of the area roar, thump their chests, and charge forward.

Lancelot goes off to the left and starts dealing with a herd of them over there. I don't pay him much attention, really, and instead simply charge into the midst of the attacking monsters. Half a dozen of them jump directly into combat while the others hold back, and with that, I go into battle mode.

The first ogre swings a club. I leap back, and the weapon carves around and whacks another ogre in the face. It grunts and staggers back, and I take the opportunity to stab the first ogre through the heart with the Enlarged Dagger. When I rip the weapon back out, the hook does its job, and a great deal of blood begins to leak down the front of the monster. It snarls and drops the club, throwing several quick punches. *That* surprises me, and I'm knocked backward several feet. It draws a deep breath, takes a step forward . . . and falls flat on its face.

Good. One down, five to go. Another runs at me, squaring its shoulders rather like a football lineman. I leap to the side and feel the wind as it races straight past. Another comes forward and tries to flatten me with an overhanded blow, but I manage to step out of the way of that too. A third swings a sword; a fourth attacks with a frying pan.

At this point, I'm mostly just dodging, but I know the situation can't remain this way. I wait just a moment longer, then race forward. The one with the sword swings at me again, and I flip the Enlarged Dagger around to block. The blades catch and ring out loudly, and I quickly pull downward. The hook catches on the sword, yanking it down as well, which makes that particular ogre stagger forward. With that, I jump up and stab it in the neck with my Rainbow Dagger, causing another eruption of flame.

Before anything else can attack me, I swing around and slash my Enlarged Dagger through the neck of another ogre. It doesn't take the head clean off, but it severs enough of the neck that I'm confident the thing won't be healing. With that, I spin onward, hacking and slashing with all the force I can muster. For not having any special effects, the Enlarged Dagger is *quite* powerful, and I find myself enjoying it a great deal.

It only takes a few minutes more before there's only a single ogre left in the bunch. I duck around and behind it under a blow, then stab the thing just under the ribs. As I pull the weapon back out, though, the hook gets caught on a rib. The monster falls forward, landing with a loud *thud*, and rips the weapon out of my hand. The motion pulls me off-balance, and I find myself looking up at the business end of an ogre sword.

More of them are coming in from the sidelines.

I know I have two options: abandon the Enlarged Dagger and yank another one out of my inventory or find a way to get to the Enlarged Dagger. I opt for the latter. I grip the dagger with all my might and pull just as hard as I can. There's a *crack* of bone, a squelch of flesh, and the dagger is ripped clean out of the body of the monster. It then flashes up and parries the sword quite perfectly, knocking the sword to the side. Before the new monster can react, I leap forward, stabbing it in the chest. That one drops as well, and I spin toward the remaining creatures.

"Alright, pets," I say softly. "There's enough room for you here. Let's show them how it's done. Burnie, Bjorn, you're up."

My pocket dimension flickers and opens, and Burnie comes flashing out. Lancelot turns and looks at them, admiration flickering in his eyes as the two creatures fly into action.

FOOOOOOOM!

Burnie lets out a jet of heat and fire that blasts the closest ogres back into the wall. Bjorn follows, jumping up and grabbing the wrist of the first one with his teeth. He pulls sharply downward, yanking it off-balance, and I run forward and aim a slash at its neck. The second ogre snarls and, recovering from the blast of fire, readies itself to attack Bjorn.

And that's when Bjorn howls.

Ice spreads across the surface of the monster and, before it realizes what's happening, penetrates down to the bone. The ogre lets out a pained gasp before freezing entirely solid. A single breath escapes its mouth, and I punch the statue in the chest as hard as I can. Slivers of frozen ogre explode throughout the room under the attack, and I move forward yet again.

Together, the three of us clear the right side of the ogre town. As we come to the last one, a great pot-bellied beast wielding an entire cauldron, Burnie lets out a great blast of flame that melts the pot, splattering the ogre with the molten metal. It shrieks and falls backward, only for Bjorn to snarl and freeze the metal in place. It hardens all across the monster, locking several limbs in place, severely limiting its range of motion. I open my pocket dimension and draw out Blub, who expands to his full size. With all my might, I throw him into the monster's face.

KA-BOOM!

The explosion ripples across the town, and the ogre falls to the ground, dead. Blub bounces back into my pocket dimension, and I let out a long, satisfied breath.

"Good show!" Lancelot walks up next to me, nodding at the dead ogres all around me. "A bit of a fight, but apparently nothing you couldn't handle. If Arthur is still alive once we get out of here, I'll recommend you for the table."

"I'd certainly appreciate it." I smile, then gesture at the broken door. I don't know what we'll find behind it, but I'm hopeful that it will provide the key for me to get out. Maybe it'll even provide answers for why I'm here in the first place.

That might be too much to ask, but I've got to at least give it a try.

CHAPTER FOUR

Lancelot and I slowly approach the broken doors. They stand slightly open, and a massive crack runs from the upper left-hand corner of one down to the lower right-hand corner of the other. Lancelot sheathes his sword, Ascalon, as we step up to the threshold.

"You know, I remember the first time I found this place. It was quite the task, really. I had been hearing this grumbling and growling from other points in the dungeon, but I couldn't quite find it. Finally, I made a map, as accurate as I could, and marked out where I could hear the sounds the loudest. Using that as a guide, I was able to pinpoint the location precisely, though it still took me two more weeks to actually find the way down here."

Lancelot seems quite jolly, and as he walks inside, I follow. The interior of the room is subsequently lit up as a handful of torches around the edges all blaze to life, revealing a large skeleton lying across the ground. It looks like a larger version of the wyverns, with the notable distinction that it only seems to have two legs.

"Ah, Grendel." Lancelot chuckles. "Beowulf will be upset I got to it first. You know, everyone thought he killed the creature, though it was a closely guarded secret among the knights that he only injured the beast. It slunk into realms unknown, and, of course, I managed to slay it after that. Quite a good show, if I do say so myself."

[FireStorm: I still can't tell if he's being serious or not.]

[ShadowDancer: And who's this Beowulf guy? He's not listed in the register of warriors either. Is there some sort of secret network we don't know about?]

[RazorEdge: I seriously can't believe you don't know who Beowulf is. If Lancelot can defeat a monster that he can't, then . . . Wow!]

[GrendleH8tr: Wow, indeed. *slow clap*]

[Originalgoth: You're just jealous, GrendleH8tr. I think this could be called poetic justice.]

I shake my head and ignore the chat once more. I'd really appreciate it if Originalgoth would just bug off, but every time I block her, she just appears in the chat once again. Not that she's being terribly disruptive at the moment, but in general, she drives me nuts. "Alright, then. Help me look around. Did Grendel drop any loot when you killed him?"

"A few dragon scales, which I promptly disposed of. Dragon's scales are just as cursed as their treasure." Lancelot crosses his arms. "A bit of gold, also disposed of. There were a few weapons, which I could only presume came from heroes he had devoured, so those were buried with all due respect. The only thing I've kept is this."

He opens his inventory and pulls out a dagger, which is the color of blood and gleams in the light. I gasp, sensing the power contained therein.

"This was Beowulf's dagger, according to the name given to it. It's a powerful weapon, one that I'm not worthy to wield." Lancelot lifts it up, then sighs. "When I get back to our world, I plan on trying to find his line of descendants. I know he had a wife and a son, so I can only assume that his line continues somewhere."

"Incredible." I nod at him. I'm certain there's a story there, and frankly, I'd be quite interested to hear it in another circumstance, but for the moment, we really need to keep moving. "Now, I want you to think. Did you see any sort of a crystal while you were down here? It would have been about yea long"—I hold up my hands to demonstrate—"and it probably would have radiated power."

"It doesn't sound familiar, no." Lancelot shakes his head. "Why is it important?"

A third voice cuts into the conversation. "Because it's the only way out of here."

I spin just in time to see a massive creature jump down from a small ledge, behind which is a darkened cave entrance. The creature is yet another ogre, one dressed in long tattered black robes. It looks to me like he's a mage of some sort, and he slowly raises his hand. A ball of energy starts to form, and I brace myself.

"Allow me at this foul creature, and I will bring an end to him." Lancelot stalks forward, but I hold up a hand.

"Wait! I have a feeling he wants to talk."

"Your feelings are correct." The mage chuckles, then opens

up his inventory while keeping the ball of energy pointed at us. With a pop, a dungeon crystal appears in his hand. "One-time use. It'll get you out of here, right back where you came from. Defeat me and it's all yours."

I give a nod. "That shouldn't be too hard."

"We'll see if you still feel that way in a moment."

I race forward with Bjorn at my side and Burnie flashing through the air. The ogre mage simply flicks his hand, and the ball of energy detonates. I brace myself against the impact, expecting a bit of pain but otherwise expecting to shrug it off.

Bzzzzzzzzzzzzzzzzzzzzew!

The energy hits me, lifts me off my feet, and flings me across the room like I've been hit by a sledgehammer. I come crashing down, then, groaning, climb to my feet again, only to find the mage preparing another attack. Lancelot runs forward to meet the beast, Ascalon flashing in his hand.

"Foul creature! You will pay!"

The ogre doesn't move but puts the crystal away and launches another blast from his hand. Lancelot is knocked backward as well, and the ogre lifts both his hands above his head. I roll out of the way as lightning shoots down from the ceiling, blasting away at the stone as if it were nothing but sand. Particles sting my face, but I ignore it as I charge at the monster, drawing my weapons as I do so. The Enlarged Dagger sits in my left hand, the Dagger of Damage in my right. It's a slower build, of course, but boss battles always take a while, so I figure it's probably worth it.

Lancelot seems slowed by the lightning, as his armor turns him into a bit of a lightning rod, but I ignore the lightning as it flashes down all around me. The ogre mage snarls and balls his meaty hands into fists, and I know this is going to hurt. The lightning stops, and dark energy begins to pulse around his body. It looks sort of like portal energy, but—

Bzzzzzzzzzzzt!

Sure enough, dark strands of portal energy explode off him, flashing through the air brilliantly. I drop to my knees and slide under one of the blasts, which makes the air tremble just above me. As I stand back up and leap forward, he launches another blast that hits me in the chest.

It's hard to describe exactly how the attack feels. As the energy pulses through me, my entire body grows cold. It's like I'm having the life sucked out of me. My health plummets, and *fast*, and I stagger a bit as I reach the ogre mage. Still, as the attack ends, I have the presence of mind to duck underneath a massive blow from the monster, and I stab him with the Enlarged Dagger right through the heart.

"*Gaaaak!*" the ogre mage gasps, staggering back a bit. I rip the weapon back out, inflicting an immense amount of damage and carving a long gouge down his belly. As a great many bodily fluids leak out, the ogre begins mumbling some sort of healing spell. Light flashes across the wound and stitches it back shut. Clever, and probably helpful, but I don't intend to give him a chance to benefit from the healing.

Before the ogre can move, I leap at him, attacking with both of my daggers just as fast as I can possibly move. My Dagger of Damage begins to inflict more and more and more damage, scaling upward with each hit. The ogre quits healing after a moment and closes his eyes, and I tense. I quickly stab him under the armpit with the Dagger of Damage, causing him to howl and jump out of the way. Fire flares around him in a sort of twisted halo, and he flings a great fireball at me. I try to evade, but it hits me in the chest and knocks me down to the floor.

Shing!

Lancelot leaps forward, Ascalon blazing in the light of the flame, and chops the ogre's left hand clean off. The monster snarls and spins, splattering blood across the floor, but Lancelot doesn't stop. His next blow is aimed at the ogre's neck.

Unfortunately, it never lands.

Unleashing a great blast of magic from the stump of his wrist, the ogre hits Lancelot with a powerful concussive blast that flings the knight backward. The ogre then quickly raises his one good hand and causes cracks to spiderweb across the ceiling. Stone comes crashing down, flattening Lancelot under a metric ton of stone and rock. Lancelot groans from somewhere underneath the pile, but the ogre isn't done yet.

"Get away from him!" I recover myself and charge at the monster as he stalks toward the pile of stone where Lancelot is trapped. The ogre glances over at me, huffs, and raises the stump of an arm once more. I have a flash of insight and spin out of the way as a concussive blast of energy tears through the space where I had been standing. It doesn't hit me, though it *does* blast a rather large chunk of stone out of the wall, but then, that wasn't the ogre's intention. It prevents me from getting between the ogre and Lancelot for a few key seconds.

With a grunt, the ogre waves his remaining hand and makes all the stone roll away. Lancelot smiles and springs back to his feet, but before he can do anything, the ogre draws a sword out of his inventory.

[DarkCynic: Wow! That's a cool sword!]

[RazorEdge: Wait . . . Haven't we seen that sword before?]

[ViperQueen: YEAH!! That dragon person thing down in the Pumped! factory was wielding it!]

[ChaosRider: Either that sword, or one identical to it.]

The sword is made of dragon bone and has a number of rather evil-looking runes carved into it. The last person who wielded it told me that the weapon steals the life force of anyone injured by it. Personally, I'd rather not find out firsthand just how accurate the claim happens to be.

"Foul creature, this makes me pleased! Let us duel!" Lancelot cries out.

"Wait!" I hold up my hand. "It's a trap!"

"I know, my boy, but where swords are concerned, I have somewhat of an advantage."

Lancelot isn't concerned and leaps into battle. I'm forced to draw up short as the two of them crash together. Quickly, I change out my daggers for the sword of light, which has a much longer reach—handy, if I should get involved. I take my stance and call Burnie to come down for support as well. He lands on my shoulder as the two warriors clash in front of me.

Ascalon glows with a brilliant and purifying light as it crashes against the dragonbone sword. Meanwhile, the rune-covered sword seems to extrude evil as a warped and twisted energy grows around it. Suddenly, the ogre lets go of the sword altogether, and it begins to fight by itself, simply hanging in the air as if being wielded by a ghost. My jaw drops . . . and with a crackle, a shape takes form.

The dragonspawn warrior, the one I killed in the Pumped! factory, suddenly appears. He doesn't look a bit different from when I fought him, and he snarls and presses the attack. Shaken, Lancelot is forced backward, and that's when disaster strikes.

The ogre mage, while both of us were distracted by the sword's magic, had crafted a small trap behind Lancelot's foot. With a crackle as Lancelot steps backward, a stone boot grows up around his right foot, climbing all the way to his hip. He growls and smashes out of it, but not before his stance is affected. With one mighty lunge, the dragonspawn drives the sword into a chink in his armor, just above his left hip.

Dark energy flares, and I can see energy being sucked out of Lancelot and into the sword. The dragonspawn smiles, then dissolves into smoke, which is sucked into the hilt of the sword a moment later. The ogre grunts in satisfaction, then turns to me.

"And now, for—"

I don't hesitate a moment longer and spring forward at the beast. I was distracted momentarily, but that's gone now. My sword of light carves through the air, and I open up the ogre's neck. Turns out, I wasn't the *only* one distracted. The ogre staggers back, blood flowing down from his neck, and his eyes go wide. I have an inkling of what he's going to do, and I jump forward to stop him.

"No!"

He leaps at the sword, rips it out of Lancelot's body, and throws it on the ground. The sword tilts itself up, letting the point gleam in the light, and with that, the ogre flings itself upon the weapon. There's a sickening *crunch* of bone, and the monster crumbles into dust. The flesh withers away, leaving only the bones, and then even the bones dissolve into smoke and are sucked into the weapon. With that, a portal opens, and the sword is drawn away.

[You have leveled up!]

[Congratulations! You are now Level 37!]

[Item Acquired: Portal Crystal]

[Item Acquired: Crystal Ball]

[Item Acquired: Magic Focusing Device]

[. . .]

A long list appears in the air, showing me everything I got from the ogre, but I ignore it for the time being. Instead, I rush over to Lancelot's side. He's lying on the ground, weak, and I kneel next to his head.

This isn't how I expected things to go. How . . . how did the ogre manage to get the drop on Lancelot?

"What was that thing?" Lancelot asks, his voice weak. "I've never . . . I've never seen anything like it."

"I've only seen it once before. I don't really understand what it is, myself," I answer quietly. "Only that it absorbs life energy."

"It certainly got a good bit of mine." Lancelot sighs. His head falls back against the stone. "I . . . I had the highest honor . . . I had the highest honor fighting alongside you."

Then his head falls against the stone floor, and his body grows cold.

He's dead, and I'm alone in the dungeon once more.

CHAPTER FIVE

It takes me a moment to process the fact that he's dead. Just like that? Gone? How? Then, with a flicker, dark energy begins to pulse all around him. His armor rusts and crumbles away, his body turns into dust and smoke, and he's sucked into a little splinter of the dragonbone sword, which falls to the floor. I bend over and pick it up, holding it up to the light. It's just a tiny bit of bone—you'd hardly notice it under most conditions. His armor must have caught a little bit of it. In any case, lodged in his body, it continued to drain him away, even when the rest of the sword was removed.

[ShadowDancer: What *is* that weapon? I've never seen anything like it!!!]

[GoldenShield: It's not listed in any of the official guides I can find.]

[FireStorm: I mean . . . there's a *lot* of stuff not mentioned in those guides. It is still being written, after all.]

I sigh, then stick the sliver into my inventory. I don't want it—please don't get me wrong—but I can't take the chance that something comes back for it. I'll dispose of it once I'm back on Earth, and that's all there is to it. Suddenly, though, my eye catches something.

Ascalon.

The great sword just lies there on the ground, brilliant in splendor. I slowly reach out and pick it up, feeling an immense power contained therein. It's incredibly strong, A-Ranked at least, and I slowly place it in my inventory. I don't know if I'll use it yet, out of respect for the dead, but . . . wow. Then, fingers trembling, I reach out and pick up Beowulf's Dagger.

Now *this* one is going to be hard to keep from using. I give it a bit of a swing, and it just seems to *fit.* This one is S-Ranked and simply seems to shiver with energies. Leather has been wrapped around the hilt, holding the blade firmly in place. It's the most powerful weapon I've yet encountered—of that, there can be no doubt. Slowly, I place that in my inventory as well.

In any case, as I stand back up, I open my inventory once more and do a bit of scrolling. I pull out most of the items that I got from the ogre and drop them onto the dungeon floor. A Crystal Ball is only going to cause trouble. Most of the Magical Focusing Devices are very clearly for dark magic, which isn't something I want to deal with in the slightest. Finally, I'm down to nothing but the Portal Crystal, which I activate.

"Open."

With a flicker, a dark portal forms in front of me, and I take a deep breath. I slowly walk forward, stepping through the rift in space and time, uncertain of where I'll land.

Dark energy washes over me, and I'm sucked on through. Now, I know I've described this before, but I *hate* portal travel. It's not just simply stepping through a doorway, it . . . Well, first you get hit with this jolt of electricity, and then it feels like you get just sort of slurped up through a straw, or maybe a siphon tube, and shot across interdimensional lines like a smoothie being sucked along through a machine. Then, you're shot out the other end, and you're not quite sure if the material that's now making up your head once came from your feet, or vice versa.

Anyway, I digress.

I fall through the portal, then come out the other side with a dull *whump*. I find myself standing in Central Park, near the gates where the last vestiges of civilization gathered. Now, it's much more open and lovely, with cars driving by—mixed, of course, with steeds that have been pulled from the dungeons—and pedestrians walking about. The sun is rising in the sky. I'd wager a guess it's around ten o'clock, and I sigh.

"Jason!"

Ali's voice echoes through the air, and I turn as she comes running up, her face awash with delight. I smile, and she gives me a quick hug before stepping back.

"You're alive! You're actually alive!" She sighs. "Oh, you have no idea how glad I am to see you."

"Why?" My eyes suddenly narrow. "Is something wrong?"

She suddenly looks a bit less excited. "That . . . that sort of depends on your definition of the word *wrong*, but . . ."

I slowly cross my arms. Suddenly, I'm missing the straightforward battle of the dungeons. "What exactly is happening?"

Before she can answer, chopper blades begin to echo in the

distance. In this day and age, life itself runs just as fast as the internet my life is being broadcast on. That chopper almost certainly signals the arrival of Mr. Wang, which means I'm about to be hired for something again. Slowly, I turn my eyes to the sky, ready for whatever's about to come.

The helicopter soon arrives and takes Ali and me up into the skies over New York City. As we fly, I gaze down upon the strange new world where we find ourselves. Portals flicker and open here and there, and monster battles happen on the same streets where people are sitting and enjoying a good cup of tea, or even having a video conference where they talk about the bottom lines and rates of exchange. It's a strange new world, but one we're all getting used to quickly enough.

Somehow, I'm not surprised when the helicopter takes us to one of the tallest buildings in the entire city, landing on a helipad on a sleek, modern-looking structure that twists and rises to a height that's truly remarkable, even for New York. As we climb down, Mr. Wang is already waiting for us, alongside John. He waves us toward a set of doors that lead through a great glass wall, where a massive club overlooks the city. The club is empty now, save for a single robotic bartender standing behind a counter near the back. Four chairs have been set up near the glass, which I can only presume are for us.

"Welcome, Jason, Ali," Mr. Wang says as we walk into the club. "What do you think? Just bought it last night."

"It's impressive." I glance down at the floor, where I'm clearly tracking a good bit of dirt mixed with monster blood. "Uh . . . Sorry about that."

"Nothing to worry about! We're all in this fight together.

You three are always welcome up here!" Mr. Wang sits down in one of the chairs, then motions for us to do the same. We obey, though we're all a bit confused about it. I glance at Ali and John, who simply look back at me and shrug. Mr. Wang is an interesting sort of character, to be certain, and not one that any of us would have ordinarily associated with back in the old world. Not because we were snobbish or anything, mind you, but folks of his class don't usually mix with commoners like us. After a moment, he folds his hands and starts to speak.

"Last night, the three of you went and cleared out a Pumped! restaurant that had been set up in a dungeon rift. Columbus lured you there with the intention of using stardust to send out cursed food to humans. Is that right?"

"That's correct. He told us that he had managed to send out a little bit of the cursed food, but I was hoping he was joking." I pause for a moment. "Has there been an outbreak?"

"Indeed." Mr. Wang gives a nod. "I used all my resources to try to track down the shipments, and I thought I'd managed to shoot down all the food that was actually cursed, but it would seem that some of it slipped through my fingers. Now, the outbreak is contained for the time being, which is why we aren't rushing, but that's where you'll be heading next. It's about an hour's flight from here, on a cruise ship out in the ocean. The surviving passengers who are still human have barricaded themselves into a safer area, but the infected passengers are rapidly trying to break in. You're to save the human passengers and get them back to port."

"We'll do our best." I give a nod, then pause. "If you don't mind my asking, what's the situation beyond that? You obviously called us here for a reason, and I doubt it was to discuss a simple mission."

"Yes, indeed." Mr. Wang pauses. "I wanted to ask you about last night. I don't like things that I don't understand, and whatever happened in the early parts of this morning very clearly fall into that realm of things."

"Actually, I'd like some answers on that front too." I nod to Ali and John. "I was asleep, and then . . ."

Ali gives a small nod, then glances at John. He gestures at her, and she turns back to me.

"The short version of the story is that at about four o'clock this morning, I woke up to someone calling my name. Now, that's not unusual—I *am* supervising a lot of things right now—so I jumped up and ran out into the hall. When I got out there, though, there was no one. I went up to the lobby, but even there, they didn't know what was happening, so I went back down. By the time I got there, everyone else was gone. My chat told me that you were alright, so . . . I didn't worry about it too much."

John quickly gives a similar story. "I woke up. I thought someone was tapping me. When I sat up, I was certain I heard Ali calling my name from the hall. I stood up, trying to be careful not to wake you up, and slipped out. From there, I could see a figure at the end of the hall waving at me, so I went after it. Before I got there, though, the person I *thought* was Ali slipped into the stairwell. I went on a wild goose chase, and by the time I got back . . . well . . . you'd been sucked into the portal."

"We both went to a computer so we could watch you," Ali offers. "That was about the time you were in the pit, trying to fight your way upward. We asked around, but everyone just said that yeah, portals can technically form anywhere, so . . . I don't know. We figured you were probably okay."

"And neither of you put together the fact that you were lured out of the room?" I scowl at them.

"When I ran into Ali, I just thought I'd finally caught up with her. It wasn't until later that we got our stories straight." John pauses in thought. "It just doesn't make sense to me. Why get us out of the room just to drop you into a fairly straightforward dungeon? There wasn't a trap to try and catch you, you know?"

"In some ways, it was straightforward. In other ways, it was actually . . . different." I pause for a moment. "That Lancelot character—there's something about him that I can't quite place."

"I agree," Mr. Wang says. "There was something about the whole of the dungeon that felt off to me. It didn't seem quite like a normal dungeon. It seems like you were brought there for a reason."

"The only question is *what* reason." I pause in thought. "My best and only guess at this moment is that it has something to do with that sword the ogre had. I've seen it wielded once before, and more importantly, that very creature appeared at the end of the fight once again."

"That was my thought as well," Mr. Wang says. "I don't really understand why, or what the sword actually does, but I have a team working on figuring it out."

"Much appreciated." I nod and then slowly shake my head. "It's got me flummoxed, and I'd rather like answers before they come back to bite me."

"Agreed." Mr. Wang claps his hands and stands up. "Well, as per usual, it's been wonderful getting to meet with you again. You have your orders, I'll have the jeticopter get you out to sea just as quickly as you can. Once you're done with the ship, we can get on with other things."

"And what's our cut of the profit?" I flash a small sly smile at him as I climb back to my feet. Mr. Wang never does anything for free.

"Oh! My apologies." Mr. Wang bows his head. "This one is something we're doing for free. I suppose that means that any of you can bow out if you choose, but I assumed you'd be good to help out."

"Free?" I raise an eyebrow. "Now that's something I don't hear come out of your mouth very often."

Mr. Wang pauses for a moment, and I get the feeling that he has a great many things he *wants* to say. After he's done thinking, he meets my eyes.

"Unfortunately, you were lured into a rift that was actively attacking the human world. I've had fun the last few days clearing dungeons out for corporations, but the fact of the matter is that this war is beginning to grow more intense. I'm still running those jobs and earning a lot off of them, but I'm taking the profits and using them to recruit new hunters so we can enter more dungeons, training and growing more powerful. I also have contacts in other countries doing the same thing."

A realization begins to grow in my mind. "You're building an army."

"Yes, indeed." Mr. Wang gives a nod. "The other side of this war, the dungeons . . . they aren't unified. All the infighting among dungeon bosses tells us that much, but they're also still held together by a common bond: hatred of the humans. That bond will serve to be our downfall unless we can manage to prevent it, and for that, I will spare no expense. You three, if you consent, will become my top soldiers, my shock troops that will go into places no one else dares to venture."

"You're really sounding like quite the general!" I laugh as we all start walking toward the door.

"I wanted to make an enormous profit. In doing so, I accidentally set myself up as the best framework possible for taking down the creatures facing us in our world today," Mr. Wang answers. "They say that with great power comes . . . Oh, I don't remember the second part. What I know is that a lot of people are counting on me." He pauses and flashes a smile. "Plus, the government said they would tax my income at ninety percent unless I did something to help."

We all laugh, and with that, we make our way out onto the landing pad. Engines roar in the distance, and I brace myself.

I've never been on a cruise before.

Something tells me that after this one, I'm not really going to be in the mood to do it ever again.

CHAPTER SIX

The jeticopter, as it turns out, is a little jet airplane whose wings can rotate, allowing it to fly both vertically and horizontally. Two of them come roaring up, and one lands on the helipad while the other hovers nearby. Ali, John, and I all hop into the one sitting there, and it lifts off while Mr. Wang waits for the next ride. Only a moment after we take off, the wings snap into position, and we go roaring forward so fast that we're pressed back into our seats.

"ETA in fifteen minutes," the pilot calls back as we shoot out across the city, leaving sonic booms in our wake. We flash over the top of the Statue of Liberty and out to sea, and I peer out through the front window, looking for our destination.

The sea below us is a giant mess—of that, there can be no doubt. Broken husks of ships float about, some in the process of sinking, others simply listing to the sides or bobbing around like rusted corpses. Great oil slicks cover massive swaths of the waves, while cargo containers slosh about here and there. I catch glimpses of more than a few people waving their arms and homemade banners, but we have no time to try and help.

"Don't worry!" the pilot calls out. "There are rescue operations being launched now! Mr. Wang has a handful of warriors who specialize in fighting sea monsters. They'll be able to get those people to safety."

That does, indeed, settle my mind, and I lean back in my seat. Suddenly, a hologram springs to life in front of me, and I lean forward as the pilot speaks up once more.

"Alright! This is the ship you'll be entering." The hologram takes on the form of a massive cruise ship, which seems to be listing slightly to the side. I don't really know which side—I'm not terribly familiar with nautical terms—but if you were facing out from the front of the ship, you'd be tilted to your left. "There's a small anti-aircraft battery on the top of the cabin. We've managed to disable it slightly, but it's still rather powerful. You'll be jumping down onto the prow—the front of the ship—where you'll land next to the swimming pool."

"Let me guess," I mutter dryly, "that's right in the middle of the infected portion?"

"You got it," the pilot calls back. "The survivors are in the rear engine compartment, down by the rudder and the propellers. The bulkheads are really thick there, to help keep water contained in the event of a breach, which has slowed down the monsters. Problem is, you've got to go through a whole ship full of the things in order to get there."

"So long as I keep leveling up, I'm not too particular." I slowly stand up and bounce on the balls of my feet. "Is the ship actively taking on water right now?"

"It is," the pilot confirms. "Now, we don't expect it to sink entirely for another twenty-four hours or so, but the tilting will get worse over the next little bit, and, of course, if anything gets damaged, it could sink faster. I don't know the exact length of time it's expected that the survivors of the crew can manage to stay alive. I know the leaking compartment isn't far from their position, so they might have significantly less time, or they might have almost that full twenty-four hours. Sinking ships get a bit tricky."

"I'll take your word for it," John says, standing up and walking over to the door. "Just tell us when to jump."

"I'll be coming to a halt just over the insertion point here in thirty seconds," the pilot answers. "I'll come to a stop for exactly five seconds. That's all the time we have before the anti-aircraft weapons are able to get a lock on us. After that, I'll be gone. It's possible we could get back to you sooner, but our plan at the moment is to have a pickup arriving here in five hours to get the passengers out."

"Got it!" Ali calls. "Let's do this!"

We both stand as well, and the jeticopter slowly comes to a halt. I hear distant booming, though it's fairly quiet over the roar of the engines. The door flies open, and the three of us jump.

I don't realize until we're in the air just how *high* the pilot was flying. I was expecting a drop of a hundred feet or so, *maybe* two hundred. No. We're a good thousand feet up, with the cruise ship visible *way* below us, looking rather like a little bath boat. We tumble down through the air, spreading our arms and legs as we try to control our downward motion. I've never been skydiving before, so it's not a skill I come to easily.

In any event, the booming grows louder, and white-hot

bullets flash through the air as the guns on the cruise ship fire up at the copter. Jet engines scream, and I see it shooting off into the distance. Good. As we drop lower and lower, I try to keep an eye on our trajectory and brace for impact as we flash down to the pool area.

Ali is lucky, as she lands in the water. A great explosion of water and foam shoots up into the sky under her impact, and she emerges a moment later, grinning from ear to ear. John doesn't do too badly for himself either and lands in a small fenced-off area full of pool floatation devices. Me? I slam right onto the wooden deck, cracking the wood beneath my feet. My health drops to almost 50 percent, and I groan as I slowly climb back to my feet. Ali comes splashing up out of the pool, and John smashes his way out of the area.

"Everyone alright?" I open my inventory and pull out a Pumped! drink. My health starts to refill as I chug the whole thing in one gulp, then toss aside the glass bottle.

"Right as rain." Ali takes out her bow and fits an arrow to the string. A bit of fire flickers to life on the end of it, and she looks around. "Now, where's the party?"

John flexes his fingers, and I glance down at the bone claws that slide out, ready for a fight. Both of my friends are formidable opponents, which makes them quite fun to fight alongside.

"We also need to decide on a plan," I murmur as I draw out the Enlarged Dagger alongside the Dagger of Doom. High above us, I can see dark forms moving about behind darkened glass, and below us, I can hear feet skittering about. "Are we going to cut straight to the passengers, are we going to try to clear this place out first, or . . ."

"I think we ought to at least clear out the control room,"

Ali comments, "or the bridge, whatever you all it. As long as it's still in place, they'll be able to fire those guns and any other defenses the ship happens to have, and that's going to make things difficult as we try to get everyone out of here."

"True." I nod to John. "What do you think? Head up, clear out the bridge, and then go from there?"

"Works for me." John nods. "We just need to make sure we do it fast."

Kraaaaaaaaaaaaaaaaaaaaaaw!

The noise sounds just like a kraken call, and with a great rumble, a creature rises up out of the pool. It's a massive lizard, something rather like a T-Rex, with large spines coming out of its back. The monster roars once more, and all around us, I can feel the ship shaking. There are all sorts of things coming for us, and, suddenly, I realize just how exposed we are.

"We need to make for those doors." I point to a set of doors on the opposite side of the pool, which leads into the bulk of the ship. "Out here, we're just going to get swarmed. Ali will be a bit more hampered inside, but our combat styles will both be better in closed spaces."

"In the middle of a fight, monsters coming from everywhere, I'm not going to be all that much better out here," Ali says. "I'm way lower in levels than the two of you."

"Then it's decided," I confirm. "Let's get inside!"

The giant lizard . . . I can't decide if it hears our conversation and decides to put a stop to it, or if it simply decides to try and crush us. Either way, the thing lets out another roar, then lumbers forward, snarling and gnashing its teeth. A great blast of fire erupts from its open mouth, and the three of us dive out of the way.

As we come out of our roll, John charges forward, flexing his claws. As he reaches the edge of the pool, he jumps upward and punches the thing in the stomach. It staggers backward, then grabs him with its arms, which are just about the only thing not proportioned like a T-Rex. With a snap of its wrist, it throws John backward across the area, and he bounces several times.

Ali draws back her bowstring and fires an arrow into its face. Flames explode across the monster's scales upon impact, and the beast snarls. It turns and looses a gout of flame at her, and she dives out of the way.

In the meantime, I brace myself, then run at the thing, drawing my Dagger of Doom and Dagger of Damage. I, too, leap up into the air as I reach the edge of the pool. Water slows you down, and I'd rather not be fighting such a monster in its native environment. In any case, I slam into the creature's knee and stab it with the Dagger of Doom.

[Dagger of Doom has discovered a [lightning] weakness.]

Electricity crackles from the blade—admittedly, not a ton—and I glance down at the water beneath me. Water and electricity don't mix well, which puts me in a greater amount of danger than I might otherwise like. In any event, the creature jerks backward, and I tumble down into the waves.

The moment I go under, a great deal of chaos breaks out. I can't tell if it's trying to sweep me with its tail or stomp me with its feet or *what*, but there are bubbles everywhere, things whack into me, and I feel rather like I just got thrown into a washing machine.

[FireStorm: Hey, Jason! I can't see a thing!]

[ShadowDancer: Yeah, if you could get to a better point of view, I'd sure appreciate it!]

[DarkCynic: Guys, let him alone!]

Something whacks me in the chest, *hard,* and I'm launched up and out of the pool to land on the deck. John has just come back into the fight, throwing two pool tables at the thing like discuses. They whack the monster in the head, making it reel, and I grit my teeth. Ali fires another arrow, and I look around.

Suddenly, I see the monster's spines. Ideally, I'd love to run a cable from an electrical room and just zap the thing into oblivion, but that's not practical. Moving quickly, I run forward, jump once more, and catch hold of one of the spines. The thing is smooth and wet, and I have to brace myself against its scales in order to avoid falling down into the pool once more.

"Jason! You okay?" John throws another pool table, but the monster launches a fireball that melts it into slag.

"Yeah! If you have any electricity, hit it with that! Otherwise, I'll be doing my best!"

I brace myself a bit better, then begin stabbing the monster with the Dagger of Damage.

[Damage Dealt: 1]

[Damage Dealt: 2]

[Damage Dealt: 4]

[Damage Dealt: 8]

[Damage Dealt: 16]

[Damage Dealt: 32]

The damage starts to climb. The monster doesn't notice at first . . . then suddenly begins to howl and buck about. As I top one thousand, it snarls and spins, tossing me back to the ground. Blood gushes down the back of it . . . And with that, it truly shows its colors.

With a mighty roar, the thing leaps up out of the pool,

abandoning its watery origin. Flames pour down from its mouth, a torrent of fiery energy that blasts away poolside umbrellas and old chairs. I race away from the flame, then spin and throw the Dagger of Damage with all my might. It hits the beast right under the chin, opening a gaping wound across its throat. The monster staggers, and I give a nod.

"John!"

John runs up from the side and leaps into the air to punch the monster in the side of the head. It staggers and falls back into the pool, and I open up my pocket dimension. Bjorn steps out, unbidden, and gives a mighty howl.

A layer of ice grows across every surface I can see, rippling outward from the Frost Wolf. As it hits the pool, the whole thing turns to ice and freezes the monster in place. Only a single hand remains outside the thick layer, and as we stand there, it twitches a few times before growing still.

"And . . . that's done." Ali lowers her bow and gives a nod. "Can't say as I'll complain about that."

"Not in the slightest." I shake my head. I keep Bjorn out of the pocket dimension and call Blub out as well, just for the sake of it. The Living Bomb hovers just behind my head, and I turn back toward the doors.

Smash!

Metal splinters and bends as two werewolves smash through, eyes gleaming. Behind them, I can see a great many more creatures as the halls fill up. Behind us, the deck begins to splinter as creatures claw their way up from below. We've suddenly become the center of attention and spent *way* too much time fighting off the sea monster. I glance around, then point down the deck, leading along the side of the ship.

"That way!"

Things shriek all around us, but we ignore them and charge forward. A cruise ship full of monsters, survivors down on the very bottom, and the whole thing actively sinking?

What could be more exciting than that?

CHAPTER SEVEN

The three of us race down the immense deck. The bulk of the cruise ship rises up to our left: cabins and bunks and engine rooms and dining areas and concert halls and all sorts of other things. Behind us, the werewolves snarl and charge along, their claws tearing into the wooden deck as they throw themselves at us pell-mell. One of them leaps forward, and John spins and punches it clean off the side of the deck. Another comes up, and I spin and chop off its head with my Enlarged Dagger. The weapon, while far from the flashiest one in my inventory, is rapidly starting to become my favorite.

"Right there!" Ali points ahead and to our left. There, the ship extends outward slightly, allowing space for a number of elegant, and now rather tattered, tables to spread out across the overlook. A glass wall stands just behind it, where a restaurant seems to be relatively well-preserved. Actually, aside from a few food spills, it looks entirely intact. I nod and run along in that direction, even as I see things moving high above us.

"You hold them off!" John puts on a burst of speed. "I'll get us inside!"

"Works for me." I glance over my shoulder, where three of the werewolves are right on my tail. Next to me, Bjorn glances up to meet my eyes, and I give a nod. With that, we spin around, and I hold out my free hand. Blub lands in my open palm, and Bjorn lets out a howl.

A great sheet of ice explodes outward, hitting the werewolves head-on. The leaders are frozen in place, while the ones further back all come to a screeching halt at the edge of the ice sheet and even start to back up as it spreads. Bjorn lets his voice stop after a moment, and I throw Blub with all my might.

KA-BOOM!

Blub explodes powerfully and shatters the frozen werewolves into slivers. As their body parts rain down all around me, I snatch up my Living Bomb and take my stance. Ali, meanwhile, begins firing arrows at something I can't see, higher up on the ship. Things start to rain down, thunking to the deck behind us, but I don't pay it much attention.

"And . . . Got it!" John calls.

With that, I turn and run. The werewolves lunge forward as well, and Bjorn lets out another blast of cold. He stands his ground, staring defiantly at the red-eyed monsters.

Back behind him, John, from what I can tell, has used his finger to pick the lock. As Ali and I run inside, he pulls the door sharply shut, then grabs the metal door handles. His muscles bulge, and he twists the handles together into an impromptu lock that certainly doesn't look like it'll be opening anytime soon. With that, Bjorn steps back into the pocket dimension, and the werewolves come charging forward.

A dozen of them, maybe more, throw themselves against the glass of the door and of the wall, but it does no good. Pounding frantically, scratching and tearing, they're unable to breach the glass. I let out a sigh of relief, and we turn away.

"Are you the rescue party?"

I blink in surprise as a waiter, fully dressed in his evening attire, steps out of the kitchen. I sheath my Enlarged Dagger and give a small nod.

"That's the idea." I gesture upward. "We're trying to get to the bridge right now, then we'll be heading down to rescue everyone."

"Good." The waiter smiles, relief showing on his face. "You know where everyone is trapped, then?"

"We've got a pretty good idea," I confirm.

"Could you tell us the fastest way to the bridge?" John asks.

Before the waiter can answer, Ali cuts in. "Or he could just tell us how he's alive! I'm sure he'd love a bit of compassion and companionship after all this."

The waiter gives a small smile. "While I'll admit that I've been somewhat lacking in human company, it's only been a few hours—one horrid night. I'll survive, unlike so many of my patrons, and I'd much rather not waste your time jawing. If you must know, when I heard the chaos on the deck . . . Well, most people on board weren't all that worried about the monsters. They thought the portals were only a land-based problem. I locked the doors tightly the moment I sensed something was wrong. The few people I had with me at the time all left, hoping to find their families. I haven't heard from them since. I've just tried to stay out of sight, watching and waiting for my chance to strike back."

"I'm glad you made it through." Ali smiles. The waiter does seem to relax, but only for a moment.

"Right! You need to get to the bridge." He pulls a napkin from a nearby dispenser, remaining incredibly calm even as the werewolves outside continue to bang on the doors and window. "Go out the back doors. You'll enter a servant's corridor. It's remained relatively quiet through all of this. Head straight back, and you'll come to a broad, elegant sort of hallway. There's an elevator there that will take you straight up, and if the elevator isn't working, you can take the stairs." As he speaks, he draws a map. "Now, if *that* doesn't work, there's another option that might be a possibility as well. There's a side door right over there that opens into a music hall. There's actually a whole chain of entertainment rooms that you could pass through. It's a bit more piecemeal, but that might also provide some more places to hide."

I glance up at the werewolves. Some of them are slinking away, though it doesn't seem to me like they're giving up. No, it looks to me like they're looking for another way inside.

"Would you like to come with us?" I offer. "They're sure to find you if you stay."

"Ah, I'm nobody. They won't care about me, and if they do, at least I've done you a service," the waiter answers. "If I were to come along, I'd only slow you down and perform quite a *dis*-service. I'll wait right here, and I'll be just fine. You all run along, now."

"It's been good meeting you." John shakes his hand.

"And we'll make sure to get you out of here with us," Ali says.

The waiter doesn't say anything but bows his head, then leads us to the back of the restaurant. There, he gestures at a small set of doors, which seems to open into a small hallway. They've been barred with a fire axe, and I slowly step up and take the axe away.

Wham!

The door flies open, whacking me in the face, and I'm thrown backward. I come crashing down on a table, where I slide on the tablecloth and flip off the other side. It's not dignified in the slightest, but I leap to my feet as a werewolf comes stalking through.

More come from behind it, but that doesn't slow us down. John leaps forward, punching the werewolf in the face. His mighty fist crushes the monster's nose into pulp, smashing it back against the rear wall. I run forward as the monsters enter the room and draw out the Enlarged Dagger. With all my might, I swing the weapon at the creature's neck. My aim is true, and I cleave straight through the spine, leaving the head to clatter to the ground several feet from the body.

Ali has an arrow fitted to the string before the werewolf has fallen, and she fires a bolt of lightning into the next creature. Fur burns and hisses as the lightning arcs through the whole row of attacking monsters, knocking them to the ground. I stab the first one through the heart, and John grabs the next one, which is lying in the doorway, and swings it out of the way, smashing its head into the wall so hard that it leaves a dent behind. I quickly slam the doors shut, and the waiter calmly hands me the axe. An instant later, the door has been barred shut again, and the waiter sighs. "Hmm. Perhaps this will be trickier than I thought."

Snarls and howls echo from the other side of the door as werewolves begin throwing themselves against it, trying to break through. *This* door has quite a bit more give to it than the other doors, which makes me worried. "There's a freezer in the kitchen. I'll hide in there," the waiter says. "The power has been cut, and there will be enough air for me to survive for some time. Just don't forget about me."

"Will that be safe?" Ali asks.

"According to several tests performed, if the ship were to sink, a person could hide in the fridge and have it serve as a life capsule for a short time." The waiter shrugs. "They won't be able to touch me."

"Then we'll go the other way and hope to see you soon." I wave at him as he runs for the kitchen. The three of us wait just a moment until we're certain he's safe, and then we run for the side doors.

These doors have been locked and barred with a security bar, which John pulls away and sets to the side. Quickly, we push our way through, then glance around as the doors fall shut.

Only a few flickering lights illuminate the interior of the music hall. We're off to the side of the stage, where the seats slope down gently from the top. At the entrance, the doors are wide open, and a number of dark figures stare in at us. There's a brief pause, and then they charge forward. We do the same, racing for the doors on the other side of the room, which lead to the next area, whatever that might be.

Clackackackackackack!

Half a dozen of the strange creatures, which look rather like humanoid crabs, come charging down to meet us. One of them leaps at me, and I spin and lash out with the Enlarged Dagger.

Crack!

The weapon smashes into the hard exoskeleton of the monster without doing anything more than cosmetic damage. It lets out a hiss and begins to snap at my face and arm. Pincers clack down around my right arm, squeezing impossibly hard, and I grimace in pain.

"Oh, lay off, will you?" I raise my Enlarged Dagger and stab the thing in the face, right between the mouth mandibles. The blade crunches loudly, and the monster lets out a squeal as I push as hard as I can. Blood trickles out the open mouth, and I shove it away, letting the corpse fall to the ground.

[You have leveled up!]

[Congratulations! You are now Level 38!]

Wham!

Another pincer whacks me upside the head, sending me reeling. A *much* larger version of the creature lunges at me with half a dozen arms clawing at me all at once. I parry them as best I can, but I stagger back into John, who kicks away another one attacking him. I can't see Ali, but I hear an explosion that I assume is her.

"Get ready," I call out. Both of our monsters prepare to attack. "And . . . Switch!"

We spin around at the same time. John lashes out at the crab attacking me, throwing an uppercut to hit it in the chest. Meanwhile, the *other* monster lashes out with its pincers, trying to stay out of John's reach. I respond by lashing out with my Enlarged Dagger, hitting it in the gap in its armor.

The claw falls to the floor with a clatter, and I call out, "Now, Blub!"

Blub, who had remained outside my pocket dimension

following close behind, flashes forward. I brace myself as he hits the monster and explodes violently, filling the air with smoke and flame. Bits and pieces of crab rain down around me, and I run forward, now with a free shot toward the next door. There, I see Ali trying to pick the lock with an arrow, keeping an eye on the entrance. As another of the crabs steps through, she nocks an arrow to the string and fires, hitting the monster in the eye and killing it instantly. The others fall back, and she returns to picking the lock.

"No time for that!" I brace myself. I know my strength is a lot higher than it used to be—though, with John always right next to me, it's hard to know *exactly* how much stronger. Gritting my teeth, I throw myself into the door as hard as I can.

Crash!

Metal folds around me, glass shatters, and I crash through into the next room. Ali steps through and gives an approving nod, then screams. I turn around just in time to be smashed in the face by a chair.

This room appears to be a more casual stage setting, with tables and chairs scattered around in front of a small setup. Of course, it's filled with more of the crab things, and I climb back to my feet as a monster swings another chair at me.

"Not today." I raise my Enlarged Dagger and parry the chair, strange as that is to say, then stand up and stab at the creature's belly. There, a handful of plates interlock to form a shield, and I slam my dagger into it with all my might. The blade finds a small gap and sinks in up to the hilt, and the monster snarls and falls back.

An entire table flies through the air a moment later, thrown by a particularly large beast near the door. I grit my teeth, then swing the stabbed monster around, using it as a shield. The table smashes into its back, and with all my might, I rip the dagger back out. It falls to the ground, and with that, John comes charging inside.

Side by side, the three of us run toward the door on the opposite side, cutting through what few monsters bother trying to stop us. John smashes through *this* door, leading into what seems to be a stage for an orchestra. There are still violins and fiddles and cellos lying about, and we leap over the ruined instruments in our mad dash onward.

All around, the cruise ship rages, but onward we go.

There are people counting on us—a lot of them.

Failure simply isn't an option.

CHAPTER EIGHT

John, Ali, and I continue to fight our way forward until, finally, we punch our way into a long red-carpeted hallway. As we run toward a set of elevators not far from our position, we suddenly notice that there are no monsters watching us. Noises come from the stairwell, and, ready for a bit of rest, we all spin and duck into a restroom that catches our eye. It's a family room, big enough for all of us, and the door slowly clicks shut behind us as the first of the monsters chasing us steps through the previous, ruined, door. I press myself up against the exit, trying to steady my breathing, knowing that the moment they detect us in here, we'll be caught like fish in a barrel. Well, *armed* fish in a barrel.

"Mr. Wang said there was an outbreak," Ali gasps, sitting down on the floor on the other side of the room. She fits an arrow to the string of her bow, ready to fire the moment she sees something, but otherwise relaxes. "It seems like the whole *ship* turned. Do they infect you when they bite you or something?"

"I sure hope not." I glance down at my arm, where a long cut bleeds into my shirt. I decided to take a moment to heal and open up a bottle of Pumped! to get the wound to stitch itself back up. "My guess is that the delivery out here was just *really* big. I mean, this cruise ship has probably been floating ever since the portals opened, right? That has to have been a good week or two now."

"I can't keep track of it, but something like that, yeah." John nods. "They were probably on rations by this point, so if a cargo crate of fast food suddenly gets dropped onto your ship, you're going to want to eat it."

"Fair enough." Ali sighs and lets her head fall back against the wall. After a moment, she pushes herself up and draws a deep breath. "Alright. Are we taking the elevator shaft or the stairs?"

"I think we have to take the stairs," I answer. "The power on the ship is out, I'm sure of—"

The deck shivers under our feet. We don't hear the noise so much as feel it, but I recognize it instantly. It's the sound of tearing metal, of something breaking. The ship tips a bit more to the side, and I gulp. It only moves a degree, maybe half a degree, but it's enough to feel. I give a nod, and John steps up.

"One. Two."

On a silent "Three," John runs forward and smashes through the door. He catches the side of one of the humanoid crab monsters, spins, and throws it into a werewolf not far away. Dozens of eyes, some on stalks, some blazing red, some fiery with anger, all turn toward us.

"Hey-o!" Ali steps out and fires a lightning bolt from her bow. It arcs from monster to monster, flashing back and forth across the whole area. A few of them collapse, dead, but the majority of them simply stagger under the attack. Quickly, the three of us run past, angling for the stairs. A werewolf stumbles forward, and I hack off his head with the Enlarged Dagger, but he's the only one I touch. With that, we crash through the door and into the stairwell.

Screeeeeeeeeeeeeeeeeeeee!

As we look up, a great many tentacles begin to unravel, crashing down through the stairwell like a cascade. We blink in surprise, then step back into the hall where the monsters are recovering. They were once human, so the fact that we can deal out a ton of damage isn't lost on them, but they do start to snarl and walk forward. Several spider-like creatures appear at the end of the hall, and climb up to walk across the ceiling, angling toward us slowly and purposefully. We're surrounded, and they know it.

"Alright, then," I murmur. "In ordinary circumstances I'd say let's go take out the tentacles. Now I say we take the elevator."

"I agree," Ali murmurs back. "John, you go first. We'll cover you."

"Right."

John quickly steps to the elevator, slips his claws between the doors, and starts forcing them open. His fingers dent the metal, and, slowly, he peels them apart. With that, all the monsters around come charging forward, and Ali and I dive into the fray.

I throw Blub once more, blasting away a large number of them, then start attacking furiously with the Enlarged Dagger. A werewolf lunges from the side, and I slam the weapon deep into his chest, then rip it out just in time to cut the head off one of the crabs. Several spiders jump down from the ceiling, trying to bite me. One of them lands on my back, wraps its legs around to the front of my face, and bites me on the neck. I flick my dagger around and chop it in half, and a status appears.

[Condition: Poisoned. You will lose 10 HP per second for the next 00:00:30.]

I grit my teeth as a great deal of blood begins to cascade down my back, and my health drops sharply. Something growls at the end of the hall, and I glance that way to see a bear, a massive and rabid one, snarling and pawing at the ground. It charges forward, pounding across the floor, snarling and gnashing its teeth. A crab standing in its way is flattened beneath its feet, and I brace myself.

[LunarEclipse: BRUTAL!!!]

[ViperQueen: If you defeat that guy, Jason, you're going to be a LEGEND!]

[FireStorm: Guys, have you seen the things he's beaten before? This will be a piece of cake!]

I grit my teeth, spin, and chop down a werewolf jumping at me, then open my inventory and pull out a Pumped! bottle. With my free hand, I pop the cap off, chug the drink, and then spin and throw the bottle through the air. It smashes into the bear's face. It's not enough to stop it, but it's enough to slow it down. It snarls and rears upward, waving its claws, and John calls out, "Elevator's ready!"

Ali quickly ducks inside, then lets a blast of electricity fly. Once more it arcs through the whole area, staggering everything trying to get to us, including the bear. I run into the elevator, where I find that John has ripped a hole in the ceiling and has a hold on the cable that helps lift the elevator. He starts to pull downward, manually lifting us upward. He's good, but he's still a bit slower than the monsters outside the elevator, which are starting to eye us. The bear in particular snarls and runs forward, and Ali shoots another lightning bolt into him to slow him down.

"Blub!"

With a flicker, the Living Bomb appears in my hand. He inflates, and I throw him with all my might. A resounding *boom* shakes the ship as he hits, and the bear is knocked backward. He returns to my hand with a bounce, and I call out Bjorn and Burnie as well. Burnie perches on my shoulder, and the bear snarls as he recovers.

"Burnie!"

My Phoenix spreads his wings and exhales a piercing blast of fire that streaks across the deck, hitting the bear squarely in the face. Hair is burned away across its whole body, and the monster snarls and backs up. As the fire dies away, I nod.

"Bjorn!"

The resulting howl sees a sheet of ice grow across the weakened bear, and I give another nod. With that, John hauls us upward, and up we go.

Ali and I stay at the ready as we continue to climb. The next two floors we pass have the doors closed, so while we can see plenty of shadows flickering around on the other side, none of them can see us. I hear the bear roar and snarl off in the distance, but it's quite a ways away, so I don't worry about it altogether too much. I have a feeling that we'll face the bear again before we leave the ship, but I'm willing to deal with that when the time comes.

When we reach the third floor up, we find the doors open. Blood stains the deck, while bullet holes mar the walls. I can see several chewed-up guard uniforms and shudder a bit. Things snarl and snort off in the distance, but nothing can be seen directly. I don't dare poke my head out into the hall.

Crash!

The doors burst off the stairwell right next to us. The only reason I know that, of course, is because one of the doors lands on the hallway floor just in front of the elevator entrance. John hauls us along a bit faster, and I see something dark and furry race out. It spins, and I look into two hard and pained eyes before we're drawn up ever the more. It snarls and spins back around, and I brace myself.

This time I can hear something crashing along through the stairwell, which is just on the other side of the wall from us. When we reach the fourth floor, the doors are shut, but something slams into it hard enough to dent them inward. I wince, and claws punch through the gap and start straining to open them.

Bear claws.

"Alright," John mutters. "With those doors dented inward, I'm not going to be able to keep pulling this upward. Hang on to me, alright?"

"Why should we—?"

I take hold of his bearskin cloak, and Ali does the same on the other side. With that, he swings up, pulling himself and us upward, hand over fist. We actually go up much faster than before, and we quickly swing through the top of the elevator car and up into the darkness. Below, the bear rips the door open and lumbers into the elevator, staring up at us.

"Alright, everyone off!" John swings Ali over to a small ladder that runs up the elevator shaft, then sticks me on the opposite side.

[FireStorm: Ahh! Jason, don't fall!]

[IceQueen: I think I know what's about to happen . . .]

[DarkCynic: Don't spoil it!]

With that, he swings over to the side directly opposite the doors, where he simply catches hold of a beam. The bear snarls and starts to climb upward . . . and John simply lets go.

Cables whir, and the bear and the elevator drop like a rock. Down, down they go, until a resounding *boom* countless floors below signals their destruction.

"And there we have it." John nods. "One fewer bears to plague the world. Let's get climbing."

"Uh . . . John?" Ali ventures. "That's going to be a little difficult."

John and I both look upward to see a number of insects are climbing down. I can see praying mantises, spiders, ants, and more.

"Difficult is my middle name. Come on!"

Ali nods and starts climbing the ladder. I go upward as well, climbing as best I can. There's a network of beams and rods that I can use, and I make good time. John is faster, of course, with his claws and things, but I certainly make a good account of myself. As we reach the bugs, we launch into one of the strangest battles I've yet fought.

A large ant snaps its mandibles and skitters down at me. I quickly grab hold of a bar with my left hand, draw out my Enlarged Dagger, and stab it in the face. There's a sharp squeal as it dies, and I use a flick of my wrist to fling it down into the depths. With that, I lift the blade and stick it in my mouth—rather like a pirate—and keep climbing.

Two more of the bugs come down at me, a mantis and something like a grasshopper. This time I hang on with my right hand, slash the mantis's head off its fragile stalk, then spin and cut down the grasshopper. More of the insects come down from my right, and I'm forced to toss the blade into the air, grab hold of a support with my left hand, and then catch the blade with my right.

"Ooh. Aren't you fancy?" Ali calls out from the opposite side. She hooks her elbow around the ladder and whacks a mantis with her bow, then slings it off down the shaft.

"I'd like to see you do better," I call out, rather in jest, then stick the blade back in my teeth and climb faster.

"Alright. Watch and learn." Ali hooks her legs and feet around the ladder, then leans back until her torso is completely horizontal. As bugs swarm down, she fires a lightning bolt upward, striking dozens of the creatures all over. Charred insects rain down like . . . well, rain. With that, she rights herself and starts climbing once more.

"Fair. Fair." I laugh and climb faster once again.

The bugs keep coming for almost three floors while we steadily carve our way through them. It's a difficult fight. More than once, I almost fall as I forget that I have to hold on to the wall to keep from falling. In any case, though, we pass out the far side and climb up a bit more steadily. At that point, I switch over to the ladder, which is *far* easier to climb than the wall.

"Alright, I think we're getting near the top," John murmurs. "Better hang back for a moment. Let me check this out."

John springs on ahead and soon climbs all the way to the top of the shaft. There, he climbs around to the elevator doors, hooks a claw through the narrow gap, and twists it open just a bit. Ali and I climb up next to him, and slowly, he pulls it open.

The hallway is dark, and John cautiously steps through. He waves after a moment, and Ali follows with me bringing up the rear. As I step into the hall, I glance around, trying to get my bearings. There's a large couch at one end of the hall and a set of red doors at the other end. A small plate next to the door clearly announces the bridge, and I slowly step toward it.

"And this is our destination. Come on, we should—"

Rrrrrrrrrrrrrr!

The noise is soft, and I spin back around to the couch. With a snarl, it starts to push itself up. The bear, scarred and injured, slowly takes a step toward us, then another.

"Good bear," John soothes, drawing out a bone dagger. "Quiet bear. Let's—"

The bear roars, then charges forward. John runs to meet it, and I see his dagger flash in his hand as he hits the thing. The dagger sinks in up to the hilt, but the bear is relentless. It slams into him, all thousand pounds or more, and launches John back into the elevator shaft. John screams, and below, there's a loud crash. With that, the bear turns toward Ali and me, and I run forward to face it.

"Ali! Lightning, now!"

A blast of lightning hits the bear, which makes the whole thing shudder. That small delay allows me to pull out Blub, and I bounce him in the palm of my hand.

"Skill: Duplicate!"

With a flicker, I suddenly have *two* Blubs. I throw the first one, and the explosion shakes the room. The bear is knocked backward, and I throw the second one a moment later. *That* blast launches the monster clean out the back of the hall, and for a moment, there's nothing but silence.

I slowly walk up to the new hole as both of my Blubs bounce back into my hand. They fuse into one, but I don't care. Far below, the body of the bear lies on the rear deck, not moving. Dozens of monsters look up at us, and I give a nod.

"Alright, come on." I turn away, back toward the door. "We need to get moving, and we need to do it now. We're going to be overrun here in just a few seconds, and I'd rather be long gone by the time that happens."

CHAPTER NINE

"Wait!" Ali shakes her head. "What about John?"

"He'll be on his way up." I glance over the edge of the elevator shaft. "Chat? Anyone know how John is doing?"

[ShadowDancer: Oh yeah, he's doing great!]

[ViperQueen: I wouldn't say *great*, but he's alive. He caught himself on an I beam and is climbing back up. Looks like he's taking his time to heal, though.]

I turn and nod to Ali. "Yeah, he'll be here in just a moment. Might be better to have him show up suddenly, you know?"

"I suppose." Ali nocks an arrow—it looks to me like an exploding one—as I step toward the door. "What do you think we'll find in here?"

"I haven't the faintest idea." I grab hold of the door handle. "One. Two . . ."

On "Three," I pull the doors wide open. Inside, I see a large number of instrument panels set across a wide white floor. A long glass window allows for a wonderful view of the front of the ship, as well as the sea beyond.

And, of course, I can see the captain strung up in a net hanging from the ceiling. He seems quite conscious, though rather terrified of all the monsters standing at the instrument panels.

The creatures there are unlike anything I've yet seen. They look like wraiths but physical. They wear long dark rags, have bony fingers and misshapen faces, and magic crackles in their hands. Most of them stay at their posts, but as Ali and I enter, four of them turn away and slowly start walking toward us. Their empty eyes stare holes through me, and they wordlessly draw swords from beneath their robes.

"Ah! I knew a rescue party would come!" the captain says, finding his voice. "Wonderful to see you! Watch out, these things are powerful!"

"I've taken down bigger prey." I settle into my stance. "Ali? Light them up."

Ali lets an arrow fly, hitting the first of the monsters in the chest. The arrow explodes and knocks the monster backward, though it doesn't seem to kill it. I race forward, my Enlarged Dagger flashing in the air, and come up to meet the first of the monsters.

It swings its sword, and I parry it with ease. My reach is shorter than the creature's, both when considering the length of my blade and the length of my arm, but I don't expect that to be an issue. It attacks with fury, rapidly swinging the weapon with wide, imprecise attacks. I let several go past me simply because I can tell that they won't hit. I parry a few more, and then, as the creature oversteps slightly, I lunge.

My blade flashes through the air, and I stab it deep in its chest. Withered bone and flesh crumbles to dust as I find its heart, and the creature lets out a scream before collapsing, dead. Now *that* gets the attention of all the other monsters in the room.

Shing!

Just about every single sword in the entire room is drawn in one smooth motion, and I brace myself.

"Alright, pets, I could use some he—"

With that, all the monsters attack, and I throw myself into a desperate fight for survival. Half a dozen of the monsters attack me at once, and I dodge some blades while parrying others. Knowing I'll never survive at the center of a ring of the creatures, I run forward, bowling between several of them, knocking them aside as I try to get to a better position. I spin and cut the head off one of them, only for another to hold out a withered hand.

I don't really know how to describe the sound that comes next: it's a sort of hissing, withering noise. Strands of twisted energy leap from the thing's palm and wrap around me, pinning my arms to my side and tightening around my legs. The spectral ropes burn with a cold, yet fiery energy, and I try to avoid screaming in pain. One of the monsters runs at me, sword at the ready, intent on chopping me into hash.

"No . . . you . . . don't!"

I flex my muscles and push with all my strength. The bonds snap and send a blast of rebounded energy back upon the wraith that cast it. The monster is blasted into dust, and I lash upward with the dagger. My first stroke bats its sword out of the way, knocking it up to the ceiling. My second slashes through its chest, ending its cruel existence.

[You have leveled up!]

[Congratulations! You are now Level 39!]

I have to blink in surprise. It feels like I'm leveling up way faster than I've done in the past, and I can't quite figure out why. In any event, Ali runs past me a moment later up on top of one of the instrument panels. She looks almost like an elf as she fires an arrow into the mass of creatures. A flash of light emerges, and the foul creatures shriek and fall back. I blink in surprise, then switch out my Enlarged Dagger for the Photonic Dagger. As it comes into view, the monsters shriek and fall back, only to rally and come charging forward.

"Alright, then. If that's the way you want it!"

I transform the dagger into a sword, then lunge forward to meet the creatures. The weapon leaves long trails of light through the air as I crash into the darkened monsters, hacking and slashing with all my might. Now, *they're* the ones parrying *my* attacks, and their strength is a good bit less than mine. One of them stands up to me, and I swing downward as hard as I can. Its sword is battered from its grasp, and I stab it through the heart.

Suddenly, a great many more of the energy-ropes flash down around me, tying me tight. I grit my teeth, but at least three of the monsters are casting the ropes now, which makes them a *lot* stronger. Another of the wraiths flashes forward to stab me while I'm tied up, and I take a deep breath.

As it swings its sword at me, I pull to the left, letting the blade pass beside me. With that, I headbutt the thing just as hard as I can. It hurts me, don't get me wrong, but it hurts the wraith more, and it lets out a shriek and swings its sword at me again. I duck this time, then sweep its legs out from under it.

Thwick!

An arrow flashes over my head and hits one of the wraiths casting the spell, killing it instantly. As that rope dissolves, I take a deep breath, then spin as hard as I can. The effort severs the other two ropes, and blasts of energy ripple backward to kill those two wraiths as well. Good. I'm making progress. I stomp on the skull of the one that tried to stab me and slowly lift my blade.

"Alright. You guys aren't going to—"

Screeeeeeeeeeee!

A massive, visible shockwave of screech energy hits me and knocks me backward against a console. Several of the wraiths raise their hands, which begin to crackle with lightning and energy. I grit my teeth and push myself away, even as bolts of lightning flash through the air to blast my surroundings into oblivion. Several of the lightning bolts hit me on the shoulder and scorch down my body, but I ignore the pain and charge forward at the culprits. One of them flings a ball of lightning at me, but I catch the lightning on my sword, spin around, and fling the lightning back into their midst.

"Jason!"

I spin to see Ali pressed up against the window of the bridge. Several of the creatures have her cornered. She's wielding a knife in either hand and is doing a fair enough job of parrying their attacks, but she *is* also a good bit lower-leveled than me or John. I grit my teeth, then slash the head off a nearby wraith, leap over a computer, and run toward her.

Before I can get anywhere close, a hand comes up from beneath the window, as if something is climbing up the outside of the ship. Claws slam into the glass and begin to grind through. Cracks spiderweb across the whole of the window, and with a mighty crash, one of the panes of glass shatters and falls away. With that, John swings up into view once again and snorts.

The wraiths around Ali pause as they're distracted by John's entrance, and I decide to take advantage of it. "Ali, duck!"

Ali obeys, dropping down to her knees, and I swing my sword. It cuts through all three of the creatures in a single blow, causing a good amount of dust to dribble down onto Ali. She grimaces and stands back up, and John walks over to join us.

"Sorry about that. Got a bit lost. You know how that goes."

"Not exactly, but I'll take your word for it," Ali answers with a grin. "I've never before gotten lost on a cruise ship and wound up climbing the outside of it, but . . . you know."

John smiles. One of the wraiths snarls and flings a rope around him, and he simply reaches out, grabs the rope, and pulls. The wraith flies out the window, screaming, and we turn to face the last of the monsters together.

A few moments later, the last of the monsters have fallen to the floor, dead. John walks over and pulls the doors to the bridge closed, then twists the handles together to prevent anyone else from following. Meanwhile, Ali and I climb up to the captain, who's been watching everything with a terrified expression.

"I really can't thank you enough." The captain wipes his brow as we help him down from the net. He lands on the floor with a *thunk*, slips and falls, and then slowly pulls himself up. "When those things broke through the door, they killed the rest of my crew. They forced one to eat a hamburger, and he transformed, and . . ." The man shudders.

"Why didn't they kill *you?*" I ask.

"They needed someone who knew the ins and outs of how to run the ship," the captain answers. "It's really as simple as that. The one that transformed forgot how to do everything almost instantly, which meant that they needed someone to remain human. I'll be the first to admit that I'd rather survive a situation than die a hero, so . . . I helped them figure out pretty much everything they wanted to find."

"A coward. Great," John grunts. He turns away, but Ali takes the captain's hand.

"That's easy for you to say. You can bench-press a Boeing."

John chuckles a bit at that, and I nod at the captain.

"If you don't mind, we need some help. First off, how do we shut down the anti-aircraft batteries? We have a transport on the way to get everyone free, but we're going to need to do it without being shot down."

"Ah, yes. Right this way." The captain waves us to the rear of the room, where he gestures to a rather small station. It only has a few basic controls and reminds me of an arcade game, really. "I've never actually seen it fired before, but we do sometimes pass through pirate-infested waters. It gives us a bit of security since, otherwise, we're a bit of a target."

"That makes sense to me," I murmur. Frankly, I've been dying to know why a cruise ship would have such massive guns, but if you're running a giant luxury ship through oceans where pirates are known to live . . .

"Before we were taken over by the things, we actually used the guns to shoot down a dragon." The captain grins as he presses a few buttons. With a flicker, the control panel shuts down. "There we go. That ought to fix it so no one can fire them again."

I nod, then motion everyone back. As they retreat to the other side of the room, I take Blub out of my pocket dimension and throw him at the little station. The resulting explosion blows out the back side of the bridge and opens a hole into the captain's quarters, but it removes the station.

"That'll *definitely* fix it so no one can fire them again." I nod with finality. "Alright. We need to get down to the survivors, and fast."

"If you like . . ." The captain waves us over to another section of the bridge, where he snatches up a small tablet. He hands it to me, then steps up to a working computer and hits a few buttons. A three-dimensional map of the ship appears on the tablet a moment later. "You can use this to track things through the vessel. As you get lower and lower in the ship, it sort of turns into a maze, as you can see from the heat detectors we have spaced throughout the vessel . . ." Little red dots begin to blink across the model. A great many of them are clustered in the engine room, with a handful of others spread throughout the rest of the area. "You can also use this to track the location of all non-infected humans."

"You keep tabs on your people?" I look up at the captain in horror.

"Well . . ." The captain shrugs. "It helped with tracking down pirates when they boarded. Also, every now and again, guests will get adventurous and try to see the maintenance areas for themselves. This helps find people when they go missing. More importantly, it let us know that the infected individuals have a much lower body temperature than us non-infected folks. You're welcome."

"This will be very helpful. Thank you." Ali takes the tablet from him. "Now, should we get going?"

"Yes, we should." John nods. "Every second we spend here talking is another second those passengers risk either drowning or being eaten."

"Wonderful!" The captain claps his hands. "Well . . . then . . . lead the way!"

CHAPTER TEN

The four of us quickly make our way out of the bridge. The captain takes us back into his quarters—which to me look like they were rather messy *before* everything fell apart, but that might be a rash judgement call—where he leads us to a small locked door at the very back of the area. There, he pulls out a key and unlocks the door, then slides it open to reveal a narrow staircase.

[LunarEclipse: WHOA!!! Secret staircase!!!]

[DarkCynic: That's the best thing ever!]

[FireStorm: I bet it's infested with monsters! Big, gross monsters!]

[ChaosRider: You know, I bet Astrid would work really well on a cruise ship. She uses ground magic, and the ship is made of metal! She could just open up rifts and drop things into lower levels, or crush things, or . . . If I were in your shoes, I'd be using her.]

[DarkCynic: I hate to correct you, but if you use a monster

like that on a cruise ship . . . I mean . . . that's not going to end well for you. You'll probably just sink the ship.]

[ChaosRider: I'd be careful.]

The chat begins to argue, but I mostly ignore it. I take the lead as we head down the staircase, our feet making metallic *bongs* that echo loudly in the still air. As we go downward, I can hear monsters moving about on the other side of the walls, but none of them seem to take any particular notice of us.

"Where exactly does this go?" John asks the captain quietly, in the rear.

"Down to the maintenance tunnels," the captain explains. "That'll be on the main deck, level with the pool and such things. From there, we'll be able to make our way down to the lower decks."

I start to feel a bit uneasy about that. The werewolves first came out of a set of doors that certainly *looked* like they belonged to a kind of maintenance area, which makes me nervous. Still, though, I'm also expecting us to have to fight more monsters—that's sort of my job—so I'm not too concerned.

"What can you tell us about what happened here?" Ali asks after a moment. "We talked to a waiter on the main deck, but he didn't know much more than the fact that it had happened."

"Indeed." The captain shrugs. "The gist of it is pretty simple, really. We've been out on the water ever since the apocalypse started. For the first couple days, everyone on board figured that it was safer on the water than on land. Then, once everything started to settle down and we got communication back, the harbor clogged up. The harbor authority is working on clearing out the harbor for docking, but it'll still be a little while before they really get things tidied up enough that anything of our size will be able to make landfall."

"I see," I murmur thoughtfully. "And then you started to run low on food."

The captain gives a nod. "We ordinarily keep enough food on hand to keep us for a week. It's been longer than that at this point, and . . . well . . ." He chuckles. "You don't typically come on a cruise if you're the sort of person who's used to skipping meals. We started rationing, which didn't make people happy, and since we weren't in active danger, we were pretty low on the priority lists of the people running the rescues."

"I'm sorry to hear that," Ali says comfortingly.

"Thanks," the captain sighs. "In any case, we survived, but it was difficult. Then, last night, word comes that a helicopter was dropping a shipping container full of food. We told them where to drop it, and down it came. It wasn't until they actually had the thing on the deck that I noticed it was a dragon making the delivery and not a helicopter. We managed to get off a few shots at it as it flew away, but by then the crate was already deposited. I sent guards to keep it closed, but by the time they got there, the starving masses had already ripped it open. The rest you can probably figure out. Wasn't pretty."

"I see." I nod slowly. Ahead, I can see that we're coming to the bottom of the staircase. "I'm terribly sorry you had to deal with something like that, but you're safe now. I hope."

As I come to the bottom, I find another door. It's locked as well, though several large dents inward seem to indicate that the monsters were certainly trying their hardest to breach the door. I press my ear up against it but hear nothing. Quietly,

I hold out my hand, and the captain passes down his key. It takes me a few moments to get the door open since the monsters bent the lock slightly when they dented the door, but I do manage to get it open.

At that point, we step out into a hallway that just feels like it belongs on a ship. I mean, think of a stereotypical navy ship hall, and this is it: bulkheads every few feet, everything made of metal, incomprehensible script scrawled all across plaques that sure *ought* to be telling us where to go. I glance back at the captain, and he nods off to my right.

"Go that way." His voice is quiet.

"Thanks." I turn in that direction, then slowly start creeping forward. The hall gets darker this way, and I can see shadowy forms moving up ahead. Thankfully, if we do encounter more werewolves, they're not the trickiest things in the world to get rid of. They're not the nicest things either, but beggars, choosers, and all that.

Anyway, I continue to creep onward and see another open door not far away. I can't tell exactly what's through the door, but it almost looks electric to me. I slow down, then carefully creep up to glance through the gap.

Inside, I see a handful of cylinders rising up from the floor in a large room. Computers line the walls, displaying a large number of statistics and charts and graphs and other such things. Pulses of electricity flicker from coils on top of the cylinders, zapping and flickering here and there.

Oh, and, of course, there are a handful of werewolves prowling about.

I take a deep breath, then step through the door. "Hi, everyone! Is this the officer's club?"

Every werewolf in the place turns and looks at me. Now, I didn't describe them perfectly earlier, so I'll do it now. Though they have the form of a wolf, each one of them *does* walk on its hind legs and stands about seven feet tall. Their front hands are still human-looking, with opposable thumbs and fingers, but with long claws at the end of each finger. And their eyes glow red. Anyhow, that sums them up, and as I stand there, they snarl and start to stalk forward, slowly and purposefully.

"I guess not." I draw out my Photonic Dagger alongside my Enlarged Dagger. "You know, you all should really be more welcoming of guests!"

I know it's not the greatest banter in the world, but it keeps them distracted. Two of them snarl and race forward at me, and in such closed quarters, I know I'm going to be in a much tighter spot than usual. One of them sweeps out at me with a massive paw. I try to slash off its wrist with the Enlarged Dagger, but as my blade hits, I'm simply knocked aside. The massive claws slash across my chest, opening rather large wounds, and I do my best to keep from crying out.

[RazorEdge: Ouch! That looks painful!!!]

[ViperQueen: Jason! You've got to watch yourself better!]

[DarkCynic: I'd have known that a simple dagger wouldn't be able to cut through a werewolf's wrist.]

I reel backward from the attack, and the werewolf springs forward. That's its big mistake. I still have the dagger in my hand, and its underbelly is a whole lot less protected than its arm. It snarls and tries to bite me, but I duck underneath its head and stab it deep in the gut. The blade sticks in up to the hilt, and with all my might, I rip it back out. The werewolf staggers, and with that, I spin to the next one.

This werewolf is smarter and doesn't give me a chance to get in close. Alternating claws, it rushes at me, slashing and snapping at me faster than I can possibly follow. I'm forced backward, and I see another werewolf coming up from behind me. Thankfully, both of them are so distracted that they don't see an arrow flash out of the hallway to finish off the werewolf that I stabbed.

That means that everything is going according to plan—or is at least enough.

The one behind me lunges, and I duck under its attack before spinning to slash up at it. My intention is to chop its head off, but it's too fast and backs up, so I only land a wound across its neck. The other werewolf snarls and lunges as well, and that one I'm not quite fast enough to dodge. I'm knocked backward into a computer but push myself away before it can take advantage of the situation. As it is, it leaps forward and throws a massive punch at me, and I only narrowly manage to dodge to the side. Sparks fly as it smashes a fist into the computer, and with that, I slash at the thing's face. My blade lands a strike over its eye, blinding it on its right side, and it snarls and slowly turns to me.

Thwick!

An arrow hits it in the shoulder, though it doesn't seem to take much notice. It slowly takes a step toward me, snarling . . . and then explodes. Bits and pieces of werewolf rain down around me, and I give a nod of satisfaction. The other werewolves in the area all glance over at Ali, and they charge forward, snarling and gnashing their teeth. One of them leaps . . . and that's when John steps into the battle.

He emerges from the hall and throws a massive punch,

hitting the lead werewolf in the face. That blow knocks it backward into the cylinders, and electricity explodes all across it. Another werewolf jumps at the two of them, and John catches it by the wrist, spins, and smashes *it* into the cylinders. This time the blow causes metal to crumple around the beast, destroying two of the odd devices. The roar of electricity is impossibly loud . . . and then entirely quiet. I let out a breath as one lone werewolf, crouching on the other side of the room, watches us with glowing eyes.

Suddenly, I become aware that it seems to be growing slightly larger, and its fur turns from brown to black.

[ShadowDancer: Hmm. That's not good.]

[ViperQueen: Are we about to see the end of our Jason???]

[FireStorm: Nah, he'll come through!]

With a snarl, the thing lunges forward, though not quite in the way I was expecting. Instead, it jumps to the side and digs its claws into the computer. Moving rapidly, it actually runs on the walls, racing around the side of the room. I spin to counter it, only for the monster to jump off the wall as it reaches the corner. It lands on the floor, springs, and hits me with the force of a freight train.

There's just no way to sugarcoat it: I'm slammed back into the far wall. I groan in pain as the werewolf snarls and slashes at me, and I take more than a few hits. Suddenly, I hear another growl, and fire flickers to life across the werewolf's coat. It pauses, then turns around to see Astrid standing there, snarling softly in the light.

[ChaosRider: I KNEW Astrid would work well here!]

The werewolf springs at Astrid, and she reacts instantly, ducking under the blow and biting the monster in the leg. It howls in pain, and she gives it another chomp, sending fire rolling up its torso. It breaks the lock and steps back, limping slightly, but I don't give it time to recover. Instead, blood dripping from several claw wounds, I run straight past Astrid and throw myself at the beast.

The two of us come together, my daggers flashing against its claws. I stab it in the chest, the gut, the arms, the legs, and slash it in a dozen other places. The werewolf, though, just *won't* go down and claws me in several places. It flips around and bites me on the left arm, but that only puts it in a good position for me to stab it behind the ear. I grit my teeth against the pain as I rip my dagger out, and the monster staggers as it draws back.

"Alright, Astrid," I murmur. "See what you can do."

Astrid nods, then growls. The metal plates of the deck begin to shiver, and the computers around the room all go dead. Suddenly, the remaining cylinders crumple up into balls and discharge massive blasts of electricity across the monster. It howls and falls to the ground, where a good portion of the deck peels up to fold itself around the creature. The werewolf thrashes as it tries to escape, but the deck only folds itself tighter and tighter, compressing the werewolf more and more. Within an instant, I can't see it. An instant later, blood begins to leak out through the rivets and gaps, and the beast falls dead.

"Good. That's done." John walks past me toward the other side of the room. "We need to keep moving."

"Uh . . ." The captain steps into the room, staring in horror at the carnage. "This isn't good."

"Why not?" Ali asks.

"Because this was the ballast room," the captain answers quietly. "Those generators powered the central gyroscope, and these computers coordinated the readings of the gyroscope with the rudders and pumps and weights and other such things."

"What are you saying?" I ask, even though I have a pretty good idea. Suddenly, the ship tilts just a little bit more, perhaps another half degree. I hear something crash in an adjacent room. This isn't good and is rapidly getting worse.

"Without this room, and with the fact that we're already taking on water, I estimate that the time until we sink has decreased rapidly," the captain says. "We need to get to the survivors, and we need to get to them *now*."

I give a nod, then turn in the direction we need to be heading. "Then let's do it and hope that our ride gets here in time."

CHAPTER ELEVEN

The four of us quickly leave the ballast room behind and continue to head down the maintenance passageway. I don't see any other werewolves, which is good, though I certainly see plenty of signs that monsters have been about. Claw marks on the bulkheads, blood staining the decks. Here and there, tattered uniforms lie about, though I don't see any bodies. I don't know if that means that the injured crew were eaten or transformed, and, frankly, I don't know which is worse.

"Hey, chat!" I call out as we reach another door at the end of the hall. "Can some of you get in contact with Mr. Wang? I need to know what the plan for the extraction is, if he can be here in time, that sort of thing."

[RazorEdge: We'll get ahold of him, don't you worry!]

[ViperQueen: Yeah! For sure! Happy to be of help to our beloved Jason!]

[DarkCynic: I'm sure he'll be here in a jiffy!]

I smile and nod in thanks, then step up to the door and nod at the captain.

"When you go through this, you'll be in the foremost engine room," the captain explains. "The survivors are all in the rear engine room. It's a big place. Don't be fooled—lots of places for things to hide." He's starting to look a bit more nervous. "Oh, I wish I had my gun with me."

"If it's any help, it wouldn't do you any good." I slowly turn the wheel set in the door, retracting the latches. "Now, let's check this out."

Slowly, I push the door open, and we all step through. The inside of the engine room, all things considered, is about as stereotypical as you might expect. From wall to wall, it's as wide as the entire ship, and the walls slope inward toward the bottom of the room, matching the curve of the hull. The very bottom of the room, where the walls meet, is filled with a massive engine. It's a twisting hive of tubes and pistons and burners and all sorts of other gadgets I couldn't even begin to understand. The catwalks of the room run around above the engine, with stairs and ladders leading down to it here and there. At the back of the room, the far opposite end from us, a massive shaft runs through a wall. I whistle softly as I look it over, then cross my arms.

"Quite a place you have here." I nod to the captain. "What sorts of monsters do you think are living here?"

"I haven't the faintest idea," the captain mutters. "Hopefully, nothing, but—"

Hissssssssssssssss!

The noise isn't a snake's hiss, but it certainly comes from a monster. I don't have any hope that the engine room is abandoned, since Mr. Wang clearly told us that the monsters were trying to get to the remaining civilians. Indeed, the single door

I can see leading into the rear engine room is heavily dented and scratched, though it *does* look like they were unable to breach it. Small miracles, I suppose. Carefully, I start walking out along the catwalk, gesturing back at the others.

"Ali, you hang back with the captain. Keep him protected and cover us as you can," I order. "John, you come along with me but hang back a bit. Keep an eye on everything, alright?"

"Got it." John flashes a thumbs-up. Slowly, I start forward and notice a handful of beady-looking eyes peering out of the darkness. I'm being watched . . . The only question is, who's doing the watching and what are they going to do about my presence? The hissing noise begins to grow louder . . . And, as I cross the halfway mark, shadows race forward from the engines.

Rats.

Big rats.

The monsters, just like their smaller counterparts, swarm up the ladders, the stairs, even the sides of the hull as they decide that I'm worth taking out. The things are *huge*, at least for rats, though they're admittedly a good bit smaller than your average human. Each one is probably two to three feet in height and has sharpened teeth that flicker in the light.

Oh, and they also have a *lot* of weapons—mostly tools used to work on the engines.

I brace myself as they come charging forward. The first of the creatures throws a pipe wrench at me, which I narrowly dodge. With that, I slash my Photonic Dagger through its neck, dropping it to the ground. The rest of the rats don't take notice, though, and they simply swarm forward with all their might. Holding the Photonic Dagger in one hand and the Enlarged Dagger in the other, I throw myself forward into their midst.

Rarely have I ever hacked or slashed quite as fast as this time. They come so fast, climbing over the bodies of the dead without a moment's pause, flinging themselves upon me without abandon. A hammer comes crashing down on my head. A pipe cutter latches down on my leg. I grit my teeth against the pain and spin around and around as I try to cut through the creatures.

"Ahhh!"

Bong!

John, swarmed with the beasts, punches one into the air, then grabs another around the neck, spins, and throws it into the hull hard enough to dent it. His punches come fast, but as the creatures swarm all over him, it doesn't look like he can really get any good leverage against them. Ali's arrows come fast and thick, but even she can only do so much. Slowly, John is forced backward as he flails against the beasts.

Suddenly, teeth slam into my ankle, biting *deep*. I gasp in pain as they chomp down on the bone itself, grinding down into the base of my foot.

[Condition: Sick. You will experience some symptoms for the next 00:01:00.]

Almost instantly, a wave of nausea hits me, and I vomit across the deck. More of the creatures spring up onto my back and knock me down, and I find it almost impossible to resist them. My entire body feels cold, achy, and my nose begins to run. I stand back up, only to sneeze in the face of one of the rats. Now, my augmented sneeze is powerful enough to knock it backward, which is entertaining, but I'd much rather have just chopped its head off.

"Jason! Are you okay?" Ali calls out.

"Right as—"

Before I can finish, tiny hands grab me. I suddenly feel myself lifted up into the air, and without preamble, I'm thrown over the side of the walkway. The world spins around me, and with a mighty *crash*, I come down hard on something sharp. Metal things stab into my back, and I groan and roll off, only to fall down to the curved hull just next to the engine itself.

[Condition: Sick. You will experience some symptoms for the next 00:00:15.]

Fifteen seconds or thirty minutes, it all feels the same. I slowly climb back to my feet as the monsters start leaping down from the catwalk above, throwing their tools at me. A screwdriver slams into my arm, an entire toolbox bounces off my head. I sway . . . And then, finally, the effects wear off.

"There we go!" My strength returns, and I reach out and grab one of the creatures by the tail. With all my might, I sling it around and around, then throw it at another of the monsters. They go down in a heap, and I turn to the engine and start climbing.

It takes me a mere instant to clamber up onto a large block, which contains a large number of pistons and such things. As I take my stance, the monsters come swarming up all around me, and I transform my Photonic Dagger into a sword. I need the range, that's for sure.

The sword of light blazes with brilliance as I slash it back and forth, cutting down the creatures as they try to climb up. Dozens emerge from the depths, all desperately trying to get to me, but I drive them all back. Sometimes I kill them outright, sometimes I'm only able to wound them, but none of them manage to lay a finger on me.

And then . . . And then I start to feel the air grow cold around me.

There are only a few reasons that ever happens, and it's usually because I'm about to be attacked by a spectral creature. I spin around and find a wraith hovering just above the engine block a few feet away. It lets out a scream, then transforms into a dark cloud and flashes forward, hitting me in the chest. I'm knocked clean off the engine block, only to tumble down into a mass of gears and pulleys. As I start trying to climb out, the wraith flashes into the machine itself, and everything comes to life.

Gears grind, pulleys whir, and I suddenly find myself in *quite* a predicament. A normal person would have been killed instantly. As it is, I'm sucked down into the guts of the machine, where I'm battered about rather like a toy before being spat out the other side. My health has fallen to a mere 50 percent. I groan and slowly rise back to my feet.

Wham!

The wraith hits me again, tossing me up into the air. I come down on top of the pistons, and the wraith dematerializes and flashes down into the engine. Suddenly, a large chunk of metal slams into me from underneath, knocking me back to my feet. The pistons are starting to move, and I'm right in their midst.

As I stagger backward from the initial impact, I fall right into the next piston, which smashes me up into the air. I come down hard, meeting another one that's erupting straight up to meet me in the face. Groaning, I desperately stagger to my feet and try to find a way to escape, only for the wraith to flash out of the machine and hit me in the chest again. This time I come down on the flywheel that turns the enormous shaft. The thing begins to whine, and with all the titanium fins that the flywheel possesses, I'm certain that it will kill me. Desperate, I jump backward, only for more of the rats to begin jumping down onto me.

The wheel spins to life, and I punch the closest rat in the face. It staggers, and I sling it into the flywheel, a bit gratified as it turns into a little red mist. I snatch out my dagger and stab several of the other rats, but more are coming. I'm being forced backward by the sheer volume of them, pushed ever closer to that spinning wheel, pressed ever closer to my doom.

"I . . . will not . . . go down this way!" I bite out. With all my might, I reach out and catch hold of a small tube. It's not much, and it's *burning* hot, but it steadies me. With all my might, I swing myself upward and onto it. It rattles about, unstable, but I'm away from the rats. I see shadows flickering about and know that the wraith will emerge in a moment, but . . . this time I'm ready for it.

As the wraith erupts from the engine, I grab it with my hands. It's tricky, and it can shapeshift, but it's not *entirely* incorporeal. The monster screams and thrashes about, nearly knocking me into the flywheel, but I maintain my grip. Then, with all my might, I begin to pull. I stretch the wraith as hard as I can manage, and . . . finally . . . it snaps.

Boom!

A resounding detonation shakes the hull, and I'm thrown backward to slam into the wall. I slide back down toward the engine, but as the flywheel winds down, I don't care nearly so much. As I slid up to the edge of it, I groan and force myself upright, then stagger toward a ladder. My health is sitting at 20 percent, which isn't great but isn't terrible either. I open up a Pumped! and start to drink it, allowing my health to rise. Meanwhile, the rats all around me begin to shrink back down, black smoke trailing up from their fur. Apparently, these weren't crew but were simply ship rats being manipulated by one of the monsters. Interesting, indeed.

By the time I've climbed back up to the walkway, the rats have entirely reverted to their natural form, and the battle seems to be over. John walks up to me and helps me the last of the way up, and Ali walks over to join me as well. The captain's eyes are wide, and he seems more than ready to get out. Suddenly, I notice a notification blinking in front of me.

[You have leveled up!]

[Congratulations! You are now Level 40!]

[Please accept from the following rewards:]

[. . .]

I decide not to focus on the reward at that moment and, instead, turn my attention to the bulkhead before us. The monsters are dead, at least in this area, and that means we can get out of here.

Now, we just have to make sure there aren't any *other* complications that we're forgetting about.

CHAPTER TWELVE

As I walk up to the bulkhead, I can hear muffled voices behind. I knock a few times, letting a loud hollow sound echo through the air.

"Hello? Can anyone hear me?"

There's a long pause before anyone dares to answer. Finally, a young woman's voice comes warily through the metal.

"Yes, we can hear you. Who are you?"

"My name is Jason Lee. I'm here with a small group of hunters. We're going to get you out." I hold my breath, hoping that she believes me.

"This isn't the first time someone has tried to get inside. Only a few hours ago, a member of the crew tried to convince us that *he* was a rescue party. The only reason we got away alive was because one of his co-workers recognized his voice and knew he was being manipulated. I won't risk anyone's life in here."

"Then you know you have no choice but to trust us," I

answer. "The ship is taking on water; you can feel it tipping. We don't have long before this place goes under."

There's a terribly long pause. Finally, the woman's voice comes back.

"We'd all rather drown than be eaten."

I sigh, closing my eyes for a moment. "Is there anything we can to do prove to you that we're not monsters?"

"Nothing comes to mind." The woman is frank. "We're on a cruise ship in the middle of the ocean. No one is going to care about us, not when the whole world is being overrun. We're not upset or angry about that fact, and we're not going to simply give up and *let* ourselves die, but we've also accepted the fact that we're *going* to die. That may not make sense to you beasts, but if you had a soul, you'd understand."

"No. No, that makes perfect sense to me." I sigh deeply. "There's something entirely human about it, I think. You have to face the reality handed to you. Fighting it will only cause problems. That said, you aren't going to do anything that violates your humanity or your dignity." I pause in thought. "Now, you have to understand where *I'm* coming from. Mr. Wang sent us here with explicit instructions to get everyone out, and a great many people are watching my every action. Plus, you know, I'm not going to just leave you here to die. I can't promise I'll get everyone out of here alive, but I can get some of you, and if you stay here, you *will* all die."

There's another long pause, and I know they're discussing it among themselves. Finally, the voice comes back.

"Did you say Mr. Wang? What's his first name?"

"I wish I knew," I answer, glancing at Ali and John. They

both just shrug. "But if I *did* know, I'm sure he'd make me pay him a hundred bucks or something for the privilege."

There's another muffled discussion. A moment later, the sound of a wheel turning echoes through the air, and the door pops slowly open. The captain runs past me to leap inside, and I step through with the other two hunters.

The rear engine room is far less spacious than the front engine room. It's only twenty or thirty feet long and has a *lot* more machinery packed inside. Only a few dim bulbs light the place, which show almost a hundred people packed in there. They're all covered in grease and dirt, oil and muck. Water stands on the ground, rising almost imperceptibly. The ship tilts again as I stand there, this time almost by a full degree, and I grip a handrail to steady myself.

The woman who was doing the speaking pushes a bit of hair back out of her face and shuts the door behind me. "So, you're real."

"We are indeed." John flexes his hands, then begins clucking his tongue. "Interesting."

"There's a lot of them," I say. "This is going to take some work. It's good, don't get me wrong, but that's going to be a long trail of people, and there are a *lot* of monsters between here and the deck."

"If we take the forward hatch, I think we can get there faster," the captain says. He's now standing with several other crew members, all of whom look just as beaten down as everyone else. "These men say that they managed to seal it off before the monsters got there. Once we make it through the forward engine room, we ought to have a clean shot up to the deck."

"That's the best idea I can think of," I say, glancing at Ali and John. "Any objections?"

"None that I know of." John shakes his head. "We just need to know if the transport is here yet."

[Riftwatch: A Mysterious Benefactor has sent you a gift!]

I blink in surprise at the notification, then open the interface. With a flash, a small cell phone appears in my palm, which almost immediately starts to ring. Slowly, I lift it up to my ear, and I'm somehow unsurprised when I hear Mr. Wang's voice.

"Hey! Looking good!" He sounds pleased. "You got to the survivors! Tell me, is there a girl named Akira anywhere among them?"

I slowly lower the phone. "Akira? Is there an Akira here?"

A young woman not far from the door, a girl who looks like she could be Mr. Wang's twin sister, slowly steps forward. "That would be me."

"She's here," I confirm.

"May I talk to her?" Mr. Wang sounds excited. "She's my twin sister."

"So *that's* why you wanted us to come take on this cruise ship." I suddenly understand things a bit better. Oh well. We're rescuing people, so I can hardly complain. "I'll pass the phone to her, but before that, I need to know a few details. When is the transport getting here?"

"About thirty minutes. We're loading up a few hunters to protect the plane when it lands on the deck and to help get everyone inside. We'll be launching in five minutes, and then it's just a matter of getting there. You went a good bit faster than I was expecting."

I lower the phone and glance at the captain. "How long do you think it'll take us all to get to the deck via that route you mentioned?"

The captain frowns in thought. "To get everyone there? Ten minutes."

"Then we'll leave the engine room in twenty." I turn my attention back to Mr. Wang. "Much appreciated. Here's your sister."

I pass the phone to Akira, who happily accepts the phone and lifts it to her ear. As they start to talk, a few of the other passengers start to grumble about not getting help from *their* relatives, but I ignore them—mostly. Instead, I slip over to the captain, along with John and Ali. We keep our voices low, but in the near silence of the engine room, every noise we make echoes so that everyone can almost certainly hear it.

"What now?" John murmurs. "We just run up and out, and that's it?"

"I think so." The captain nods, then sighs. "Honestly, I wish we could just blow the whole place up. I'd sure hate to leave this wreck for someone else to come along and find, you know? Even pirates don't deserve to be eaten by werewolves."

"The ship is actively sinking." I raise an eyebrow. "Won't that get rid of things well enough?"

"Yeah, but I reckon that some of these guys can swim. We're hardly in the arctic." The captain shrugs. "Besides, in the passenger part, there are plenty of things that can float. Beds, doors, you name it. If the ship keeps sinking nice and slowly, they'll all just be able to float away without any issues. Now, if we were to blow the place up . . ." He mimes an explosion.

"Do you have the ability to do that?" I ask, hardly daring to hope.

"I reckon so," a man next to the captain says. "As long as the anti-aircraft guns haven't been emptied, we should have a handful of shells leftover from that. Aim one or two of those at the fuel tanks, and this place will vanish in a fireball like you've never seen before."

I stroke my chin. "And how would we do that?"

"I could come with you, tell you where to aim," the man says, shrugging.

"We destroyed the gun computer on the bridge."

"But we could just do it manually," the man continues, protesting. "It could work."

"But what about all the people left on board?" Ali asks. "The waiter, and the others shown on the tablet? If we just blow the thing up, we're saving lives at the expense of lives. That's not math that adds up."

"I agree," I say. "That said, if we could give them all a chance to escape, we could make it work."

"And how could we do that?" The captain snorts. "This ship is *crawling* with monsters."

"We draw them off," the other man says, speaking up once more. "Jason and I will go up to the gun. I'll start working on it, and Jason will do something to draw the attention of the monsters on board. We'll use the intercom system to make an announcement. The monsters can't understand human speech anymore—we're pretty confident of that. They'll all come back to try and kill us, and then Jason fights them off while I set up the gun. When everything's ready, I fire, and we escape along with everyone else."

[LunarEclipse: That sounds like the most epic thing I've ever heard of!!! DO IT!!!!!!!!!!!!]

[FireStorm: Yeah! I'd love to see a cruise ship explode!!!]

[ViperQueen: I mean, that's a good plan even without the gun. If you don't draw the monsters away, you'll be leaving people to die.]

"I like it," I say. "The only issue is with how to draw the monsters away. Making noise will only attract the ones that can hear us." I take the tablet from Ali and open it up. While the vast majority of the survivors on the ship are clustered in the engine room, I can see a dozen more spread throughout the rest of the vessel. "We make an announcement on the intercom telling everyone to run, but . . . we need something more. Something the monsters can't resist. Some sort of monster bait."

"The only monster bait I've ever seen would be ordinary humans," John answers. "They can't seem to resist attacking any that they see, or smell, or otherwise sense. The issue is getting that bait to them in the first place."

I nod, then frown. "Alright, then. New plan. I can take this tablet and personally run past every single one of these rooms. I'll draw away any monsters, just from these locations. That way we're not trying to attract the whole vessel."

"That's too much for one person." Ali shakes her head. "What if we all do it? There aren't supposed to be any monsters along the route that these people will be taking."

"Not *supposed* to be is too much of a risk. Besides, if any of them happen to notice a group of a hundred people, it's going to be mighty hard to deter them without a show of force."

"Ahem."

The voice is soft and elegant, and I jump slightly as I notice Elrith, my elven butler, standing at attention just next to me. Not a bit of the dirt or grime from the engine room seems to touch him, and he gives a small bow. Others flinch back from him as well, though more than a few others suddenly seem to show a great deal of interest in him.

"Forgive me, but it would seem that there's an easy solution." He gives a bow. "Jason is in possession of a number of *very* capable creatures that could easily assist. Bjorn, Astrid, Burnie, Lightfax, Ratatoskr, and I would all work quite well for such a thing."

"I thought you were a pacifist," I comment wryly.

"I am indeed. I will not lift a hand against the foul beasts, but if I can draw them away, I would be happy to assist." Elrith nods, pausing. "And, of course, the others wouldn't hesitate to sink their teeth into those grisly, dark monsters."

There's a long pause while everyone considers the options.

[RazorEdge: I like it! It sounds like a great plan to me!]

[IceQueen: And that's only two survivors per pet! That's totally doable!]

[LunarEclipse: It's the best plan I can see!]

I have to agree with LunarEclipse. There are flaws, to be certain, but I don't really see any other options. "Alright." I shrug. "We'll just have to do it."

"How much longer do we have?" the captain asks.

I check the clock on my interface. "It looks like we have about twenty-five minutes before our transport gets here, which means you have fifteen before you need to get out of here. I'll leave right now with . . ." I glance at the man next to the captain, who introduces himself quickly.

"Carter."

"Carter." I turn toward the door. "We're going to have to time this right, everyone. We won't fire the gun until we're sure everyone's on board the plane. Just make sure that we get on it too, alright?"

Heads nod across the engine room, and I quickly slip toward the exit. As I get there, I find Akira still talking to Mr. Wang, a wide smile on her face. She gives me a thankful nod, and with that, I step out through the door into the forward engine room. This is going to be tricky, but it's definitely feasible.

I only hope that it costs as few lives as possible.

CHAPTER THIRTEEN

Carter and I quickly step out onto the walkway, and the survivors pull the door shut behind us. The clock is ticking, and we have a lot of ground to cover. I'm reminded of the giant tentacle thing in the stairwell, and I really hope that we don't have to go up to that particular area. In any case, I quickly open up my pocket dimension, and all the monsters taking part in the operation come out.

"Here." I flip around the tablet so they can see what I'm looking at. "Find these people. Get them to safety. You can decide among yourselves who you'll be taking, but make sure that they make it to the upper deck, alive, in exactly . . . twenty-three minutes."

My pets all give me a nod, or as close to it as they can manage, then turn around and race off. As they vanished through the doors at the other end, Carter takes off at a run.

"What's it like having all those things constantly at your beck and call?" he asks.

"It's nice. They're good and loyal." I flash a small smile. "And it keeps me humble. Or humbler, I suppose. John can just punch his way out of any situation he wants. With the help of my pets, I can deal out more damage and take on larger groups of monsters than he can, but only because of their help."

"I sure wish I had something like that," Carter says as we run back into the maintenance halls. I see the body of a werewolf, a new one, covered in scorch marks. My pets aren't pulling their punches, it would seem. "I have a gerbil back at home. Well, had. Once we get back to the mainland, I'm heading to my apartment for a week's rest if it's still there. I sure hope he's alright, but it'll depend on whether or not my house-sitter is alive and still taking care of him—or whether the *house* is still there or not."

"I'm sure everything will be okay." I smile at him. "And hey, if you did lose him, maybe I can get you a giant gerbil of fire and destruction or something, eh?"

Carter laughs. "Now *that* would be epic! I'd have a way to impress girls, that's for sure."

The two of us continue to banter as we make our way through the lower portions of the ship. Suddenly, I hear something ahead of us, and I slow to a walk. Carter drops behind me, and I creep forward. We're nearing the section where we'll have to start climbing upward, and I don't expect that it will be easy.

Ahead, there's a larger cross hallway, though it's still one for the crew. I slip into the shadow of a bulkhead as we approach and hear a growl from the other side. Slowly, a monster stalks past: one of the black werewolves. I can't tell if it's alone or not. Ordinarily, I'd just fight the thing, but here, all my pets are helping other people, and John and Ali are elsewhere. I have no backup, and on top of that, I'm trying to actively protect someone else. The beast stops and sniffs the air, and I steel myself for battle. Then, with a snuffle, it moves on, and we're left alone.

"Where are the guns located?" I ask quietly.

"Just above the bridge," Carter whispers back. "Our best bet is going up to the bridge, then taking the stairs there up to the top. Do you know how to get to the captain's private staircase?"

"I think so." I poke my head out into the hall. The werewolf is still there, but its back is turned, and it's a good fifty feet off. We need to head in the opposite direction, which is good. "Alright. You lead the way. Move slow, but if I tell you to run, you do it."

"Got it."

Carter quietly steps out into the hall, then starts walking in the right direction. I follow, and together, we creep along quietly through the depths of the ship. I don't quite know what alerts me to trouble, but suddenly, the hairs on the back of my neck prickle up. I glance over my shoulder, and, sure enough, the werewolf is watching us.

Just like us, it's creeping along, hardly making a noise. It's maybe twenty feet behind us.

"Run! Now!"

Carter springs forward like he was shot from a gun. The werewolf does the same, and I draw out my Enlarged Dagger. There's not enough time for anything more, as the creature body-slams me with unfathomable force. I'm slammed to the ground. Claws dig into my shoulder . . . And then, with a mighty spring, it leaps over me.

"Carter!"

I call out his name and have the presence of mind to reach up and grab the monster's tail. Bones pop in both my arm *and* its tail, and it slams to the ground a few feet away. As I jump back to my feet, the black werewolf spins around, spittle flying from its jaws, and it lunges forward at me.

I respond by stabbing upward as hard as I can and hit it underneath the jaw. The blade slams up into the roof of its mouth, and it snarls with anger. It punches me in the face, then slashes its claws across my chest. I stagger backward, and it reaches up, rips the dagger out of its own body, and casts it to the side. I brace myself and run at the monster, drawing out my Photonic Dagger. It transforms into a sword just as I hit the werewolf, and I slam the blade into its belly.

The glowing tip of the sword comes out its back, and I spin and shove it off. It falls to the ground, though it's not dead yet. Slowly, its hands tighten, and it starts pulling itself back up.

I simply grit my teeth and chop off its head.

As the werewolf collapses to the ground, I glance around for my dagger, but I don't see it anywhere. Ahead, I see Carter pull the door open and step inside, letting out a scream as he does so. Behind the door, maybe a hundred feet in, I can see another of the black werewolves snarling and charging forward.

"Skill: Speed!"

The world around me slows, and I race forward just as fast as I possibly can. The werewolf doesn't slow nearly as much as I'd like, but its speed is reduced to a jog instead of a sprint. We both reach the doorway at the same time, and I slash my dagger through its neck before stepping inside and pulling the door shut. The world speeds back up, claws scrape across the entrance, and on the other side of the door, there comes a loud *thud*.

"I don't think it's dead, but it *is* slowed down," I call to Carter as he pounds up the stairs. "Move!"

The two of us are moving at top speed as we come to the top of the stairs. Down below, I hear a mighty crash as something gets the door open. Carter flings the top door open, only to step back in fear. I run past him, knowing that we don't have time for delays. Unfortunately . . . Well, the bridge, which we so painstakingly cleared, is now rather infested once again.

A great many of the humanoid crab monsters have now taken it over and are picking their way through the rubble and wreckage that we left. They all turn to face the two of us, and I quickly pull Carter through and slam the door shut. "You get to the next staircase. Leave the rest to me!"

He bolts along the side of the wall, and the crab monsters rush at him. I run forward to intercept, throwing a punch at the face of the first one to reach us. It doesn't kill it, but it does make the thing reel backward slightly, which is enough for me. Another steps clearly into Carter's path, and I throw my dagger as hard as I can. The weapon hits the monster in the shoulder, right between two plates, and it screams and spins out of the way. I snatch the weapon back out of the thing as we pass, and Carter reaches the next door.

Wham!

The rear door is blasted clean off its hinges as the black werewolf comes stalking through. Its eyes burn with an inner fire, and it looks upon the two of us with unbridled fury and hatred. One of the crab monsters runs past, and the werewolf simply reaches out, grabs the thing, and crushes its skull in a single movement. Carter gasps, and quickly flings the doorway open.

I follow, then pull it shut. I can't spin the wheel fast enough to lock it tightly behind us.

WHAM!

The werewolf smashes into the other side, denting it rather badly. Quickly, I open up my pocket dimension and draw out my last creature, the Living Bomb, Blub. I hold him up to let him inflate and hover in front of the doorway.

"When that thing gets through, you let him have it. Come find me afterward."

Blub-blub! Blub!

The words echo in my mind, and I nod and race up the stairs. At the top, Carter throws open one final door, and the two of us stagger out onto the highest position on the cruise ship.

KA-BOOM!

Smoke billows up from below, and I glance down into the turmoil. I can't tell for sure what happened, if the werewolf was killed or not, but if it's alive, it's sure to be wounded. I watch for a moment, then turn my attention to the antiaircraft battery.

It's a collection of four barrels, all in a line, with an automatic loading mechanism that pulls shells up from below. The thing is enormous: each barrel is twice as long as my body, and big enough around for me to crawl through. I whistle softly as I look it over, but Carter simply runs up to a small set of hydraulic levers.

"The people who built this wanted to be able to fire it even if we got shut down." Carter starts pulling levers, and the barrels of the gun slowly turn away from the sky. "The pirates sometimes try to jam our systems."

"And it can be turned to shoot down at the ship?" I ask. Sure enough, the fitting where the gun is mounted actually sits fairly high off the ground, and the barrels slowly lower to point almost straight down.

"It was determined that if pirates ever got the ship, destroying it was preferable to allowing them to steal it away entirely," Carter mutters, trying to focus. "The captain told us that we were never, ever to actually do it, but . . . desperate times, and all that."

Something echoes up the stairs, and I turn in that direction as something slowly emerges from the smoke. It's the werewolf, charred and bleeding from a dozen cuts but still very much alive.

"You *again?* I thought if anything, I'd have to fight off some of the crab people." I draw out the sword of light. In the daylight, the effect is somewhat diminished, but it's still an impressive weapon, nevertheless. "Alright. You want to dance? Let's—"

Something skitters on the ground behind me, and I risk a quick glance to see several spiders climbing up over the edge of the roof, eyes gleaming. Their fangs glisten with venom, and I draw in a deep breath.

"Alright, Carter. You stay on those guns and keep your eyes closed."

Carter nods and squeezes his eyes shut, and the werewolf lunges forward. I slash upward at it, landing a long cut from its gut up to its chest, then punch it in the side of the head. That sends it reeling, and I lap back, slashing one of the spiders open as I go. More of them are coming, and as the werewolf charges again, I run in a circle around Carter, slashing at the spiders with everything I have.

The next several moments are complete and utter chaos. I slash at the spiders just as fast and as hard as I can, knocking away the attacks of the werewolf whenever it comes close. By now, the beast seems mad with pain, and it claws at the deck, tearing long gashes in the metal. I cut yet another spider in half, then charge at the werewolf. As it swings at me, I drop down, slide underneath it, and stab the thing in the gut. It howls and staggers, and as I come up behind it, I stab the sword deep into its back.

That really does something. Blood drips down out of its mouth as it spins away and rips the handle of the blade out of my grasp. I quickly open up my inventory and draw out the Enlarged Dagger in one hand and the Seeking Dagger in the other. I haven't used the Seeking Dagger in ages and quickly fling it almost straight behind me. It vanishes, and I lunge forward just as fast as I can go. The werewolf snarls and leaps . . . and the Seeking Dagger hits it in the side of the neck.

Blood spurts across the deck as the weapon bites deep, and the werewolf staggers and falls headlong across the metal.

[You have leveled up!]

[Congratulations! You are now Level 41!]

I nod grimly, then leap over the body to hack away several

spiders that are coming quickly. Carter suddenly opens his eyes and looks up, and a grin comes across his face.

"There's our ride!"

I follow his gaze, and, sure enough, a large plane is shooting across the waves, flying low, angling toward our position. Several small dragons fly along behind it, though guns from the plane keep them at bay. As it approaches the cruise ship, the wings tilt upward and bring it to a hover. Smaller jet engines roar to life underneath the belly of the plane as well, helping the wing engines in their task. Slowly, it lands—at least partially—on the deck of the cruise ship. Monsters come surging out of the ship's doorways even as hunters leap down from the plane to fight them back.

"There they are!" I point as a hatch pops open and John climbs up. He starts helping people from below, one after another after another. I hold my breath, watching closely as each and every person gets free. I don't see my pets, but it's very possible that they went back into my pocket dimension on their own terms once they got the survivors back to the main group.

The battle is fierce across the deck. I see two hunters fall, victims of poisoned barbs shot by a group of ape-men, but those are the only casualties. Ten minutes pass, and with a roar, the plane slowly takes off. It rises into the sky, slowly and carefully, and then starts to drift over toward me and Carter.

"Alright." I give Carter a nod. "Time to light this place up."

"Sounds good." He glances at me. "If we don't make it out, know that it's been a pleasure knowing you."

"Do you think we'll—"

BLAM!

The guns go off, all four barrels, with unfathomable force. Up close, the noise is simply incredible, and the fact that the shells punch straight through the roof of the ship and down through layer after layer of construction only adds to the noise. The briefest of pauses follows, only a fraction of a second, and the shells all explode.

The ship is tossed wildly about. I'm slung clean off the roof, but I manage to grab hold of the railing on my way over. Carter is tossed into the gun itself and knocked unconscious in an instant. Below me, flames erupt across the whole of the ship faster than I can blink. A powerful heat hits me, and, slowly, the ship begins to list.

Already beginning to sink, the ship lists faster and faster, soon falling to a solid forty-five-degree angle. Carter starts to slide toward the edge of the roof—the opposite side—and I grit my teeth, pull myself up, then leap forward and slide down just as fast as I can. I grab hold of his wrist just as he goes over the edge and only narrowly manage to grab hold of the railing with my other hand.

And . . . there I am: hanging from the railing as the ship tips over on top of us. Fire roars everywhere and even spreads across the ocean itself as burning fuel begins to float across the waves. Monsters scream and begin to leap into the sea, flailing about as they burn and drown at the same time.

"Jason!"

A rope falls down right next to me. Helpful, to be certain, except that both of my hands are in use at this exact moment. I consider trying to bite it to see if *that* works.

[RazorEdge: Oh, no!!! How's Jason going to get out of this one???]

[DarkCynic: He should just let go of Carter. Better only one of them die instead of both of them.]

[IceQueen: How can you be so heartless???]

An idea pops into my head to let go of the railing, push off, and grab hold of the rope. It's a desperate plan, sure, but it just might work. Suddenly, though, John slides down the rope and holds out his hand.

"Here! I've got you!"

He grabs hold of my arm, his claws digging into my skin a bit, and I gratefully let go of the railing. With that, we swing away from the ship, and the plane slowly begins to pull up into the sky.

There I am, dangling above a burning ocean. As the ship fades behind us, one final explosion sends fire and smoke billowing upward in an immense cloud, and I sigh in contentment.

Another problem solved, another day done.

Now it's time to go back home, wherever that is, and relax.

CHAPTER FOURTEEN

The plane soon comes roaring back to New York, where it lands at the airport. The survivors come staggering off the plane as first aid workers come racing over to help them. John and I shakily drop to the ground, and I pass Carter off to a paramedic. Ali jumps down from the plane as well, right alongside Akira Wang. A jeticopter comes roaring down only a few feet away, and it isn't long before we're well on our way.

In any case, none of us really talks until we arrive back at the club that's now apparently serving as our base of operations. There, Mr. Wang greets us with a wide smile. He and Akira embrace, and the two of them lead us back inside, where the robotic bartender has already served up a handful of drinks, along with a number of steaks, hamburgers, and other food.

"Now *this* is a club." John sits down at the bar and begins to eat without preamble. "Do you have any water? Sorry, need to stay hydrated."

Ali laughs and sits down next to him. She picks up a hamburger, and I suddenly realize just how hungry I am. I join the two of them, and Akira leaps up next to us. Belatedly, I realize that she's probably the hungriest of all of us, having been stuck down in the belly of that ship for so long, and I slide her the platter.

"Well, I simply can't thank you enough." Mr. Wang sits down at the end of the bar and sips a martini as he watches us. "You rescued my sister, along with a hundred other civilians. Well done, well done."

"Just glad to help," John says around a mouthful of food. "You could have told us that your sister was there, though."

"I didn't want you to worry about her," Mr. Wang answers. "I knew you would do what needed to be done to rescue each and every survivor. Not that you've shown such inclinations in the past, but if you knew ahead of time that one of them was related to me, it might negatively affect your performance. I wouldn't want that."

"My brother sees the bigger picture better than anyone I know," Akira says. "Sometimes he has funny ideas about how to get it all to fit together, but you can usually be pretty confident that it *will* all come together."

"Here, here." I chuckle. "In any case, another battle won. Hopefully, that's the last we hear of the stardust and the cursed food."

"I've been checking my scanners and contacts while you were inside, and I do believe that we've seen the last of it," Mr. Wang confirms. "I'll certainly let you know the moment we learn anything else. In the meantime, are you all ready to dive back into another dungeon, or do you need a rest?"

"I'd like to go check on my assorted projects," Ali says. "I want to make sure that the portal that sucked Jason away last night didn't do any damage. From what we can tell, it was targeted, so I *assume* it's all fine, but dark energy can do some nasty things. I also just have some general administrative work to handle."

Mr. Wang nods, then turns to John. "And you?"

"I'm afraid I need a bit of a break as well." He shrugs. "My sister has been DMing me about coming over to see her. I don't need much time, just a few hours, but I'd like to pop over and make sure she's okay. In today's world, a day's time can make quite a difference."

"Indeed. Well, my jeticopter is ready to take you anywhere you desire." Mr. Wang nods, then adds, "Within reason, of course."

"Of course."

With that, we all tuck into the food with a bit more gusto. As we all finish up, John and Ali wave goodbye and walk away, and I'm left with Mr. Wang and Akira. We retire to the chairs overlooking the city, and I fold my hands.

"Well, Jason, if you're up for it, I can have you a new project in just a few minutes." Mr. Wang pulls out his phone. "There are over a hundred businesses in my queue, all with dungeons that are affecting their operations. It would be worth a pretty penny, if you're interested."

"I've got enough money for the moment." I pause in thought. "That said, if you could take what I already have and buy me something, I'd sure appreciate it. I didn't spend much time there, but the apartment was nice back before it got blown up."

"But of course." Mr. Wang smiles. "I'll get you the nicest—"

"Really, it doesn't have to be much," I say, holding up my hand. "I'm really fine with something nominal. Frankly, before all this started, I lived in what would be considered poverty by a lot of people."

"Ah, but you forget!" Mr. Wang waves his own hand. "We have to be able to land the jeticopter wherever you're staying! That requires a certain level of space."

I sigh but give a nod. "Fair enough."

"If you don't mind my saying so, there seems to be something on your mind," Mr. Wang says. "Is there something that you're looking to pursue? An angle that I haven't considered?"

"Possibly." I give a small nod. "Did you watch the livestream where I was fighting my way through the dungeon I fell into this morning?"

"I'm afraid not. I was on a defense call with the Ministry of . . . Oh, I suppose that's not important." Mr. Wang takes a sip of his martini, then folded his hands. "No, I didn't. What happened?"

"At the end, there was a sword that appeared," I explain, "made of dragon bone, covered with runes. I've seen it once before, back in the Pumped! dungeon."

"Really?" Mr. Wang crosses his arms in concern. "That dungeon is actually doing quite well for me. We just opened it in Chicago, and we're running almost five hundred visitors at any given time—more at lunch and dinner hours."

"You opened it *this morning,*" I counter. "Dinner hasn't come yet!"

"Yes, but our projections are good." Mr. Wang shrugs. "Now, is there danger in that dungeon still?"

"I don't think so." I shake my head. "The sword was being wielded by a dragonspawn. When I defeated it, it killed itself with the sword. At that point, the sword seemed to absorb the dragonspawn and then flew through a portal. The same thing happened in the dungeon this morning, only . . ." I pause for a moment, uncertain of how exactly to explain it. "The monster that was killed with the sword *last* time appeared alongside the ogre mage today, helping him fight."

"Curious. It absorbs souls, then?" Akira asks, hazarding a guess. "And then the souls can come back out to fight if they need to?"

"That's sort of my working theory," I confirm. "Anyway, the fact that the thing showed up twice . . . I don't know. It makes me nervous, and I'd love to be able to look into it."

Mr. Wang picks up his phone and starts scrolling. "Ah-ha! Here's a picture of it. Hmm. Creepy-looking thing."

"I know, right?" I hold up my hands. "Like it's just going to kill you by looking at it, or something."

"Let me see . . ." Mr. Wang types a few more things into his phone. After a moment, he gives a nod. "We've got a hit."

I stand up to come look at the phone, but before I can, he hits a button and the glass wall darkens. The room goes pitch black, and then, with a flicker, a video appears on the glass.

"And there we go. Screen share," Mr. Wang murmurs. "Let me just get the sound . . . And then . . ."

The video begins, and I watch in horror from the first-person viewpoint of someone wielding two swords. They seem to have a small party with them, a healer and a tank, and are in a dungeon approaching a set of double doors.

"Alright! Patricia, hang back! I need to be healing at least ten HP every second," the voice calls out. It's male, so I can set that much in stone, at least. "Rodger, you're in front! I want this thing taken down. We've been chasing it for too long."

The video pauses, and Mr. Wang explains, "This video comes from the end of a several-hour chase sequence that took place while you were clearing out the cruise ship. Okay, moving forward."

The video starts again, and the tank, Rodger, runs forward and smashes through. The double-sworded man runs through the doors after him, and . . . There it stands.

Something holds the dragonbone sword firmly, a shadowy figure that seems to be made out of liquid darkness. The runes gleam with a dark reddish hue, and the enemy slowly takes its stance. It's trapped. And then, suddenly, it lunges forward.

I can hardly even see it move, but I *can* see the sword punch straight through Rodger's armor and out his back. He dissolves into smoke and dust in the blink of an eye. With that, the shadow moves forward again, shooting straight past the screen. The unnamed man spins around just in time to see the shadow cut the healer, a rather beautiful woman, clean in two. She dissolves into dust as well, and the monster turns to face the screen. It feels like I, myself, am staring deep into the beast's dark eyes.

"You . . ."

The unnamed man lets out a great many words that have been bleeped out—the streams are intended to be for all audiences, after all. The shadow lunges forward, and with that, the screen goes dark.

"That took place about thirty minutes ago." Mr. Wang puts down his phone, and the windows become transparent once more. "The dungeon isn't far from here. I could have you there in . . . oh, I'd say about twenty minutes."

"Do it." I nod in confirmation. "I need to get to the bottom of this. I can't imagine that it's a coincidence."

"I'll have the jeticopter on its way as soon as it finishes dropping off John." Mr. Wang stands up and puts his phone to his ear. With that, I lean back in my seat, only to blink in surprise.

"Right! I haven't gotten my reward for leveling up yet!"

Akira suddenly seems interested. "What does that entail? I'm rather fascinated by you hunters, the way you can just kill anything and everything that comes your way."

"It's actually pretty boring." I open my inventory and do a moment of scrolling. "Wow. That cruise ship was *brutal.* I lost three of my best weapons."

[ShadowDancer: Wait, what? I didn't see that!]

[DarkCynic: I saw you lose two!]

[FireStorm: Wait, WHAT???]

I smile at the chat, then give a nod. "Yup. I lost the Dagger of Damage, the Seeking Dagger, and the Photonic Dagger. And since the Photonic Dagger could turn into a sword, I suppose you could say I lost four weapons." I quickly lay out the rest of my weapons. "All I have now are the Dagger of Kings—which is just a fancy, decorative thing—the Dagger of Doom, the Rainbow Dagger, the Enlarged Dagger, and then . . ." I pause as I see Beowulf's Dagger. I don't really know whether to claim that one or not. Right alongside it is Ascalon, which I slowly draw out into the light. It shivers with internal energy, and Akira whistles.

"Now *that's* a weapon."

"Problem is, I'm not really a sword user." I slowly place the weapon with the others. "I don't mind them, and they're useful every now and again, but it's not ever going to be my main weapon. Alright, here we go. I got a reward at level forty. Let's see what we're looking at."

My inventory opens with a ding, and a message appears.

[Please accept from the following rewards:]

[Weapon]

[Monster]

[Skill]

My chat immediately fills with suggestions, but for me, it's a pretty easy choice.

"Weapon."

With a flash, a small silver box appears in my hands, and I slowly pop it open with a little bit of fanfare. Once more, light flashes through the room . . . And when it clears away, I have a new dagger in my hand.

No . . . two new daggers?

The thing seems to flicker and shift in my hand, and I grip it tightly. As I lift it up, it leaves a ghost trail behind, sort of like old cursors on some computers. I swing it around and around, watching the trail flash through the air spectacularly.

[Phasing Dagger]

[Rank: B]

[Details: Impossible to block. Ignores damage resistance.]

"Now that's going to be nice." I give the weapon a toss and practice catching it even without knowing exactly where the physical part of the weapon is. It's tricky, as my eyes don't exactly like to follow it—which, I suppose, is what makes it impossible to block. I stick it into my inventory, along with my other weapons. As I pick up Ascalon, though, I pause in thought.

"I really need a sheath for this." I frown. "I'm always switching out my other daggers as the need arises, but it'd be really handy to just yank out the sword when I need it—which is *usually* when things are starting to spiral and I don't have much time left."

"What about a sheath that goes on your back?" Mr. Wang walks back up to the chairs, even as a jeticopter arrives and lands on the small helipad. "Here, you can have this one."

"Why do you have that just lying around?" I catch the item he's tossed at me and blink at it a few times.

"Ah, you never know when it might come in handy. I have all sorts of random things like that on hand." Mr. Wang shrugs. "Now, get it on, and let's go!"

I nod and smile, slipping the sheath onto my back. The straps fit around my shoulders, holding it firmly in place on my spine. It takes me a couple tries to get Ascalon to slide in, but as it clicks in place, I can feel its power flowing into me. I clench my fists, and Mr. Wang gives a nod.

[Hidden Skill Activated: Bearing of a Knight]

[+25% Charisma]

[+10% Strength]

[Extra Bonuses upon experiencing peril.]

I'm not exactly sure what *peril* might mean, or when that effect might kick in, but I suppose that it's a good thing. With that, I follow Mr. Wang out onto the helipad, giving a final nod to Akira as I go.

I don't know exactly what I'm heading into next, but I'm certain that it's going to be *quite* a fight. I only hope I can come out the other side of it with some answers.

CHAPTER FIFTEEN

The jeticopter roars as it takes off, and we're soon shooting off over the city, angling to the south. As we go, Mr. Wang leans forward to hold out a tablet.

"Here are the schematics of the dungeon so far." He shows me a map of some tunnels. "It's an underground one. No fire, no ice, though there are some carved-out structures: a handful of rooms. The explorers didn't get terribly far before they encountered the shadow, at which point they pursued it deep into the dungeon in a manner inconsistent enough that we weren't able to form a proper map." Mr. Wang gestures at a small undefined area of the dungeon. There are other undefined areas on the map, too: likely places that the party saw but didn't have time to explore. "My experts think it's likely the back end to a temple of some sort, but we aren't confident in that."

"I'll keep all that in mind." I nod. "What are we looking at as far as monsters are concerned?"

"Mostly magic," Mr. Wang says. "Golems, and some nasty ones at that. There were a few wraiths, though not many, and then of course that shadow thing. There were some cloaked figures that we think might be monks of this religion, or maybe just worshippers, but we can't be sure. They were located here." He points at a larger room, not far from the main entrance. "Like I said, our best guess at the moment is that this is a temple, but we just don't know for sure. I don't know where you'll find the sword. No other warriors are entering for the time being."

"Probably a good thing." I nod in confirmation. "Alright, then. Where's it located, as far as Earth-based coordinates are concerned?"

"It's in a park. Nothing fancy, just a little park in the middle of a subdivision." Mr. Wang shrugs. "It opened up this morning, right as some of the local moms were staging a meet-up there. Nothing came out, which is unusual enough. That's why they sent for that team you saw get torn apart."

"Wonderful," I mutter. "What level were they?"

"I believe all in the upper twenties."

"Alright, then." I slowly stand up as I hear the engines shift. "I suppose I'll just have to take over the operation from here."

[ViperQueen: Yeah! That's our Jason!!!]

[ShadowDancer: So epic! No fear, just muscle and grit!]

[RazorEdge: Oh! Oh! Do a jump!]

"We'll have you down there in just a moment, and you can get right into it." Mr. Wang gives a smile.

"No need." I shake my head. "I can make it from here."

[RazorEdge: YEAAAAAAAAAAAAAAH!!!!]

Mr. Wang shrugs, then pulls the door open. I take a

deep breath, then run and jump through the doorway. Unfortunately, my jump is a bit too hard, and I wind up jumping right into the backwash from the jet engine. I'm shot straight downward as if I had been fired from . . . well, from an anti-aircraft gun pointed at the ship it was built on. I have only a moment to blink before I slam into a carousel ride, crushing it into nothing but a metal pancake. My health drops a good bit more than I might like, but I stand back up and manage to shrug it off like it's nothing.

"And there we go." I hold up a finger. "That, kids, is why you never jump without a parachute. Also, these spinning rides are considered *very* dangerous, so you're welcome! I just saved someone a broken leg."

The chat explodes with laughter, and I smile and look about. The park is a rather lovely one, with a handful of trees and an impressive amount of green space. The playground area is actually rather small. The flickering portal stands about twenty feet away from a large slide, crackling and swirling, beckoning people to come inside. I open up a Pumped! bottle and drink it as I slowly start walking forward, readying myself for whatever might come next. As I reach the portal, I draw in a deep breath, then step through.

Sometimes I think portal travel will get easier with time. It never does. Just like always, I'm sucked along, twisted, and turned all about, and then spat out the other side into a dark cave setting. A handful of flickering torches light the area, casting long shadows wherever they come in contact with the sparse objects lying about. I can see a few openings, mostly off to my right but also ahead of me. It's large and open, though not particularly tall.

And then . . . I hear chanting.

I don't know whether to run or to attack. Slowly, though, a long line of red-robed figures marches out of one of the open doors. They have large hoods drawn over their faces, and they walk straight toward me. They don't make any signs of excitement. They don't draw weapons. They simply chant and march.

[ChaosRider: This has to be one of the creepiest things I've ever seen!]

[IceQueen: What are you going to do, Jason??? You can't just kill a monk in cold blood!]

[ViperQueen: He can if the monk is going to kill *him* in cold blood.]

[GoldenShield: Yeah, but then it's not cold blood.]

I ignore the debate in the chat as the figures march ever closer. Mentally, I draw a line across the floor. They can come *that* far and no closer. Eerily, the first one comes to a stop just at that line and gives a nod of his head. The other figures spread out, taking up their positions just on the other side of my imaginary boundary, and stare out at me with impunity.

"Why do you come here?" the first one asks, his voice booming through the room. "Do you come in peace or hatred?"

"That depends," I answer. "There's someone among you who has a sword, a sword that's killed a lot of people and attacked me twice. I'd kind of like to get it out of commission. If you're protecting it, I'm probably not going to seem very peaceable."

"We know," the voice says back. "He is our leader. The sword came to him in a vision this very morning. Then, just as he was told, people came to attack us. Brutal people."

"They're just trying to defend their homes," I answer.

"Perhaps. Then again, all we are doing is defending our home."

I cross my arms. Honestly, I can't decide what to do here. I'd sort of just like to attack, but as IceQueen said, I really can't just go and kill a monk without good reason.

"What did the vision tell him to do with the sword?" I ask. "I do need to see it. You can either stand aside, or you can defend yourself."

"The vision did not give him explicit instructions, only instructing him to wield it." The monk slowly unfolds his hands and raises them. As they come free of the voluminous cloak, I can see that they're withered and bony, black and vile.

The monks are undead.

"To wield it?" I reach into my inventory and draw out my Enlarged Dagger. Somehow, I don't think the Phasing Dagger will work well here. They don't have anything to try and block me with, anyway, and I doubt that their damage threshold is all that high. "Who's he wielding it against?"

"Anyone who comes in here."

"Care to take me to him?"

The leader, as I now recognize him to be, lets out a hiss, and all the monks unfold their hands at the same moment. Dark energy begins to swirl about them, and I know my time is short.

[ShadowDancer: You've got this, Jason!]

[LunarEclipse: Yeah, we're all behind you! Teach them a lesson!]

The leader suddenly gives a sharp flick of his wrist, and strands of dark energy, almost like black lightning, explode through the air. I spin out of the way and charge forward, feet pounding across the ground just as fast as I can go. The leader lets out another hiss, and, suddenly, all thirteen of them attack at the same moment.

Countless strands of energy flash this way and that, and I scramble to get through it. One hits me on the right shoulder, and a great stab of ice seems to flash down through me, growing colder and colder as it plunges into my core. I gasp, and suddenly, more of the strands of energy are hitting me, pouring over me, and freezing me solid. I grit my teeth, coming to a stop only a foot or two in front of the leader. I can't even move my arms, or my fingers, to change my grip on the dagger.

Needless to say, this isn't good.

"And now, you see, that was easy." The monk slowly reaches up and pulls back his hood, revealing a desiccated face. There's still a tiny bit of flesh clinging to the skull, which twitches back and forth as his mouth moves. "You will die, and all your works will come to naught, and—"

My pocket dimension flickers open behind them, and Blub comes floating out, already expanded. It closes a moment later, and the monks stare at the Living Bomb as if it's little more than a giant booger. In fairness, the likeness to snot *is* sometimes rather extraordinary.

KA-BOOM!

Blub explodes violently, knocking the monks backward. The hold on me is broken, and I stab forward with the Enlarged Dagger. My blade punches through his back and out his chest, and I rip it upward, cutting clean through the rib cage and out the shoulders. Now, to be clear, I wouldn't be able to do that with most creatures, but as the monk *is* already dead and rotting, it's not the most difficult thing I've ever done. The monk gasps, then slowly becomes rigid and collapses, crumbling into dust as he hits the ground.

"You fool!"

The voice echoes in my ear, and another of the monks grabs me around the throat. With some sort of superhuman strength, it lifts me off the ground, then spins and throws me into a wall. I see short swords beginning to appear in their hands, simply falling down out of their sleeves to land in their palms. Magic still crackles around them, and they march forward, advancing on me. Before I can do anything, they form a semicircle and pen me in, stone on one side, death on the other.

I stand back up, only to see dark energy arcing between them, almost forming a living sort of barricade. I lunge forward, only to be driven back by a sharp pulse of dark lightning. Gritting my teeth, I try again, only to be repulsed once more. They're using each other as energy sources, I realize, pooling their power to strike at me as one.

"You will fall!" they chant in a single, unified voice. "You will die!"

"Is that so?" I open up my pocket dimension. Blub bounces back inside, and Burnie slowly flies out to land on my shoulder. "Let's see how you do with this."

Burnie spreads his wings, and a white-hot blast explodes across the room as they continue to close on me. The flame hits their barrier and crackles against the dark energy, light against darkness. The flames spread across the whole length of the barrier, raging and snarling and trying to lick at the robes and flesh of the monsters, but nothing happens. Still, though, it does one crucial thing for me.

It gives me cover.

I don't know exactly what I need to do, but I know I need to break their chain. The only question is how to do that. I have a feeling that the sword of light might have been able to help, but it's gone now. The Dagger of Doom isn't going to help, since I can't even get to the monks to attack them and find a weakness. I need something else. I need . . .

A feel a shiver on my back, and I slowly reach up to take hold of Ascalon's hilt. The blade makes a lovely *shing* as I draw it out, and the cultists all draw back in fear. Burnie lets up on the flame attack, and the sword begins to glow, radiating light in the presence of such evil.

"I'm giving you one chance to give up," I say slowly and forcefully. "Lay down arms right now and I won't harm you."

"You can't harm us at all," one of them mocks. "We're already dead."

"Then I won't feel bad about killing you."

With that, I run forward, sword flashing in my hands. The dark energy explodes out at me, but I point Ascalon forward and slash out with the brilliant weapon.

Bzzzzzzzzzzzzzzat!

The dark energy rebounds as it hits the blessed blade, and I follow it forward. The monks don't have a chance as I throw my shoulder into them, knocking two of them backward. With that, I spin and slash my sword clean through one of their robes. Bones clatter to the ground as a flash of light erupts from the weapon, and with that, the line breaks.

The monks scream and flee, and I leap in front of them.

They're fast, but I'm faster, and in the blink of an eye, I've cut down almost half of them. The remaining six quickly form up and begin chanting, and I see dark energy swirling in their midst. I don't know exactly what they're planning, but I'm quite certain that it's nothing good. I charge forward, only to feel a wind beginning to blow around me.

That *can't* be good.

"Burnie!"

Burnie shoots another blast of fire at the chanting group, but once more, it's blocked by a torrent of dark energy. I draw back Ascalon and leap forward, swinging it at them with all my might. A shield of dark matter forms, and my shining steel hits it with a powerful, resounding *bong*. There's a brief pause as I strain against it . . . And then, with a flash, the shield gives way.

My blade carves right through the midst of the cultists, and they all collapse with shrieks and groans. I nod and step back, satisfied . . . at least for a moment.

The wind continues to howl around me, and I get the sinking feeling that they managed to accomplish whatever they had set out to do. A portal opens under my feet, and the wind suddenly seems to collapse upon me, shoving me through. I'm unable to do a thing as I find myself shot down into the portal . . . Down . . . Down . . .

Down to whatever awaits me next.

CHAPTER SIXTEEN

I tumble head over heels for a brief moment, and then the portal spits me out the other side. I find myself flashing down through the air, still falling, only to come crashing into a large pool. Water explodes all around me, closing over my head, and I fight to get back to the surface. The only problem is that I'm all sorts of turned around, and only the increasing pressure in my ears tells me that I'm going *down* instead of up.

Wham!

The noise is muffled underwater, but the pain is quite intense as I whack my head on a large white object. The light is actually pretty good, and I draw back to find myself staring at a skull.

A big skull.

It's actually not human. It looks sort of like a rhino skull, though with a frill almost like a triceratops. Or maybe like one of those prehistoric rhinos. Whatever the case, it rests on the bottom of this pool, and I quickly reorient myself, place my feet on the ground, and push off with all my might. Up, up I shoot, and then . . .

I gasp for air as I break through the surface of the water and take a moment to steady my nerves. I'm in a massive cavern now, with a great many sun crystals placed around the area to keep it lit. Slowly, I turn and flounder over to the side of the pool, where I pull myself up and onto the stone. I gasp and choke for a few moments as I try to get my bearings, spit out more than a bit of water, and slowly sit up.

The cavern, as I said, is wide and long. The pool sits on one end, which tapers down into a dead end only fifty feet or so away from my position. In the other direction . . . Well . . .

About twenty feet from the opposite side of the pool, the ground drops off sharply into a massive abyss. I can't see the bottom of it. All I know is that it's *dark* down there. There could be monsters, there could be a dark, flesh-eating mist, there could be sharp rocks, more water, ice, or magma. I don't have the faintest idea, but I *am* quite certain that I don't want to fall down into it.

Of course, there *is* a path across. Rising up from the darkness are small pillars of stone, which end at uneven heights, spaced out across the area. Small arches of stone connect several of them together, though I can see that I'll have to jump at a few places at least to get across. It's far from the most welcoming place in the world, and I shudder.

[ViperQueen: Now *that's* going to be hard to get across! Bright side: no monsters.]

[LunarEclipse: I think you mean, no monsters *yet.*]

[GoldenShield: What's going to attack him? It's a platform level, and I don't see any birds. What else could there be?]

"I can think of a lot of things." I slowly push myself upright, then slide Ascalon back into its holster. It begins to glow warmly again after a moment, and I stalk forward, walking past the pool. There's a single bridge leading out to the first pillar, about twenty feet off the edge. Slowly, I take a step out onto the bridge—testing the waters, so to speak—then nod and start walking out a bit more confidently. It's only a foot wide, but it's not wobbling around at all, which is rather nice.

[IceQueen: AHH! JASON! Don't look down!]

[ShadowDancer: I think I'm going to be sick here at my computer!]

[GoldenShield: Bleh. Bleh bleh bleh bleh bleh bleh!]

I smile, then slowly look down just as I get to the end of the bridge. The fall is immense. Now that I'm out here, I can see that it goes straight down . . . oh, it must be hundreds of feet. The light from the sun crystals isn't great—thus why I can't see the bottom—but it's enough. The chat *explodes*, and I laugh.

"Alright, alright, enough joking." I look at the next pillar, which is a bit below me and a good fifteen feet away. I have a feeling that I'm going to need to make a running jump, or possibly have Burnie serve as a foothold once more. I've done that a few times in the past, and while it's not the easiest thing in the world to manage, it *does* work. "Hmm. Sorry, guys, but I am going to have to look down enough to see the platform . . . Here . . ."

As I turn around to walk back, I'm greeted with a view of the rhino skull slowly rising up from the pool. A handful of bones—an assortment of leg and arm bones, I think—forms a hand of sorts that tosses the skull out onto the ledge around the pool, then slowly begins to pull itself upward. A whole river of bones suddenly seems to flow upward from the water, and the level of the water actually drops several feet. Suddenly, I realize that the gravel at the bottom was, in fact, just bone.

"Well, I don't know about you, but I'm not waiting around to see what that thing does next."

I turn around and run as fast as I can. I only have a few steps before the end, but it's enough, and as I reach the edge of the stone, I jump as hard as I can. My aim is true, and I come down hard on the next pillar. Slowly, I climb back to my feet and glance over my shoulder.

The mass of bones has begun pulling itself together. There are no more coming out of the pool, which is nice to know. It pushes itself upward until it's about fifteen feet tall, thick and stocky, with the rhino skull as a head. Slowly, it starts walking forward, growling and muttering.

[LunarEclipse: There's no way the bridges hold that thing up.]

[DarkCynic: Yeah! I think you're safe, Jason. That thing is just for show.]

[Originalgoth: Yes . . . show indeed!]

I bite my lip as the bone golem reaches the edge of the pit. It pauses . . . and then falls forward. The bones detach from each other and form an almost liquid eruption. The conglomeration lands on the bridge and simply flows forward, racing along toward me, carrying the rhino skull along on top. As it reaches the end, just like those rainforest ants, the bones simply connect together and build a bridge across the gap without really slowing at all.

I watch for a moment, hardly able to believe my eyes, then

turn and run. This particular bridge runs at an angle to the path of the cavern; it goes more sideways than forward. I run underneath another bridge, which is a bit disconcerting, and then leap forward as I reach the end of the path I'm on. I sail through the air once more and come down hard on yet another pillar.

The bones chase along behind me, lightning fast, and I race along just as fast as I can. I can see now that the pillars and bridges are set up something like a maze, and I don't have time to really figure out the pattern. I find myself climbing up a small ladder onto the bridge that I ran underneath earlier. The bones, rather than chasing me up the ladder, change tactics and leap across to the lower bridge. Just as I reach the top, they surge upward and wrap themselves cleanly around my path. The rhino skull is carried up to block me, even as more bones wrap around the whole of the bridge, pressing ever closer to me.

"Alright, beast." I draw out my Enlarged Dagger, then run at the thing. "Time to eat steel!"

It's not the most well-thought-out battle cry in the world, but I'm already sick of this thing. As I reach the edge of the bones, I jump up into the air, sailing over them, and slam directly into the skull. It snaps at me, but I stay well enough out of its range and knock it clean off its perch. It clatters a bit further down the path, and I jump over it as I race onward. I reach the end of the bridge and jump outward, on toward the next one . . .

And that's when I can see the path in its entirety.

High above everything else, I see the remaining path I have to travel, and as I come down, I run along with renewed vigor. The bones let out a loud, angry rattle, then drop down and begin racing along parallel to me, forming bridges as its own whims demand. Suddenly, though, I see what it's doing.

The path I'm on doubles back several times, making for a longer trip, while the bones can simply surge around to block the final jump leading to the far side. I make one more jump to land on the last bridge and find the bones snapping into the massive golem form they had taken when first leaving the water. It balls enormous hands into fists, and I brace myself.

"Alright, Ascalon," I murmur. "This certainly seems like peril to me."

There's no answer, and I don't get any new buffs. I certainly don't shoot fire from my hands all of a sudden, which is somewhat annoying. Finally, gritting my teeth, I simply run forward as fast as I can.

I don't really know why I think it's a good idea, but it's the best one I can think of. As I reach the end of the bridge, I jump up into the air and ball my hands into fists. The monster does the same and throws a punch at me. I throw a punch back . . . and with that, we come together.

Boom!

Bones crack and split around me, and I come crashing through the thing, scattering bones left and right. As I land on the ground, I look down at my hands, then slowly stand up.

[DarkCynic: Wow! Could Jason do that yesterday?]

[IceQueen: Who cares? He can do it now, and that's the important part!]

[RazorEdge: That's what comes from gaining umpteen levels in like 6 hours.]

I can't argue with the last comment. The bones all begin

to rattle as they pull themselves back together, and the rhino skull snaps into place. Slowly, it begins to thunder forward, and I run up to meet it.

All fear fades from me, and I draw out my Enlarged Dagger. As the monster swings a fist down at me, I duck under the blow, then slash out across the monster's stomach. Bones crack and rattle to the ground, and I stab it again. For a few long moments, we lock ourselves in combat. Several blows hit me, knocking me backward, but I return them with interest. Slowly, the monster begins to shrink. Suddenly, I see my chance, and I leap upward.

"*Hi-ya!*"

I swing the dagger with all my might and slam it into the side of the skull. There's a loud *snap*, and the skull is knocked clean off the shoulders, and it falls back into the pit beyond. The golem freezes, apparently confused about what to do, and I kick it as hard as I can.

Crash!

Bones explode through the air as my foot connects, and the golem, or at least most of it, falls backward into the pit. A few bones rattle down to land on the edge of the chasm, and I sigh and slowly sheath my dagger. I bend down and pick up one of the bones, then nod at the gap.

"Do you think these belonged to someone sacrificed against their will, or were these all cultists who willingly gave themselves up?" I honestly don't know the answer, but my chat is quick to help.

[ChaosRider: Mostly cultists, I'd say!]

[ViperQueen: A lot of those bones didn't even look human. Most of the hands I saw looked almost reptilian to me.]

[LunarEclipse: Yeah, my mom is a veterinarian, and a bunch of those were *definitely* cow bones. I think.]

I nod slowly. I'm satisfied enough to know that I wasn't desecrating the bodies of people martyred by the cult. Slowly, I stand back up and kick a few of the bones down into the pit, listening for the echo of an impact. Nothing happens, though, not even after a full minute. If there *is* a bottom, it's so deep that noise can't travel all the way back up, at least not loudly enough for me to hear it.

"Very good." I slowly turn away and walk toward the entrance. "Now for a couple of housekeeping items. First of all, where am I? Am I in the same dungeon as before, or a different one? Is there a way out, or am I trapped?"

The answers, thankfully, come back rather quickly.

[LunarEclipse: I've been studying that, and I'm pretty sure you're in the same dungeon. The rock layers are the same. If you look up near the top, you can see a band of red stone. There was a similar band of red stone on the walls of the entrance, though it was down near the floor. I'd say you're at the bottom of this dungeon and have to go back through it now.]

[ChaosRider: Back through? That's super cool! This will be epic!!!]

[IceQueen: Actually, it's probably going to be pretty boring. He'll be able to just tear his way through everything without even blinking.]

I smile, then wave my hand to dismiss the concerns. "Well, as long as we're convinced I'm in the same dungeon, I'm not going to worry about it too much. Watch out for more traps, and . . ." I shrug. "Let's go find that sword."

CHAPTER SEVENTEEN

I'll admit that I creep along pretty slowly as I make my way forward. Ahead of me the cave is dark, though it begins to flicker with torchlight the deeper I get. Frankly, a whole lot of thoughts are passing through my mind.

It's possible that I was thrown to the end of the dungeon and just killed the final boss, but I doubt it. It was too easy a fight. I really see two options as being the most likely. Either A: the bone golem was a mini-boss—maybe secret, maybe not—and I just defeated it, or B: the whole thing was a trap, something intentional that the cultists do to everyone, and now I'm going to be progressing through the dungeon as normal. I honestly don't know which is right, and that worries me.

In any case, the tunnel isn't long, and I soon come to a small doorway. This, thankfully, is where I get the answer to at least one of my questions.

The doorway is backward.

What I mean is that I come to a smooth stone surface,

which has a door carved in it. The only issue is that there's no doorknob. No handle. No hole. No way of opening it at all.

[ShadowDancer: Ooh! I bet this is a hidden door! On the other side there will be a bookshelf or something, and you can only open it by pulling the right book!]

[IceQueen: That would be cool to see! If only John was here. He could smash right through it.]

[FireStorm: Hey, don't be knocking on Jason! He's getting a whole lot stronger. With John always running off, Jason will be way stronger than him soon enough!]

I chuckle at the last one. Still, the conversation gives me an idea. I open up my pocket dimension and call forth Bjorn and Blub.

"Alright, you two." I hold out my hand, and Blub floats down to land in it, where he slowly begins to inflate. "Have you ever done any work in the locksmithing business?"

They both stare at me blankly, not even saying a word in my mind. I flash a smile, then nod to Bjorn.

"Freeze it."

Bjorn turns and growls, and frost begins to spread across the stone surface. There's no layer of ice that appears, which is good. I need as much of the blast as possible to hit the stone and not be absorbed by something else. As the frost spreads across the ground, I take a step back but feel a chill in the air anyway. As Bjorn finishes, I flex my wrist.

"Alright, Blub. Here we go!"

With all my strength, I throw Blub at the doorway.

KA-BOOM!

The blast fills the air with smoke and fire, and little bits and pieces of stone rain down all around. As the debris slowly clears away, I find that my goal has been perfectly achieved. The doorway has been utterly and completely demolished, along with a good bit of the wall around it as well. Blub bounces back into the pocket dimension, though Bjorn stays at my side as I slowly step through the hole.

Torches flicker to life as they detect my presence, and I whistle softly. I'm standing in what can really only be described as an underground warehouse. It's nice and square, just like a room ought to be, with shelves lining all the walls and filling up a good portion of the floor space. They're filled with crates and bags and all sorts of other things.

"Interesting," I say as I slowly turn to look at the wall that I just blasted through. It looks to me like it was grain storage. A massive amount of wheat has now been spilled across the floor, and a small fire burns in a bag of barley. "Very interesting. Food supply for the monks? But they're undead. Why would they need any food?"

My chat doesn't give me any helpful answers. Suddenly, from across the way, I hear a door creak open. Quickly, I wave Bjorn back out of the way, and he drops to the ground and slides underneath one of the shelves where there's a small opening. Meanwhile, I rather nimbly jump up the shelves, climbing up on top of some large crates. I like to think that as I'm doing it, I'm just as graceful as an elf—rather like Ali—but in reality, I'm sure it looks more like a dwarf trying to mimic an elf. In any case, I get up there and out of sight, and footsteps echo below me.

"Hmm. Lights shouldn't be on if there are no people down here," a harsh, echoing voice says. It sounds almost like sandpaper, if that's possible. I slowly peek over the edge of the crate and find that there's another monk there, though a bit larger than the ones at the entrance. It turns a corner and finds the blast mark and begins to nod slowly. "So that's where they sent the invader! Fools. Serves them right to have been cut down. They should have known that trap wouldn't hold anyone, 'cept maybe a child. Bleh. More work for me. Alright, guess I'll have to go sound the alarm."

It sighs and turns away, and I take my chance. As quietly as possible, I draw out my Enlarged Dagger and jump down on top of it.

Only thing is, it knew I was there.

As I fall down, quiet as a cat, it spins and raises a hand. Dark energy flashes out of its palm and hits me, wrapping around me in tight bindings. I gasp in pain as they pull tight, and it smiles grimly—at least as well as it can, being dead and all.

"Knew you were in here somewhere. Everyone sees all the stuff lying about and gets it in their head that they can hide and then ambush me. I've never been ambushed yet, and I've been here a long while, so you'd best—"

Wham!

A white blur erupts from underneath the shelves as Bjorn jumps out and slams into the monk. The dark energy loses its grip on me, and I fall to the ground with a loud *smack*. As I climb back to my feet, Bjorn smashes the monk into a shelf of crates, all of which come tumbling down around it. Boxes burst open, allowing ceramic jars and plates and other such things to fly out, smashing here and there across the floor. The monk snarls and raises its hands, and Bjorn yelps as he's lifted off the ground.

I don't stop to evaluate the situation. I simply throw myself into battle. With my Enlarged Dagger still in my hand, I stab at the monk with all my might. It spins out of the way, fast as lightning, and Bjorn howls. A blast of ice washes over the monk, and my blade crashes into it with powerful, resounding force.

Unfortunately, this monk isn't as fragile as the ones at the entrance. The attack shatters the ice around it and sends it reeling. It snarls and gnashes its teeth, then raises a hand toward me. I feel ice stab through my heart, just like before, and fight to keep myself standing. Bjorn howls once more, but this time the monk is ready.

A sharp flick of the creature's wrist forms a spectral shield between it and the wolf. Ice forms across that shield but doesn't penetrate all the way to the monk. I lunge forward, trying to stab it, but another flick of its finger sends the cold racing through my body more strongly. I gasp, hardly able to breathe, and fall to my knees.

"You are weak! Pathetic!" the undead monk snarls, walking toward me. "You are nothing, you are insignificant, you are—"

I reach out with the last of my strength and grab hold of the feet of one of the shelves. I give them a sharp twist, breaking them off, and with that, the shelf comes tumbling down. It lands on me, of course, but it *also* lands on the monk, which is good enough for me. It vanishes as crates and bags land upon it, and as the cold vanishes along with it, I jump back to my feet.

BLAM!

Dark energy explodes outward as the monk lets off a concussive attack. Boxes and shelves alike shatter into splinters under the force of the blast, and the monk slowly stands back up, gnashing its teeth. I'm thrown backward onto a large pile of straw that spills from one of the boxes. Fire flickers in its hand.

Foom!

It's not a terribly powerful attack, but as the black flame washes over me, I can't help but scream in pain. It cuts straight through my clothes, straight to my bone, and ignites the straw instantly. It burns cold, not hot, and I throw myself to the ground in a desperate attempt to put the flames out. Bjorn, trying to help, hits me with a cold snap, but that honestly does more harm than good. I soon have the fire out, though, and stand back up just in time to be hit in the face with a crate.

The monk laughs as objects whirl up off the ground and swirl around it. It begins to throw them with its power, flinging them at me with all its might. I dive out of the way, narrowly dodging attack after attack after attack. The few shelves in the room that are still standing quickly start to fall, crashing this way and that. It's a complete and utter mess, no other way to look at it.

"Isn't this going to get you in trouble?" I ask as I stand up. "I have to imagine that you were given the task of keeping this place *clean*."

"My superiors will be happy enough that I'm cleaning the vermin out of it," the monk sneers. "That would be you, in case you were—"

Bjorn leaps up from the side, sinking his teeth into the monk's arm. The monk doesn't really react in pain other than to spin and bring three crates crashing into Bjorn, knocking him backward and into the wall. Bjorn, on the other hand, *does* yelp in pain.

[DarkCynic: HOW DARE YOU HURT THAT NOBLE WOLF?]

[ShadowDancer: You'd better teach him a lesson, Jason!]

[FireStorm: Yeah! Here's a lesson for you! (bad guy) + (hurt pets) = dead]

[ChaosRider: I'm not really sure that math adds up.]

I run forward while the monk is distracted. It turns its attention back to me, and I slam into it with all my might. The two of us smash back into the shelves behind the monk, and I stab it in the chest with my dagger.

Quite unfortunately, it doesn't react to the attack at all.

"You fool," it whispers, then raises a hand. Another blast of energy hits me, and gravity seems to change. I find myself falling upward, and I slam into the ceiling. I groan in pain, then slowly stand up. My feet are on the stone above, and I'm staring up—down?—at the monk below.

[FireStorm: Now that's just not fair!]

[ShadowDancer: How are you going to get out of this one, Jason?]

Frankly, I don't know. I don't know if it's an effect the monk applied to me, a status condition or something, or whether it's a spell the monk is actively casting. I check my list of conditions for a moment, and, satisfied that it's *not* a condition, open up my pocket dimension.

"Alright, Burnie! Let's bring this home."

Burnie swoops out, oriented normally, and lets loose with a great blast of flame. The monk shrieks and puts its hands over its head, and I suddenly drop back to the floor. This time, though, it's to my advantage.

Just like I had intended to do earlier, I draw out my dagger and stab it in the top of the head as I land. It's smashed down into the ground, and I rip the dagger back out before kneeing it in the face. The monk's undead head is snapped back, and it slowly laughs.

"You're not bad, Jason Lee. Not bad at all."

"I'll take that as a compliment."

With that, I spin and perform a roundhouse kick to the side of its head. There's a loud *crack*, and the head is launched from its shoulders just like a soccer ball. The head slams into the far wall between a crate and a jar and explodes into dust with enough force to send out a small shock wave. The jar rattles, then tips and falls to the floor, shattering into bits upon landing. I let out a long breath, then give a small nod.

"That works for me." I glance over at Bjorn, who has just started whimpering. "Wait. Bjorn?"

Burnie flies down and lands on the ground next to my wolf. There's still some rubble lying across him, and I drop to my knees and push some of it away, clearing him off. As I do so, I find a large shaft of wood lodged in his side, just behind the leg. Blood oozes out and cakes the fur, and Bjorn slowly lifts his head.

Master, it has been an honor serving with you.

"And it's going to keep being an honor, if I do say so myself," I snap, rubbing the back of his head behind his ears. "You're not going to die, not yet."

We all have to die sometime, and my health is dropping fast.

With a flicker, my pocket dimension opens behind me, and Astrid slowly steps out. Her black muzzle nuzzles his own, and I feel my heart snapping inside of me. Then, just to top it off, Balder steps out as well. I have to blink in surprise as I see him. He's almost full-grown now, though he still does look rather like a teenager: skinny legs, just a bit on the short side, that sort of thing. Anyway, he kneels down next to his fallen father, and my whole being just melts.

[DarkCynic: Come on, Jason, you've got to do everything you can to save him!]

[ViperQueen: PLEASE PLEASE PLEASE don't let him die!]

[ChaosRider: Yeah! Do whatever it takes! And I mean *whatever* it takes!!!]

I nod at the chat, but mostly ignore it as I try to figure out a way to get Bjorn out of this alive. I know that if he can get into the pocket dimension, he'll be able to survive for a bit longer in his native environment, but that's only a delay tactic at best. I open up my inventory and scroll for a few moments, looking for anything that could help. I find my long, and seemingly endless, supply of Pumped! and slowly pull one out.

"Here, boy. Drink this."

Bjorn's face seems to take on a note of disbelief, but he opens his mouth. I pour the soda in just as quickly as I can, though I take it slow enough that he can still breathe. When I've finished the whole bottle, his eyes snap open wide, and he opens his jaws as if to vomit.

Buuuuuuuuuuuuuuurp!

I can honestly say that I've never heard a dog burp before. He shakes his head slightly, and I notice that the bleeding seems to have stopped. Slowly, he staggers to his feet, though he wobbles about.

Master?

"Yes?" I ask quickly.

The next time I have a mortal wound, I think I'd rather die than drink any of that stuff again. What exactly do you humans find good about it? I've tasted better roadkill before.

A smile flickers across my face, and I rub him behind his ears. "At least you're alive."

I am, Master. It'll be a little bit before I'm up to fighting again, but I'm alive.

Astrid barks with joy, then helps him back into the pocket dimension. Balder follows, though not before bowing to me. Burnie flaps up to land on my shoulder, and Blub floats up to me as well. I take the Living Bomb and stick him in my pocket—after deflating him, of course. He's too slow to just let float behind me, and he doesn't seem to need to do things like breathe. With that, I turn toward the exit the monk came through.

It's time to put an end to this little cult, one way or another.

CHAPTER EIGHTEEN

As I reach the door, which has fallen shut, I pause and press my ear up against the wood. For all I know, there could be a hundred of these monks on the other side, or there could be none. I don't have the faintest idea, and I'd rather not walk into a trap. Slowly, when I don't hear anything, I push the door open.

On the other side of the door is a large kitchen, and I have to admit that it gives me pause for a moment. What *is* it with kitchens in these dungeons recently? I don't have any answers, though, and I'm not here to figure it out. I glance around the area, trying to get a feel for things.

The kitchen is in an old style, one you might see in ancient times. There's a large stone oven at one end, and the flickering coals are producing heat that I can feel from the other side of the room. Cabinets and counters line the walls, with a large food-prep countertop in the exact center. Slices of meat sit around on platters here and there, while several fresh loaves of bread are in the oven cooking. I slowly step inside and close the door behind me.

[ShadowDancer: Why exactly do these monks need food, anyway? They're not alive?]

[IceQueen: I agree! There's something very fishy here.]

[RazorEdge: Be careful, Jason!]

I nod slowly to the chat, then start walking forward, glancing around for any evidence of movement. There's only one other door, and it has an ominous sort of look to it. It's hard to explain, but it just feels like the sort of door that has something hidden behind it. When nothing happens, I take a step in that direction, only for the door handle to click and turn.

Quick as a wink, I duck behind the large central countertop. The base is solid wood, which makes it easy to stay out of sight. Footsteps shuffle in, along with a handful of low muttering voices.

"Now, where did that old fool get off to? He left the bread to burn! He'll be the death of all of us, that's for sure."

"Aye, aye. If the master finds out, it'll be the altar for us. Quick, get that stuff out of the oven and onto the table. We've got to get the prisoners fed."

So, it's for prisoners. I nod in understanding. It makes sense. Cults need sacrifices for their demonic gods. If they've been capturing people, warriors, they'll need to feed them before they can sacrifice them. I grip the blade of my dagger even as two monks slowly walk around the counter over to the oven, neither one noticing that I'm there. Slowly, I stand up, then reach out and grab a frying pan with my free hand.

Wham!

I swing the frying pan just as hard as I can and whack one

of the monks on the side of the head. That particular monk goes down in a heap after one blow, skull crushed. I whistle in surprise, and the other monk spins around.

Fssssssssssssst!

A blast of dark lightning erupts from its hand and hits me in the chest, flinging me backward with extraordinary force. I'm flipped over the central countertop and come down hard on the floor beyond and groan for a moment before I spring back to my feet.

"So, you're the reason he's late." The monk flashes around the edge of the counter, moving so fast that it almost seems to be flying. It flings another blast of energy, hitting me in the shoulder this time. The blast spins me around like a top. The monk raises both hands, and spiderwebs of energy form around me, wrapping me up like a net. I gasp in pain as they dig into my skin, yank me backward, and slam me up against the back wall.

"You're weaker than I expected. I have to admit that I'm surprised. Our warehouse manager was no weakling, so to take him down . . ." The monk shakes its head. "I'd expect you to give me a better fight here and now."

I take a deep breath, then flex my muscles and push against the webs of dark energy. They strain for a moment, then burst wide open. I leap free and jump down to fling the frying pan at the monk. It raises a hand and stops the pan telekinetically, but that simply distracts it. I flash forward just as fast as I can and draw the Enlarged Dagger. It flashes in my hand, and I throw a quick stab at the monk's chest before redirecting toward its neck. It raises its other hand and fires a blast of energy to deflect the dagger but misses, and I hit it right where I intended.

Foom!

The instant my blade hits its skin, a blast of dark fire shoots out and wraps around my arm, scorching me. I grit my teeth, trying not to scream in pain, and stagger backward holding my wrist.

"You're something else," I mutter through clenched teeth.

"It's my job to deal with prisoners." The monk flexes its raised hand, and the frying pan collapses into a little ball of metal, which it then lets drop to the floor with a *thunk*. "I know how you all think. I know how you all fight. I'll not be manipulated into defeat."

"I wouldn't dream of it." I take my stance. "I don't need to manipulate. Only to crush."

[LunarEclipse: Yeah, that's our Jason!]

[GoldenShield: Hey, use Burnie! He's on your shoulder!!!]

[ViperQueen: Yeah! Go Burnie!!!]

I send a mental command to Burnie, and he spreads his wings. The monk gives a start. Apparently, it just assumed that I was a species with two heads or something. Anyway, it steps back, and Burnie lets loose an attack.

A white jet of flame erupts through the room, scorching the countertops and burning the bread quite badly. The monk staggers backward, flailing under the fire, though it manages to take a stance and form a shield a moment later. Burnie continues the attack, and I take Blub out of my pocket.

"Alright, Blub. Let's see what you've got."

With that, I throw my Living Bomb at the monk. As he hits the shield, a massive explosion shakes the room. Fire and smoke billow through the air, and the monk entirely vanishes in the chaos.

I keep my Enlarged Dagger in my hand. Suddenly, I hear the sharp scuff of a foot on the floor and see a dark figure emerge through the smoke. I swing with all my might and land a score across the monk's arm. It snarls, and I punch out with my other hand. I can't tell what I hit, but I *do* hit something, and the monk staggers backward. I follow up my attack instantly, punching and slashing with all my might. Suddenly, a blast of dark energy flares through the smoke, making it all settle. I can see clearly again, and I find the undead monk just next to me.

Shing!

I slash at the monk with all my might, hitting it in the neck. This time, as dark flames pour out, I ignore the pain and simply slash through the thing. Bone crunches, and the head comes clean off. Slowly, it topples backward and lands on the floor with a *thunk*, and the body falls forward and collapses.

"Done and done." I let out a whistle and start to turn away, only for the door to slam shut. The monk I hit with the frying pan slowly stands up, fire brimming in its hand. "You again?"

The monk doesn't answer but throws two fireballs at me. I dodge the first one . . . right into the path of the next one. Flames explode against me, and I stagger rather badly. Still, I manage to avoid falling, which is a bonus. With that, I spin and throw my Enlarged Dagger just as hard as I can. The weapon hits the monk in the chest and knocks it backward, and its cloak catches in the fire in the ovens. Flames entirely cover the monk a moment later, and I spring forward.

I've been on fire enough times to know that, while it can certainly be a fatal experience, it doesn't *have* to be, and in this case, I'd rather like it to end in death. The creature raises a hand, and the flames begin to flash off the robes to swirl around the monk's fist. I throw a punch straight through it and hit the monk directly in the face. It's thrown backward, straight into the oven. The flames grow more intense, and I let out a sigh of relief.

"There." I dust off my hands. "It's done."

There's a brief pause as the monk flails about . . . and then, slowly, it grows still.

[You have leveled up!]

[Congratulations! You are now Level 42!]

I blink in surprise. Once more, I'm leveling up *much* quicker than before. I can't be certain, but I feel like I can detect my body growing stronger faster. Out of interest, I open up my interface and do a smidge of scrolling. Earlier I received a skill that helped me level up faster, and I have an inkling that it's the culprit.

[Bonus XP (passive): Earn extra XP per kill and level up faster.]

[Rank: III]

I don't know how many ranks it has, but it's certainly been handy. In any event, I glance around the room, confirm that both of the monks are dead, and then slip off toward the far door.

This time it feels less ominous, and I slowly pull it open. The hinges squeak slightly, but nothing terrible. I find myself in a long carved-out hall with small doorways leading off to either side. Slowly, I creep forward, keeping an eye out for any trouble. As I reach the first doorway, I glance inside, where I find a small cell. There's a bed, a small altar, and . . . that's really about it. The room is empty, and I quickly slip inside as I hear footsteps in the hall.

"What's this?" a quiet voice asks. I slip as far out of the way as possible and see a quick flash of red robes move past the entrance. A moment later, there's a sharp cry, and the figure darts back in the other direction.

[ShadowDancer: Hey, Jason, why didn't you go fight it?]

[IceQueen: Yeah, now everyone will know you're here!]

[DarkCynic: Everyone probably already knows he's here, doofus.]

I nod slowly. I'm pretty sure that everyone already knows I'm here, at least all the people who matter. Quickly, I look around the room, trying to see if there's anything of use. The only thing I see is a small knife by the altar, but I'm quite certain I don't want to use anything that's been stained with that sort of blood. If dragon treasure is cursed, I can only imagine what *that* might do.

When I confirm that there's nothing useful, I walk back up to the hall and peer out into the corridor. There's no one there in either direction, and I let out a sigh of relief and slowly step out into view. With that, I move down the hall just as quickly as I can, though I do glance into most of the cells as I pass. The majority are empty, but a few of them do contain monks sleeping. Why undead monks have to sleep, I don't know, but if they're not attacking me, I'm not going to question it. In any event, judging from the number of rooms, this dungeon probably hosts around fifty monks. I killed twelve in the entryway, and then three down here, which leaves . . . well, it leaves quite a few, but I suppose I'll just have to take them as they come.

As I reach the end of the hall, a figure steps out in front of me. It has a dagger in its hand, and it raises to strike . . .

only to pause. I snarl and raise my own dagger . . . and then I, too, pause.

Deep within the hood, I can see eyes.

They're wide, and they're blue. A strand of blond hair falls out of the hood, and I glance at it. I'm not really sure what's going on here, but it has me thrown off, that's for sure.

Suddenly, a withered hand wraps around my neck even as a second one grabs my wrist.

"You got him! Good!" The monk behind me laughs. "Just what we needed from you! Return to your bunk, recruit. We'll deal with this one."

I take a deep breath, then let it out.

"Blub? I could use you right now."

KA-BOOM!

Blub, who never went back into my pocket after blowing up the monk back in the kitchen, suddenly detonates. The monk holding me staggers, and I spin, break its grasp on my wrist, and slash at its chest. It leaps backward, narrowly avoiding the attack, and dark energy brews in its palms.

"What is it with you guys and dark energy? Find yourself a new superpower or something." I grit my teeth, then brace myself and leap forward. The monk unleashes a powerful blast of the energy, striking me up and down the length of my body. It hurts—a lot—but I'm starting to realize that it doesn't actually affect my health all that much, not compared to other forms of damage. Steeling myself against the effects, I charge forward, spin, and cut off its head in one smooth motion. Two thuds echo through the hall, and I spin back to face the girl.

She looks more terrified than ever, and I nod to the dormitory right next to her.

"Inside. Now."

She nods and slips into the room, and I follow, wishing I had some sort of a screen or door to use to block off the entrance. Quickly, we slip into the corner hardest to see from the doorway and wait there.

"Hey! He's down!" Footsteps patter on the stone. "The attacker is still in here!"

"Where's the recruit? Did he take her?"

"After them!"

The shouts continue for several long moments, moving down the hallway away from our position. As they fade away, I glance over at the girl, who is starting to breathe a bit more heavily than before. She slowly reaches up and pulls the hood back, and I find myself looking at a woman, maybe a year younger than me, who simply looks terrified. Slowly, I hold out my hand.

"Jason Lee."

She shakes my hand. When she speaks, her voice trembles terribly. "Sandra."

"Well, Sandra, we're going to get you out of here," I murmur, glancing out into the hall once more. "We'll get you back to the real world, and then . . ." I shrug. "I'd like to hear every bit of the story that you're willing to tell."

CHAPTER NINETEEN

It's not really that interesting of a story." Sandra looks down at the ground. "When the apocalypse started . . . Day one, I decided that it would be fun to go into the portals even though I wasn't Awakened. I was just a stupid college student—you know what sorts of trouble you get into in those situations."

"All too well," I murmur. "So, you walked in here and got caught?"

"There were five others with me." Sandra shudders once more. "They offered us a choice: we could join their order, or we could die. The others all chose to die. I . . . I was too weak."

"Well, we'll get you out of here," I say, trying to comfort her. "Do you have any other clothes? Those robes are going to be awful hard to run in."

"I don't, I'm sorry. They took everything." A tear runs down Sandra's cheek. "Can you really get me back home? Is any of the world left?"

"Believe it or not, we're actually doing quite well for ourselves." I give a wry nod. "Things fall apart, we patch them back up. That's the American way. Granted, I think they're doing it all across the world, *but* . . ." I flash a smile, then slowly slip back up to the entrance. "Where do we go from here? We need to get you out, and I know this will sound crazy, but I need to find the guy with the glowing sword."

"Master Throm." Sandra nods. "He's usually in the high temple. It's a horrid place. I don't like to go there, but I can point you in the right direction."

"Please do," I say. "Just tell me how to get there."

"First . . ." Sandra pauses. "If you'd be willing, there's actually a dungeon in here. Like a *dungeon* dungeon, not a monster dungeon. They've captured dozens of people, Awakened and normal people alike, who they use for sacrifices. You've got to get them out while you're here."

"I'll see what I can do," I promise her. "Where do we need to go?"

Sandra points down the hall. "That way. If something happens and we get separated, turn right at the creepy statue and go down the flight of stairs. When you get to the bottom, you'll be there. Keys are usually somewhere in the area."

"Good. Let's get moving."

I slip out into the hall and slowly creep forward, moving along as quietly as I can. The hallway, after leaving the barracks behind, begins to curve softly through the stone. There are carvings on the wall here, but I can't tell exactly what they mean. They seem to be some sort of pictorial history, which I could probably decipher given the time, but I'm in a bit too much of a hurry right at this moment.

Suddenly, up ahead, I see several shadows on the wall in the torchlight. I glance around, looking for a place to hide, but there are none. An idea pops into my head, and I nod at Sandra.

"Hood up, stand still."

Sandra does exactly that, lifting her hood into place and folding her hands just like an obedient monk. I crouch down behind her, taking advantage of her voluminous robes. Feet patter on the floor, and another monk hurries into view.

"Recruit! You should be back in your cell," the monk calls out. "There's a killer about."

"I'm . . . terribly sorry." Sandra's voice is weak.

"It's alright. Events like these are always troublesome." The monk strides past, missing me. "Now, if you'll—"

I stand up, step up behind the monk, and clap my hand over its mouth from behind. I should probably mention at this point that undead flesh is *really* disgusting. It's all leathery and decayed and the teeth are rotting, and every instinct in my entire body is screaming at me to get away as fast as possible. The monk immediately begins to thrash but can only get out a small whimper. My dagger flashes in my hand, and I stab it half a dozen times in the span of a blink of an eye. Slowly, the monk relaxes and then crumbles into dust. As the body collapses in a heap, I sheath the dagger, then slowly turn away.

"You're . . . good." Sandra grimaces. "How many monsters have you killed so far?"

"I honestly don't know," I answer as I walk after her. "Hundreds, easily. I don't know if I've hit a thousand yet, but it's possible."

"Fascinating." She shakes her head. "You know, when I first started seeing all you hunters appearing, I wanted to be one of you so bad. I think that's why I entered the portal in the first place—some sort of power fantasy in my own mind. Now, I'm just ready to get back home."

A thought strikes me, and I frown. "Where exactly *is* your home? I don't recall seeing a college anywhere close to the place where this portal opened."

"Missouri," Sandra answers. "I was going to a community college there. Where are we now?"

"Right now? Who knows. This portal, though, opens up into New York City."

Sandra stops. "New York? I've always wanted to visit NYC!"

"Well, now you have your chance." I prod her ahead. "Come on. We've got to keep moving. I don't know if there's anything behind us, but we can't take that risk. We need to get down into that dungeon and out of here, and fast."

Sandra nods and starts moving forward once more. "You know, I knew Master Throm moved the portal, but I didn't know where to. It was earlier today, after he received the vision and the sword. It told him he needed to find something but didn't say what."

"Interesting," I murmur. This whole *sword* business has my head spinning, and it makes me nervous. I have some ideas about it, but I don't want to jump to any conclusions too quickly.

In any case, the hallway continues to curve until we come into sight of a large twisted statue. It looks sort of humanoid, but it has all the wrong proportions. I can't tell you exactly why I think so, but I'm quite confident that the thing is ugly beyond belief. Right next to it is a doorway, which Sandra points me toward.

"Right this way."

I nod, then slip through the door into a tightly winding stairwell, taking the lead. Once more, everything begins to feel darker, dimmer, more dismal. I take a tight hold on my dagger, knowing that I'll likely have to use it. In dungeons, jailers are always *beasts* to take down, and I have little doubt that this will be no exception.

The stairs curl tightly upon themselves, and I do my best to keep my footsteps quiet, but I soon find it impossible to maintain silence entirely. As I come to the bottom, another arched doorway stands at the ready, and I see a particularly large monk sitting in a chair. I can't see its face, only the lower part of its body. It shifts slightly.

"That you? 'Bout time you got here. The master is going to have a fit if these prisoners aren't fed soon!"

Sandra places a hand on my arm, then slips around me, adjusts her hood, and steps down through the doorway.

"Ah! You! Recruit! You know you're not allowed down here."

"I'm very sorry, but there's a commotion up there." Sandra points upward. "An intruder. He's killed . . . a lot of us."

"Hmph. Well, he won't get us here." The jailer stands up. "I'll just head up that there stairwell and make sure he can't get down here. I'll teach him a lesson if he tries to poke his dirty little head in here, and I'll—"

The monk starts to walk up the stairs, and I attack while I still have the chance. Throwing myself forward, I kick the monk in the face just as hard as I can, sending it reeling backward. As I drop to the ground, I rush it with my Enlarged Dagger. It takes another step back, bumping into Sandra. As it shoves her back, I notice that she's snatched the keys off its belt. With that, she runs over to the many, many cages spread around the room, and I face off against the jailer. I can't really spare any chance to look around, except to say that there's a lot of open space and a lot of cages, along with a few pieces of torture equipment here and there.

The monk is big: a good seven feet tall but proportioned more like a dwarf than a man. It grunts and snorts, then snatches a large mace off its belt. There's no chain; it's just a spike ball mounted on a stick, but it certainly looks like it'll hurt. The undead monk grunts and swings it around a few times, then steadies itself and lowers itself into a stance.

"You're about to be in a whole world of hurt, boy."

"Maybe." I shrug. "Then again, maybe not. Shall we find out?"

Behind it, Sandra sticks the key into the lock and begins to turn it. Knowing that there will almost certainly be a click within a matter of moments, I race forward, drawing the jailor's attention. It snarls and comes forward to meet me, and we clash together with resounding force.

It raises the mace to hit me, and I flash up and parry it with my dagger long before the monk has a chance to bring it down. That makes the monk stagger back a bit, and I slash the dagger across its oversized belly. Its robes split open, and a great deal of dust comes pouring out. The monster snarls and lunges forward.

This time it simply uses its entire mass to try and body-slam me. It works, and I stagger backward. With that, it presses the attack, swinging the mace several times in wide, sweeping arcs. Thankfully, they're fairly easy to predict, though I have to imagine that a misstep will be *very* painful. Behind the monk, I see people beginning to sneak out of the cells, and Sandra flashes me a thumbs-up before moving on to the next one.

Somehow, all my recent dungeons have turned into rescue attempts. Not that I mind, really, but it *is* strange. In any case, I'm forced to focus upon the jailer as it suddenly runs forward, brandishing the mace over its head. I leap out of the way just as the monk swings it down, and the whole floor shakes as it hits the stone. I smile and spin to attack the monk's back, only for it to spin around *way* faster than I was expecting.

Wham!

The attack hits me firmly in the stomach, and I'm knocked flat upon the ground. The jailor looks down at me . . . and then snarls angrily.

"Recruit! I knew it was a mistake to trust you!"

The monk starts to run forward, and I quickly spin and sweep its legs as best I can. It falls flat on its face with a resounding *thud*, and I jump to my feet once more. As it starts to rise, I kick it in the face just as hard as I can, making it flop over onto its back.

My dagger flashes in my hand, and I stab down at the monk. This time my aim is true, and it screams as the dagger slams down into its chest. I wait for it to die . . . only to be blindsided by the mace once more.

"*Ahhhh!*" I let out a rather undignified cry as the thing whacks me clean over its body to land on the ground with a *thud*. The monk snarls and rises, the knife still embedded in its chest, and I stand up as well. I start to open my inventory, and it twitches toward me.

"Open that up, boy, and I'll split your skull open," it snarls softly. "You just stand right there, all pretty like. Girl! Stop where you are!"

"Sandra? You keep right on going," I order. I can't see her to know how she's doing, but I'm certain that if she stops, we're all dead. Plus, you know, all the prisoners are scheduled to be sacrificed anyway, *so . . .*

"Stop!"

"Go!"

[ShadowDancer: Go, Sandra! You can get everyone out of there!!!]

[LunarEclipse: Yeah, go for it! Don't stop to listen to the creepy monster guy!]

[RazorEdge: If I were there, I'd be able to kill that fat guy in like half a second.]

The jailor looks at me, and its hand twitches. It's fast, and I know if I try to open my inventory up, I'm not going to make it. So I don't even try.

Instead, I reach up and draw out Ascalon.

The sword gleams with a divine energy as I whip it out. The monk lunges forward, but I catch the mace with the blade, batting it aside with ease. The monk screams and staggers backward, and lightning flickers from the edge of the sword.

"You're not going to get these prisoners." I set my stance. "Not now, or ever."

The monk takes in a deep breath, then opens its mouth and bellows as loud as it can. It sounds almost like a foghorn.

It charges at me once more, swinging the mace around its head. I lunge forward and slash at it, only for the monk to block me. And, with that, we lock together.

I attack as fast as I can, striking over and over and over, but it's *fast* and manages to block each and every one of my strokes. Suddenly, the momentum of the battle changes, and I find *it* attacking *me*. I'm forced backward as its blows come harder and faster. Someone more experienced with a sword may have been able to counter better, but I'm suddenly finding the weapon awkward. I keep trying to use dagger-type attacks instead of sword attacks, which the larger blade just can't handle. Suddenly, the monk lunges past my defense and smashes the mace into my face.

That *hurts*.

Blood streaming down my face, I stagger backward, and the monk raises the mace for one final blow. With that, I lash upward with the sword, hitting it in the left leg and slashing all the way up to the collar. Dust explodes outward from the hit, and the monk seems almost to deflate.

"*Rrrrrrrrrrarg!*"

Astrid, unbidden, springs past me and snatches onto the tunic of the monk. She snarls and yanks, ripping it backward, and brings the monk crashing to the floor. I lunge forward, snatch up my dagger, and stab the monk in the face. The blade sinks in up to the hilt, and with that, the monk grows still. I sigh and slowly stand back up, pull out the blade to return it to my inventory, and sheath Ascalon on my back.

"And there we have it." I slowly turn away from the fight to find Sandra unlocking the last of the cages. A collection of almost fifty people stands in front of me, a motley group of civilians and some low-level warriors. Sandra steps up to me and passes me the keys.

"I think you should have these."

"I'll do what I can with them." I nod to her, then glance at the assortment of people. "Alright, how do we get out of here? Also, what was that noise the monk made?"

Sandra gulps slightly. "That was . . . The noise was a call telling the other monks that there's trouble down here. They're probably preparing to attack this quarter right now. Sorry, I should have realized that earlier."

"Not to worry. We'll get out just fine." I frown in thought. "How do we get out?"

"The portal is this way!" a man calls out. "Right through here. We'll go up into the main entrance hall!"

"If they know we're here, they'll be fortifying that direction right now." I shake my head. "I could probably do it myself, but there's no way I could get all of you guys out of here alive. We've got to do something different. Is there another way?"

"We could go through the training rooms." Sandra points at another door. "That's probably where the monks will go to begin with to grab weapons, then leave and go a different route."

"That sounds like a good enough plan to me." I give a nod. "Alright, come on. Let's move out." I draw in a deep breath. "No mistakes, people. I want *everyone* to make it out of here alive."

CHAPTER TWENTY

The group quickly moves over to the doorway. By now, I can hear monks moving around in the distance, but as I've killed no small number of them at this point, they're not particularly eager to just come charging in, guns blazing. That, thankfully, might just work to our advantage. I slowly turn the knob and pull the door open, peering out into what seems to be a long dark hallway. Torches flicker to life as I step through, which I consider to be a good thing. It means that there's no one else there.

"Alright, come along," I whisper. "Come quickly and come quietly. Once they figure out that we're not in that room, they'll know exactly where we went."

Everyone nods. Sandra stays at the rear, ushering everyone through, while I run along ahead toward the far end. As I arrive, I find another small door, which seems to be locked.

"Interesting." I crouch down and peer through the small keyhole. It's an older style of lock, so I can actually see through to the other side. Unfortunately, I can't see much, only something that looks sort of like an eastern-style training court. Like . . . if a gazillionaire was to get it in his head that he was going to learn martial arts and fight crime, this is where he'd be sent. I watch and wait, and when I'm confident that there's no one there, I straighten up and try the knob.

Yup. Locked.

"Alright. We'll just have to get creative with this one." I draw out my Phasing Dagger, which flickers in the air. "Let's see just how much of a damage threshold you can ignore."

[ChaosRider: YEAH!!! This is going to be great!]

[IceQueen: Nah, boring. I've seen this happen a hundred times on cop shows and things.]

[FireStorm: Uh, Jason? I don't mean to be a wet blanket, but don't you have a key that Sandra gave you?]

I blink in surprise right before I attack with the dagger and rather sheepishly realize that not only was I given a key, but I'm still holding it in my left hand. I quickly insert it into the lock, turn it with a click, and swing the door wide open. I step through slowly and glance about for any sort of unwelcome guests.

Snick.

The noise is soft, and I hold up my hand. The area itself is large, maybe fifty feet on each side, with little alcoves here and there filled with weapons. Slowly, on either side, a figure steps out from one of the alcoves. One is holding a long staff. The other is holding a short blade in either hand. No, not blades. They look more like short spikes, pointed on the end and smooth on the sides. There are small prongs down at the hilt of each one, almost like a guard for a hand, but I can't tell that for certain. They look quite nasty, in any case.

"So, you *did* know we'd be coming this way." I glance at the two of them. They slowly begin to walk out, pacing around me. I should probably note that unlike the others I've fought, *these* guys look like they're built for combat. They're much slimmer, with robes carefully tailored around themselves to allow for the best combat movement possible. Their hoods aren't quite as deep, and their sleeves are tied tightly around their arms.

"We suspected. The others did not listen," the monk with the staff says. "That will be their downfall and our rise. Surrender now and we will make your death as painless as possible."

"But you'll still kill me," I clarify. "Just to make sure we're on the same page."

"Of course we will," the monk sneers. "You are nothing but a flesh-covered interloper, and you have killed many of our people. You deserve nothing but the darkness and the unending punishment that comes with it."

"I see." I don't really pay much attention to the words. I keep the monk with the staff in front of me, slowly turning as the two of them walk around me. It seems most likely that this one will be the more dangerous of the two, since it has a longer range. "Why don't you come at me, and we'll see what happens?"

There's no answer for a moment. Suddenly, the monk with the staff does, indeed, run at me, though I can tell from its stance that it's not actually intending to do any damage.

[ViperQueen: Go Jason!!! Knock these guys down a few pegs!]

[DarkCynic: He should call out Bjorn! No, Burnie! Yeah, bring out Burnie!]

[GoldenShield: I don't think bringing out Burnie would be advisable in this case. The quarters are too close, and—]

I'm forced to ignore the argument in the chat as the monk comes racing up and begins to strike at me. It unleashes a flurry of blows, rapid and strong, though they're all feints. A few of them do hit me, but it causes no damage at all, really. All it does is disorient me slightly.

Slightly, though, isn't enough to distract me from the monk charging up behind me.

Its blades flicker in the light, and I spin just as it strikes. My Phasing Dagger flashes in the light, and the monk almost seems to stagger simply in awe of it. I whack both its blades away in a single blow, then lunge forward, stabbing at the monk with my dagger. A long ghostly trail flares out behind it, and the monk raises both blades to block.

And, of course, my dagger passes straight through the blades.

In that moment, I suddenly realize a key weakness in the whole "inability to be blocked" part of the dagger's effects. Yes, no one can block it, but in turn, the moment my blade passes through the monk's blades, there's nothing to prevent the monk from attacking *me*. I stab the dagger deep into its chest just as it stabs both of its blades into my guts.

Pain radiates outward from the strikes almost instantly, and I gasp in pain. I really can't describe it—it's simply extraordinary. My vision blurs, and I feel my legs go weak. Still, I have the presence of mind to rip out my own dagger and deal quite a bit of damage to the monk. It staggers backward, pulling out its blades, and I grimace and double over in pain.

Whack!

A blow falls heavy on the back of my head, and I stagger and come crashing to the floor. I can hear the things laughing. I can hear the screams of the civilians. My blood trickles out over the floor, and my health drops rapidly.

And then, suddenly, it stops falling.

[Skill: Bearing of a Knight.]

[Peril Detected.]

[Increasing Strength by 200%.]

[Increasing Dexterity by 300%.]

[Increasing Health Regeneration by 1,000%.]

[Increasing Damage Resistance by 500%.]

[. . .]

The list of effects scrolls past my vision. It's quite long, but I don't have time to look at all of it. Slowly, I stand back up, and my health begins to rise.

Whack!

The monk whacks the staff across my face. There's a blast of light, and the staff cracks in two, leaving the monk with almost a foot less staff to work with.

[ShadowDancer: AHHHHHHHH!!! I just screamed like a girl. That's so exciting!!!]

[DarkCynic: Why didn't you tell us you could do that, Jason?]

[FireStorm: Yeah, I feel cheated!]

Strength surges through me, and I take in a deep breath. The monk staggers backward, and I leap at it with all my might. This time I switch out the Phasing Dagger for the Enlarged Dagger and attack just as hard and fast as I can.

My blows come rapidly, and the monk spins its staff around to parry as many of them as it can. It's good. It's still a bit faster than I am and manages to duck around the side of my guard after a moment. Once more, it swings the staff around to hit me in the back. The blow is hard but only makes me stagger a few feet. The monk seems to smirk, then attacks once more, flipping the weapon around to hit me in the face.

Smack!

My arm moves so fast I hardly see it myself, and I catch the staff in my bare hand. For a moment, the two of us strain, and I rip the staff down and out of its grasp with a practiced twist. The monk staggers, and I spin and whack *it* with the staff. The monk falls backward and lands with a loud *crack*, though I admittedly don't know if I've killed it or not. It's possible, but then, it could still come back.

"*Ahhhhhhh!*"

The second monk runs at me, moving at a brilliant sprint. I drop the staff and come up to meet it with the Enlarged Dagger. For a brief moment, we spar just as fast as we can. Its blades crash against my own. I'm not able to break its guard—it's far too fast—but it also can't break through mine.

As I stab at it, the undead monk crosses its weapons at the hilts and catches my dagger between the two, using the hand guards to lock them together. I grimace and try to break free, only for the monk to disengage at that very moment, redirecting me to the side. With that, it strikes and stabs me twice in the right arm. Blood gushes down for a brief moment, though it stops rather quickly as the enhancements heal me. I snarl at the monk, then attack with force once more, and within just a few steps, I break through its guard.

"Skill: Speed," I order.

[Speed activated.]

[Bearing of a Knight emergency protocols are incompatible with active skills.]

[Bearing of a Knight emergency protocols have been deactivated.]

The world slows down as Speed kicks in, but a great deal of energy seems to leave me. I shrug and charge at the monster, only for a brief flicker of light to come over it.

"Nice trick. Can you match mine?"

With that, we come crashing together once more, each moving at an enhanced speed, each desperately looking for a way through the other's defenses. I find myself blocking more times than I attack and am soon forced backward toward one of the alcoves.

[Speed will wear off in 00:00:03.]

[00:00:02]

[00:00:01]

The world suddenly speeds up again, and the monk hits me like a load of bricks. I'm thrown back into the alcove and crash into a rack of spears. The monk attacks me with a flurry of blows before stepping back. I gasp in pain as my health drops to a measly 25 percent, maybe lower. I groan and try to sit up.

"You're nothing," the monk sneers. "We've been trained for years to fight against your kind. We know all your tactics, and we're trained to adapt to ones we don't know."

"Good to know." I wince and slip back to the ground. I have a dozen wounds, maybe more. I suddenly see that the monk's weapons were designed to punch a hole into the muscle, impairing my movement rather significantly. I can't move, or not very much, and I'm in *so* much pain. Ascalon doesn't show any sign of activating again, which makes me suspect that there's at least *some* sort of a cooldown timer, though I admittedly don't know what that might be. The monk walks forward, coolly and precisely, and watches me closely for any sign of weakness. It's worried about traps—otherwise, the job would be done by now.

Suddenly, a growl echoes through the air.

The ground cracks underneath me, and a great blast of steam explodes upward from the ground. It hurts and drops my health even more, but it also conceals me from the monk. Quickly, a portal opens, and Balder sticks his head out from the pocket dimension. He has an open bottle of Pumped! in his mouth, which he tips to the side to pour into mine. His aim is terrible, and he spills as much across my face and hair as in my mouth, but it's the thought that counts. When he's finished, he draws back inside the pocket dimension, and the steam goes away. I'm once more left on the ground at the mercy of the approaching monk.

"Nice trick, but no cigar," the monk sneers. "You may have just tried to escape, but it didn't work, now, did it?"

"Well enough."

My body still hurts—a *lot*—but the little bit of Pumped! that actually got into my system is enough to heal up my wounds. I draw in a deep breath, then sit up and throw my dagger as hard as I can.

The monk isn't expecting it and isn't able to dodge before the dagger hits it in the chest. It screams and snatches at the dagger, but by then, I'm already up. I snatch out the Phasing Dagger and attack once more, flashing through the air just as fast as I can. It brings up its blades to block, but this time I'm ready.

My Phasing Dagger stabs through its guard, but I'm not in the right position to be stabbed. Instead, I jog around to the side, and I hit it in the chest just above the Enlarged Dagger. I grit my teeth and shove with all my might, and I rip through its neck and up to its skull. There's a loud *crack*, and the monk slowly topples backward, landing on the ground with a *thunk*.

"You know, when this is all over, I'm never going to be able to watch another kung fu movie again." I put my dagger away, then slowly turn to the group of survivors. "Which way now?"

Sandra draws in a deep breath, then slowly lifts a hand. "That way. It's—"

"I don't care if we're going right through the sacrifice room itself." I turn in that direction. "We need to move. Come on, let's get going."

CHAPTER TWENTY-ONE

Sandra points me toward a small reddish door covered in a great many runes, which remind me of the runes on the sword itself. That doesn't fill me full of confidence at all, and I take a deep breath.

"It's not going to kill me just by opening it, is it?"

"No, no." Sandra shakes her head, then pauses. "Well, admittedly, the only people I've ever seen opening it are the monks, so . . ."

I sigh, then, just to be safe, draw out my Enlarged Dagger and stab the door as hard as I can. Cracks erupt outward through the wood from the point of impact. Cracks that glow. A moment later, there's a powerful explosion, and the door dissolves into nothing but splinters.

"Huh. That might actually have killed you." Sandra frowns. "Interesting."

"Interesting indeed." I sigh and step through the rubble,

then start upward as fast as I can. This time I'm climbing a staircase instead of going down one. Interesting, I suppose. "Now, where *does* this lead to?"

"The central sacrifice room. The lower temple, as we call it."

My blood turns rather cold. "You're joking."

"You said you didn't care." Sandra shrugs. "For what it's worth, once we go through it, we'll be able to go right out through the main doors and into the main entryway. It should be right about there, so that's good."

"I suppose so," I murmur. Now, don't get me wrong. I'm fairly confident I can get through the sacrifice room, but these guys are getting harder and harder to beat, and I have fifty people I'd rather like to get to safety, *and* I need to make sure I can kill the guy with the dragonbone sword fast enough to take the sword from him before the sword can portal away. If I can't do *that*, then . . . well . . . this was mostly for naught. Not that saving lives is pointless by any stretch, but if I can't figure out what's going on with this sword, then a lot more people are likely to die.

Anyway, we reach the top of the stairs soon enough. Instead of a door, there's an elaborate red curtain. I hold my breath, then slowly lean forward and poke my head out.

The lower temple is massive, there's just no other way to look at it. It looks sort of like a twisted replica of a cathedral, but with dark and demonic statues instead of saintly ones and artwork drawn from blood instead of stained glass. A red carpet stretches across the floor from the doorway straight out to a stone altar, in front of which two more red-robed monks are bowing. There are candles lit, and I can only imagine that I've stumbled onto some sort of a sacrifice.

"Oh no," Sandra whispers. "They're performing a ritual designed to grant them victory in battle."

"Great," I mutter. I don't put much stock in rituals, generally speaking, but I have to imagine that this one will give them some sort of buff that makes them almost impossible to defeat. "What does that entail?"

"In about two minutes, they'll both kill themselves."

"That's good." I nod slowly.

"And the rest of them will gain indestructibility for two hours."

"That's not good." I pause in thought. "Alright, then. You guys stay back here unless something comes up behind you. I'm heading in."

"These guys are *really* powerful." Sandra grabs my arm. "I recognize them! They're both priests. Either could succeed Master Throm in the event of his death."

"Except that they'll be dead soon." I shrug. "One way or another."

"I suppose." Sandra grimaces. "Just . . . be careful."

"I will."

I draw in a deep breath, flex my muscles, and step out through the curtain.

Wham!

Almost instantly, I'm slammed to the ground as if by an unseen hand. It hurts rather badly, and I groan as all the air is driven from my lungs. Slowly, I start trying to stand back up, only to find the pressure increasing all the more.

"And just what do you think you're trying to do?"

The voice is dark and powerful, and I grit my teeth as I look up to find both priests on their feet. They're holding long, obsidian knives in their hands, and I know instinctively that it'll be very, *very* bad to get hit by those things.

"What am I trying to do?" I slowly rise up. "I've actually been trying to see your boss, but I keep getting the runaround. Go talk to this secretary, then make an appointment for next Thursday, except no one has any record of it, and I'm just done."

[DarkCynic: Good one, Jason!]

[ChaosRider: Able to make a joke even under pressure! Lol!!!]

I frankly don't think the joke was really all that good, but if my fans find it entertaining, I suppose that's good enough for me. I take one final breath and rise fully to my feet, staring at the priests as intently as I can.

"You laugh at your predicament," one of the priests snarls softly. "Soon you will be dead, and *then* you will know the true meaning of pain."

"Maybe so." I shrug. "Then again, maybe not. I have a feeling that you didn't expect me to get up off the ground."

The priests don't answer. One of them raises his hand, and I see light flaring in his palm.

That's my cue to drop, which is quite easy given the pressure on my shoulders. With a mighty *wham*, I fall back to the ground, just as a powerful piercing blast shoots over my head and hits the wall. With that, I lunge forward as best I can.

The pressure only increases as I stagger toward the two priests, and I'm brought to a halt. This is going to require some assistance.

"Alright, Bjorn. Now's your shot."

The portal to my pocket dimension opens, but instead

of Bjorn, Balder steps out. Right—Bjorn is still healing. The priests both laugh as they see the teenage Frost Wolf, and one of them raises a hand to target *him* with the deadly energy.

And that's when Balder growls.

The floor shakes, and cracks explode across the stone. Steam shoots up, scalding hot steam mixed with smoke and fire. The priests both step backward, flailing against the heat, and Balder takes a deep breath and barks.

That one bark erupts through the room like a shockwave, blasting stone from the wall. The two priests are both lifted off their feet and thrown backward, and I give Balder a nod as the pressure on my shoulders vanishes.

"Much appreciated!"

He gives an excited *woof*, which brings down a large chunk of the ceiling. As stone and rubble crash around me, I charge forward, dodging boulders as I angle toward the two priests. They start to rise, cloaked in dust and rubble, and I launch myself toward them.

"Pathetic."

One of them raises a hand, and I freeze in midair, caught by an invisible hand.

"You will die, and you will—"

I grit my teeth and throw my Enlarged Dagger at the priest, who raises a hand to bat it aside with his sacrificial dagger. But that causes him to lose contact with me. The moment my feet are back on the ground, I race forward, throwing myself into combat the instant that I can.

I don't have my Enlarged Dagger anymore, but that's all right. Instead, I draw out my Phasing Dagger and raise it as the first priest stabs at me.

Clang!

I parry his blade excellently, then stab at him. As he tries to block it, my own blade shoots straight through his weapon, and I score a mark along his arm. He staggers in surprise, and I whip around behind him, stabbing deep into his back before kicking out his knee. He gasps and falls to his knees, and I prepare to deliver the killing blow.

Except . . . well . . . that's too easy.

Wham!

A boulder smashes into me from the side, sending me bouncing across the floor. The second priest advances, using his telekinesis to fling massive projectiles. As I come to a stop, Balder steps up next to me, snarling.

A particularly large boulder flashes through the air at us, and he barks sharply. It explodes into nothing but a bit of dust. The priest snarls and slowly advances forward while throwing more and more of the stones. Balder stands strong, barking and gnashing his teeth, and blasts them all apart.

[LunarEclipse: I think I've found my new favorite of Jason's pets!]

[ViperQueen: Yeah, no kidding! This is epic!!!]

[GoldenShield: Hey, Balder! See if you can return one of those to sender!]

The second priest climbs to his feet as well, and together, they lift up a particularly large chunk of the ceiling. It begins to glow with a powerful internal energy, and it flashes toward us. Balder draws in a deep breath, then howls at the top of his lungs.

The stone stops a mere foot or two from us. Shockwaves reverberate around it and hold it back even as the priests try to force it forward. Balder's eyes are fierce, and he digs in his claws. Finally, he gives one more yap, and the hold of the priests breaks.

Wham!

KA-BOOM!

The stone is flung backward at an extraordinary speed and hits both priests. It explodes on impact, filling the air with fire and energy. Balder sways on his feet, and I give him a pat.

"That'll be enough, boy. Go get some rest. I'll take it from here."

Balder steps back, and with that, I wave my hand. Burnie shoots out of my pocket dimension along with Astrid, and together we run forward.

Burnie goes first and unleashes a great blast of fire into the smoke and dust. The light illuminates two figures, which seem to be desperately trying to fight back. Astrid snarls, and a great chunk of stone falls down and flattens them, only for Burnie to melt the stone into a great puddle of lava that flows down over the two figures. Still, they don't seem to be dying, which is a problem.

"Just how are we going to take these things down?" I scowl as I run forward. "Alright, draw back! Let me in there again!"

Burnie nods and turns, swooping away, and Astrid skids to a stop. I race forward into the smoke and dust to find the two figures just emerging from the glowing pool. They both seem to be at least somewhat blinded, and I take the opportunity to leap forward and stab one of them in the face. The priest groans and falls backward, dead before he hits the ground. As I stab at the other one, though, a red aura forms around my wrist and stops it cold.

"You will not take us," the priest snarls. "I will have my victory. We will all have our victory."

His dagger flashes through the air and stabs me in the arm. I gasp in pain. It's something truly extraordinary. It feels like my entire arm has turned to stone, and I stagger backward as the priest slowly steps up, snarling and hissing. A dire coldness seems to flow down from the wound into my fingers, solidifying them in place, then flows up into my shoulder, where it comes to a stop.

[Condition: Cursed. Debuffs have been added to all stat points for the next 00:05:00.]

Debuffs? My entire arm won't move! That's more than just a debuff!

Still, there's nothing that can be done about it. Maybe I have some healing items that could remove the curse, but I don't have the time to look for them as the priest stalks toward me. He raises a hand once more, and a concussive blast hits me in the chest, flinging me backward across the floor. Astrid snarls and drops another section of the ceiling on him, but this time he's ready, and he knocks it out of the way. Burnie swoops down, but he simply forms a force field *around* Burnie. My Phoenix lets out a massive blast of fire, but that only scorches himself, and the noble bird falls to the ground a few feet from me, smoke rising from his feathers.

"You are mighty, Jason Lee. I give you that." The priest's voice seems to mock me. "There haven't been many people who could deal out as much damage as you. You've even killed one of my brethren. No one has taken down someone of my rank in many a year, so . . . congrats." His voice is sarcastic. "However, I'm here to tell you that you've failed."

"I'm still alive, so it's not that much of a failure." I grit my teeth and force myself up. The priest raises a hand, and I feel the pressure again. Likely because of my debuffs, it's impossibly strong, and I'm smashed back against the ground.

"The key issue is that, here, you're not just trying to stay alive. You were trying to kill me before I could kill myself, which is a difficult task indeed." The priest smiles as he flips around the dagger and points it at his own chest. "Perhaps I can't complete the full ritual, and I won't quite bequeath the full effect I might otherwise have given, but I'll do enough. Good job, Jason Lee. My only regret is that I won't be around to see you fighting desperately for your life. It's almost enough to make me root for you."

[ShadowDancer: Oh no!!! Jason, you have to do something!]

I have to agree, and I think I know exactly what I need to do. Gritting my teeth against what I know will be fantastically painful, I speak a single phrase.

"Skill: Speed."

The world around me slows, and I find the pressure ease on my body. I climb to my feet, slowly and painfully, still feeling like I have a bag of concrete on my shoulders. With all my might, I run forward. It feels like I'm running through molasses, but at least I'm moving. The priest, in slow motion, sees what I'm doing and slams the dagger down into his chest.

At least . . . he tries to.

Before he can manage it, I punch outward with my numb hand. Well, I sort of throw my whole shoulder, but it's enough, and I manage to slam my frozen fingers into the blade. Given that they're frozen, or perhaps petrified, the blade refuses to cut through them, and it stops right at the priest's skin. Before he can do anything more, I punch him with my free hand, smashing my fist into his face.

The priest reels backward, and the world speeds up once more. I smile grimly and stalk toward him, even as he feebly raises a hand to defend himself.

Even debuffed, I'm not too shabby, and I'm going to kill him.

Then, I'm going to kill every other member of his little cult.

CHAPTER TWENTY-TWO

"No . . . ," the priest whispers. He doesn't seem to have any power left. I'm not exactly sure why that is, but I'm not going to question it. "Please, I—"

Thud.

The noise is soft—so much so that I hardly hear it. The room, though, grows cold, and I get the feeling that I know exactly what just happened. Ignoring the priest, I slowly turn around to find Master Throm standing tall in the midst of the rubble and destruction of the room. He has the dragonbone sword in one hand and stares at me with glowing, piercing blue eyes. His entire body is made of liquid shadow, though it does take on a mostly humanoid form. I take a deep breath and glance at the condition counter.

[Condition: Cursed.]

[Duration Remaining: 00:04:12]

That's a lot of time in the middle of a fight, especially

against a boss. I do want to talk to him, though. Maybe I can get him to start chatting? Hard to know for sure.

"The man I've been wanting to talk to." I draw myself up a bit straighter. "Master Throm, I presume?"

He doesn't react. A moment passes, and he flashes forward so fast I can barely see him move. I raise my dagger to block, but as I'm holding it with my left hand now, and because of the curse, I'm *way* slower than I ought to be. In any case, he's not even trying to hit me and instead shoots straight past me to strike at the priest. He explodes into dust as Throm's sword slashes him in two, and the shadow lurker shoots back to the middle of the room in the same breath of motion.

Wow. Okay, I might be a bit outclassed by this guy.

[DarkCynic: Hmm. Jason might have actually met his match this time!]

[FireStorm: Yeah, I don't really see how he's getting out of this one!]

[ChaosRider: Call in Balder again! It's your only hope!!!]

[ViperQueen: Oh, not his *only* hope. Blub might be useful too.]

I draw in a deep breath, then nod at his weapon.

"That sword. I'm interested in it."

There's another long pause, and the master speaks.

"And why should I tell you anything of it? I can see the duration of your curse. You're only trying to wait me out so you can have better stats."

I shrug. "Can you blame a guy for trying?" The master doesn't seem to take the joke, and I sigh. I know the only reason he's humoring me is because he can kill me in half a second right now, so waiting another minute or two won't really affect his chances. "In any case, I *did* come here to see that sword. I've been running into it for a few days now, and I have to admit that I'm a bit bothered by the thing."

"Impossible," the master snaps. "This sword was given to me by the god of fire himself, our dear patron." He utters a name in a dark tongue that I can't reproduce in English, nor would I want to try even if I could.

"No, I really don't think it was." I shrug, then pause. "Well, you never know, what with the world as crazy as it is right now. In any case, if it *was* given to you by the god of fire, it was only after that very god gave it to a dragonspawn fast-food worker as well as an ogre mage."

The master snarls softly. "Ogres are not even sentient, properly speaking. No weapon of this nobility could be wielded by a beast."

"You'll just have to take it up with your boss." I shrug. "Speaking of which . . . any chance I could meet him? If you're just a henchman, I'd really love to take things up with the big guy."

That's the wrong thing to say. The master flashes forward and strikes at me with the sword. He moves so fast that I would hardly have been able to respond in an ordinary state of existence. Being mostly petrified, I can only blink as he slashes the sword across me, knocking me backward rather powerfully. I come crashing down almost fifty feet away, groaning in pain. My health has fallen by half, which does *not* bode well for this fight turning in my favor.

[Condition: Cursed.]

[Duration Remaining: 00:03:33]

"Couldn't we talk about this?" I ask, slowly struggling to my feet. I force my petrified arm to move at least a little bit.

Maybe that means it's healing, maybe it means that I've always been able to move it a small amount. Slowly, I regain my footing. What weapons do I have at the moment? I still have my Phasing Dagger, but my Enlarged Dagger is off somewhere among all the rubble. Sure, the Phasing Dagger is a good weapon, but it's hardly going to have the reach to protect me against the reach of the dragonbone sword. The shadow lurker is simply too fast. I need . . .

I need the sword.

Slowly, I reach up with my left hand and grab the hilt of Ascalon. As I draw it free, a warmth begins to flow down through my body. The fingers of my right hand twitch just a little bit, and I touch the hilt of the sword with it.

[Condition: Cursed.]

[Status: Paused.]

[Duration Remaining: 00:03:10]

My arm gains mobility once more, and I take in a deep breath. Slowly, I start to walk forward, climbing up over the rubble toward Master Throm. The dragonbone sword glows softly with a deadly light, and he slowly starts to move forward, tensing for an attack.

In that moment, I suddenly see the briefest flicker of a pattern. The master is a shadow lurker, that much is easy to see. He can stay back out of range and then only attack when he's absolutely ready to strike, moving so fast that I don't stand a chance to react. I have to anticipate his movements, and that's all there is to it. Suddenly, the lurker leaps forward, and I swing.

My blow is far too slow, and he hits me like a ton of bricks. This time I'm blasted all the way to the far wall, where I slam into the stone not all that far beneath one of the blood paintings. The master watches me closely, his blue eyes fiery and cold.

"You will not escape my domain alive," the master snarls softly. "I will kill you."

"Then why haven't you done it yet?" I ask, glancing at my health. I have about 5 percent left, and that's it. Wonderful. "Could it be that it's because you're curious? You feel betrayed? You want to know what I have to say about this mysterious master of yours, afraid that you've been playing the fool all along?"

"How dare you speak of what you do not know?" the master snaps, though he does seem to pause at that statement. He's cautious, afraid, and I can't say that I blame him. After all, if I'm right and the sword is being passed around to other people, it might mean that his entire religion is false.

"How? It's actually pretty easy," I answer. "Now . . . Either kill me or don't."

Warmth flares up my arm from the sword.

[Skill: Bearing of a Knight.]

[Peril Detected.]

The lurker launches himself forward, and this time I'm able to react. My sword crashes into his, catching it a mere inch from my skin. He comes to a halt, and I flex my muscles and knock his sword up into the air. With that, I lash out at him, but he's too fast and flashes backward. My health slowly begins to climb, and I see a warm glow radiating out from my body.

"You have some sort of latent power," the master snarls softly. "Where you came by it, I do not know, but you are . . . strong."

"Sometimes I even amaze myself," I mutter. Then, with that, *I* attack.

My sword leaves long strands of light through the air as I

race forward, slashing and attacking with all the force I can muster. The master parries my first attacks effortlessly, but I see a change come over his eyes. Something's clicked in his mind, and he doesn't like it.

In any case, with a flare, he attacks back, and the two of us are suddenly locked in mortal combat. Sword crashes against sword, sending sparks and flares of light all across the room. My entire existence focuses upon that fight, upon that battle. This is the fight of my life, and I know it altogether too well.

With a flicker, I switch my sword to my left hand and perform an attack from another direction. It's more of a dagger move, and it catches the master off-guard. He only narrowly manages to deflect it, and I lunge forward and throw a punch into his face—another dagger-ish move, to be certain, but it works well enough. I don't actually hit anything, but it makes him dart backward out of the way, and I take my stance once more. My health is nearly back to 100 percent, and he snarls and gives his sword a swirl.

"You have tricks."

"You've noticed." I draw in a deep breath.

"Well . . . So do I."

He suddenly flickers and vanishes. On instinct, I dive forward, and a sword flashes over my head. I spin around as I come up and catch his blade on Ascalon, only a foot from my head. The master's eyes are fiery and angry, turning red even as I watch. I shove his sword away, then rise and strike with all my might. He parries, but now it's *him* on the defensive. I attack once more, then again, knocking him backward with every step. I can't tell if he's tired or running out of magical energy, or what, but I do know that I need to end this fight soon. The master vanishes once more, and this time I jump in the opposite direction as before. He appears again, right where I would have gone if I had dodged in the same direction as the first time, and slashes downward. That leaves him open, and I attack with fury. Now it's *him* that only barely manages to hold his own and is forced steadily backward.

"This isn't how this is supposed to happen!" he snarls. "This ends now!"

With that, he transforms into a black cloud, the sword suspended in the middle, and flashes forward with extraordinary speed. Suddenly, the sword is attacking me from all sides—front, right, left, back, above. Ascalon seems to take on a life of its own, blocking and parrying desperately.

[Skill: Bearing of a Knight.]

[Peril Increased.]

[Adjusting stats to compensate.]

My body moves faster and faster, matching the lurker blow for blow. Suddenly, the master disengages and flashes to a few feet away while transforming back into his ordinary self. The dragonbone sword flares with light, and it suddenly pulls itself out of his hands and points itself right at him.

"Wait!" The master raises his hands. "I've been loyal! I did exactly as you said."

The sword doesn't answer but darts forward. The lurker, though, doesn't stand still and accept his demise. Instead, he flashes to the side, and the sword carves through the empty air. The lurker then flashes around and grabs hold of the hilt once more, bracing himself against it.

"This is the weapon that was promised to my forebears. It is mine by right," he snarls. "Let me defeat this boy! If I fall, you can certainly have it back, but do not turn on me *before* I fail."

The sword seems to pause, and the master spins around. His eyes burn even brighter, like shining spotlights across the area, and he lunges forward with an almost impossible fury.

Once more, we come together in a mighty crash, sword against sword, blade against blade. I block and parry and dodge as much as possible as I look for any opening.

And then . . . I see it.

As the lurker attacks, I feint backward, allowing him to over-extend, and use Ascalon to knock his blade downward. He, naturally, swings it back upward with fantastic force to compensate, and at that point, I use my sword to knock it upward *more* as hard as I can. The sword leaves his grasp, and I slash him through the heart.

Brilliant sunbeams erupt off Ascalon's edge as the sword slashes through the shadow lurker. In that instant, I can see the contours of his body. He's a twisted and wretched creature, to be certain, filled with malice and hatred. Then the light becomes more intense, and he vanishes in a burst of cloud.

[You have leveled up!]

[Congratulations! You are now Level 43!]

[You have leveled up!]

[Congratulations! You are now Level 44!]

I nod slowly as the dragonbone sword clatters to the ground. Quick as a cat, I spring forward and snatch it up, then slowly lift it to the light. The runes continue to glow . . . and, suddenly, I hear a great many voices pouring forth.

Who has us now?

It is a being of light.

It is no one we can bond with!

Foul enemy!

A dark energy explodes from the hilt, and, caught off guard, I lose my grip. The sword falls once more to the ground, but this time, instead of clattering to the stone, it stops just a few inches above the rock. Slowly, it floats back up into the air, and I prepare to reclaim it. A portal opens just behind the thing, and I spring forward, ready to snatch it up before it can make an escape.

Fooooooom!

Fire explodes outward, and I'm reminded of the god of fire who apparently gave the sword to the cult. It hits me in the chest and knocks me backward, and with that, a figure emerges from the portal. It's humanoid but seems to be entirely made of rippling, crackling fire. Slowly, it reaches out a hand and takes hold of the sword, lifts the blade to the ceiling, and gives a nod. Black eyes peer out at me through the roaring flame, and I settle into my stance.

"Are you the true master of this sword or another puppet like this one?"

The entity doesn't give me an answer. Instead, it turns slowly around and steps through the portal. A flicker of light comes through, and with that, it's gone. The portal closes, and I'm left alone in the temple once more.

"Is it safe?" Sandra's voice drifts out of the stairwell. "It looks like it's safe."

My arm suddenly freezes up as Ascalon realizes that there's no more danger and deactivates the skill keeping me afloat. I sigh, nod, and slide the sword back into its sheath, at least as best I can.

"Yeah, it's safe." I give a nod. "We can go home now."

CHAPTER TWENTY-THREE

I quickly lead the group through the dungeon and out toward the portal. The rest of the cult members flee upon seeing us. They don't want anything to do with us, and I don't want anything to do with them. The portal beckons us onward, and I happily step through.

As per usual, I hate the process of actually being sucked through the portal, but I'm happy enough as I land on the other side. The park looks just like I left it, with the sun setting on the horizon. A handful of emergency vehicles have shown up to help with the proceedings, and more than a few paramedics run forward to help the survivors through. I, meanwhile, see a jeticopter slowly landing nearby, with the pilot waving to me. I say a few words of goodbye to Sandra, wishing her the best, and then run to the copter and jump inside. The moment I sit down, it roars off into the sky, and I lean back and try to relax.

The stars begin to come out as the sun goes down, and I

sigh in pain and exhaustion. I want nothing more than to go to bed and get some good rest, but I don't have the faintest idea if that'll be possible. Ahead, the lights of the city beckon, but I know that beyond those lights, something is waiting.

Something is toying with me, playing me.

Something that I desperately want to destroy before it manages to destroy me.

[ShadowDancer: So, who do you think that fire thing was?]

[LunarEclipse: It sort of reminded me of Harold! You remember him, all the way back from the early days of this fight?]

[ChaosRider: Ah, it couldn't be! He died!]

[DarkCynic: We didn't *see* him die. We did take a poll, and at least some people thought he might come out of it.]

I sigh and stroke my chin. The possibility of Harold had entered into my mind as well. Stranger things have happened in the dungeons. I lean back in my seat, then turn to the chat.

"Can someone run an identification scan or something on the creature? Take its dimensions and BMI or something, and then compare it to screenshots of Harold to see how they compare?"

[GoldenShield: Sure thing, Jason!]

[RazorEdge: OOOH!!! I really really hope it's Harold!]

[ViperQueen: I don't. If anyone could take Jason down, it'd be him.]

[Originalgoth: So, the plot thickens! Lovely.]

[GrendleH8tr: Kid, you're doing good. Just keep your head about you, and you'll do just fine.]

I don't necessarily disagree with ViperQueen's statement. Harold knows me and has likely been watching me. The monsters of the dungeon, even the more outlandish ones like Krak, still work on a system. They have rules they have to follow. They have laws that govern their movements and attacks and advancements. Sure, a few of them do try to buck the trend here and there, but they can only succeed to a certain degree.

Harold? If he survived the magma pit and is now wielding some sort of soul sword, there's no telling what kind of trouble he might be up to. I'm going to need to find him to put a stop to it, just as fast as I can.

The jeticopter roars back to the club, which, during the time I was gone, seems to have been renamed the Apocalypse Club. As the copter lands, I find the club lit up like a beacon in the sky with dozens of high-class guests swirling about and chatting with one another. Long ball gowns, pressed suits—it looks like something that James Bond would sneak into. I slowly hop down from the jeticopter and walk up to the doors, and a guard pulls open the door and lets me inside.

"Ah! Jason!"

A woman in a flowing red dress comes up to me. It's an elegant, older-style dress that's really quite stunning to look at. It takes me a few moments to realize that it's Akira Wang, and she takes me by the arm and leads me forward. All around, the high-class people look at me with a mixture of awe and disgust—likely from all the rubble and blood that I'm dribbling onto the floor.

She takes me up the stairs to the highest level, where the *truly* high-class of the high class are dining in the finest luxury available. Mr. Wang sits there talking to a rather large man in a white overcoat.

"Jason! I'd like you to meet Nathan Rockefeller."

I blink in surprise and hold out my hand as the man rises and shakes my hand. I raise an eyebrow. "Do I need to be concerned about assisting with a backdoor takeover of the world?"

Nathan laughs, then shakes his head. "Believe it or not, I've no relation to the famous Rockefellers. I'm a self-made man with a name that, admittedly, scares people into agreeing to business deals with me out of hand."

"Sounds nice." I smile. "What can I do for you?"

"Nothing, nothing." Mr. Wang waves his hand. "I simply wanted to introduce you. I'm considering a partnership. He's approached me about a whole line of rift businesses. If we decide to try such a thing, we'll need more Rift Crystals, of course, which is where you'll come in."

"I see." I roll my eyes. "Mr. Wang, can I speak to you in private?"

"You certainly can, but I don't see that it would do much good." Mr. Wang taps his head. "Anything you say will be broadcast on the internet, so if any of our guests decide to take an interest in it, they can just look it up."

"Of course." I give a nod. "I wasn't asking because of secrecy. I just thought that discussing battle plans might not be the most exciting thing for our wealthy guests."

"Not at all, not at all!" Nathan waves his hand. "Plan away! I'd be interested to hear what goes through the mind of a seasoned warrior such as yourself!"

I give a small bow in his direction, then turn back to Mr. Wang. "I think I've identified the owner of that sword. I can't be positive, but the entity who retrieved it this time matches the description of the entity who gave it to the boss in the last dungeon. I can only imagine that they're the true master of the sword, at least in some sense. I need to track them down."

"And you really believe the dragonbone sword to be of such great importance?" Mr. Wang crosses his arms.

"If it wasn't, it wouldn't be appearing all the time," I answer. "There's something about that sword. It's harvesting energy, and it's harvesting the energy of *powerful* people, warriors and monsters alike. I have to imagine that the owner is trying to use it for something. We need to track it down, and we need to do it before that person, or *thing*, manages to succeed."

"You think it's a person?" Mr. Wang seizes on the phrase.

"I do." I nod after a moment. "My fans are checking on a theory right now, but—"

[FireStorm: Hey, Jason, we've got it! Check this out!]

An image of Harold wreathed in flame from the battle with the undead ape suddenly appears in the chat. It has a handful of dimension readings next to it, like the length of the arms and legs, ratios, and width of the head. Another image then appears, showing the creature that took the sword. The readings and ratios are exactly the same.

"I was afraid of that." I rub my jaw. "Yeah, Mr. Wang, it's a person. Harold . . . I don't have a clue what his last name is. Was. He hates me with a burning passion. The last time I encountered him, he was offering himself as a physical body for a dragon to possess."

"Sounds like a chap you'd invite to dinner on the regular." Mr. Wang takes a sip from a glass of wine. "Do you have the faintest idea where he might be?"

"None whatsoever." I shake my head. "He portaled himself

away, so he's probably in a dungeon somewhere, but it's anyone's guess where that might be."

Nathan suddenly snaps his fingers. "That Rift Crystal of yours. Could you use *that* to find him?"

"How could that be used?" I glance over at Mr. Wang. "Do you know something I don't?"

"Yes, but only in the time since you entered that last dungeon." Mr. Wang folds his hands. "The Rift Crystal can open portals both between the rift and Earth, *and* between the rift and other dungeons. As such, it has the ability to scan interdimensional dungeon space. It took us a few hours, but we got the thing hooked up to a computer, and we can fairly accurately map out every single dungeon in the New York area. We know what bosses they contain, we know what the minions are, and we can even get hints about the ones that are about to appear. I'm working on building an app that all the hunters working for me can use. Once it's integrated, it'll be . . . Well, it's going to make me a fortune, especially if we can get some more Rift Crystals to open up other shops."

"I see." I slowly fold my hands. "You have all of that in a nice, safe place, right?"

"The physical location is so secret that not even I know where it is." Mr. Wang nods firmly.

"Good. In that case, yes, please do see if you can find him," I confirm. "If it *is* Harold, I'd really like to take him down before he becomes a problem."

"I thought he was already a problem," Nathan says.

"Well, yes, but . . . You know what I mean." I sigh. "Mr. Wang, I don't mean to put you out, but do you have anywhere I can lay down to sleep? I haven't gotten a bit of rest since being woken up halfway through the night by falling through a portal, and I really just need to get some rest." I pause. "Also, if anyone from your organization has collected any daggers that they wouldn't mind parting with, I'm burning through daggers faster than I can watch them vanish. I just lost another one in this last dungeon."

"But of course." Mr. Wang nods. "If you go right through that doorway, you'll find a handful of bedrooms. You can pick whichever one you might like. I'll wake you up in the morning with a nice breakfast and some coordinates where we'll find Harold."

"Much appreciated." I slowly turn away and stride toward the door. Suddenly, I'm experiencing every ounce of the exhaustion that I've been pushing off. The noise of the party swirls around me, but I ignore it all, and a moment later, I crash through the doorway that Mr. Wang indicated.

Monsters are one thing, but sleep and exhaustion is something entirely different. One you can fight, and one you can only hold off for a short time. I find a bedroom and slowly step inside. It's more lavish than I would have imagined was possible, with a canopied bed, a massive shower and bathroom, and more luxury soaps and towels and pillows than I would have dreamed existed in the whole of the world.

"Uh . . . Riftwatch?" I ask after a moment. "Is there a way to turn off the livestream before I fall asleep? I haven't had a shower in ages, and . . . well, I can't do that with people watching."

[Riftwatch: Livestream will deactivate in 00:00:30.]

[00:00:29]

[00:00:28]

"Alright. Goodnight, everyone." I give a small wave to the air. "I'm heading down, but I'll be with you first thing in the morning. And then"—I draw in a deep breath—"we're going to track down Harold, and we're going to kill him.

"Again."

CHAPTER TWENTY-FOUR

I hardly remember taking the shower, though I remember it being quite a pleasant experience, washing off almost two weeks' worth of grime and blood and monster gunk and dirt. When I finished, I remember staggering toward bed and passing out the moment I hit the blankets.

As my eyes flicker back open, I find Riftwatch chat scrolling in front of me, slowly powering back online.

[LunarEclipse: Hey! Hey, everyone, Jason's back up!!!]

[ViperQueen: That was a *long* time to sleep, Jason! You okay?]

[FireStorm: He was probably just tired. I mean, I get tired just sitting here watching him. I'm sure he's utterly exhausted.]

The door clicks open, and a maid appears pushing in a tray loaded up with breakfast foods. I can see eggs, sausage, biscuits, gravy, pancakes, and a whole lot more. Eagerly, I sit up only to fall backward almost immediately. Turns out that fancy beds have a *whole* lot of fluff to them. I eventually manage to get myself upright and tuck into my meal. The maid smiles, then turns and leaves without another word.

"Jason!" Mr. Wang walks into the room, a smile across his face. "You're awake! Are you feeling any better than before?"

"Much, yes." I give a nod. "Thank you for the accommodations. I really can't tell you how much I appreciate it. It's the nicest bed I've slept in for quite awhile. Just don't tell Ali." I give him a wink, and he smiles.

"Ah, not at all! I spared no expense to make sure that this was just the place for a good night's rest." Mr. Wang sits down in a plush chair just a few feet away, then frowns. "Frankly, it's a little much for me, but I'll do anything to not have my warriors put out during their short bits of downtime." He pauses, then adds, "Also, we put out a call for all sorts of daggers, but the highest value weapon that we managed to get our hands on was only D-Ranked, and you've blown way past that. So have the monsters you're fighting."

"Speaking of that, have you found anything?" I ask, spooning a good dollop of gravy onto a biscuit.

"Indeed we have. It was tricky, but we found him." Mr. Wang pulls out his phone and taps a button, and part of the wall slides back to reveal a large television. With a flicker, a map of New York appears on it with hundreds of dots all over it. Some of them are larger, some smaller, and they seem to have a color code. There are reds, greens, blues, blacks, and so on. "Right here, in the bay. I mean, the dungeon itself isn't actually *in* the bay, but that's the easiest way of representing the real-world coordinates of it, at least in a way that the computer can handle it." He pauses. "The dungeon appears to be closed off to the rest of the world, though my techs are certain that we can open a dungeon from the rift into it."

"Good," I say around a mouthful of sausage. "What can you tell me about it?"

Mr. Wang hits a button, and with another flicker, a great many stats appear, scrolling across the screen slowly.

"It's a small dungeon, which keeps it off our radar. Six rooms, no more, with an entity named FireStorm listed as the final boss."

[FireStorm: Hey, that's me!]

[ShadowDancer: Wait. Are you actually a boss just watching his progress to ensure your own victory?]

[ViperQueen: Hack him! Justice for Jason!!!]

[FireStorm: No, no! I'm just saying that that's my NAME!]

[GoldenShield: Sure you are . . .]

I have to flash a small smile at the chat, then rise and give a nod to Mr. Wang. "That sounds perfect, then. Shall we get moving?"

"If you're ready, I think that's an excellent idea." Mr. Wang nods. "The dungeon has jumped several times within the last several hours, and it could move again at any point. I'd like to get you inside it before that happens again."

I have to agree with Mr. Wang, and we quickly make our way out of the hotel room and back into the main club. There, an army of maids and butlers are tidying up, getting it so that you'd never know there had been a party there at all. A few of them smile and wave to me, and I wave back. I've never really gotten along well with high society, and I've worked cleaning-type jobs before.

Anyway, we're soon out on the helipad just as a jeticopter

lands with a roar. Mr. Wang reaches up to hold onto his hat as the jet-wash roars across the landing pad. As the engines die down, the doors slide open, and the two of us jog up to climb inside. The moment we sit down, the doors slide back shut, and the machine takes off once more.

"Alright, Jason. We're heading to the Pumped! rift, which is currently located down on Times Square." Mr. Wang nods to me. "I was afraid that if we moved the entrance, we might move the target dungeon, which would cause more issues trying to find it."

"I understand completely." I give a nod, even though interdimensional dungeon physics are *technically* a bit above my pay grade.

"Should I call up John and Ali?" Mr. Wang asks. "I notified them last night that you might be needing assistance, and they said that they would be on standby."

"I'd rather they not get hurt." I sigh. "As much as I would love their help, Harold is tricky. He's been manipulating things from the sidelines for too long now, and I don't want them getting wrapped up in things."

Now, all that *is* true. However, I flash Mr. Wang a thumbs-up down low. I don't want them getting hurt, but I also do need their help. That said, I don't want Harold to know about it ahead of time. He's going to be tricky enough as is, so it'd be nice if I could have John and Ali in reserve.

Mr. Wang gives no sign of having seen the gesture, though I'm certain that he's just playing it quiet in order to keep anyone watching from seeing and guessing my plan. The jeticopter continues to roar through the sky until it slows and begins to drop back down through the sky, aiming for Times Square.

I've only seen Times Square once before, back on the first day that this whole chaos started. Now, as we come in for a landing, I find that it really hasn't changed altogether that much. There's a huge crackling rift portal tucked into what used to be an alley, but that's really the only odd thing. Billboards are flickering with countless lights, and tourists are wandering here and there. It's really quite nice. If you like that sort of thing, of course.

We land, and Mr. Wang and I hop out. A long line stretches out of the portal, with a few guards keeping watch over it, just like at any fancy restaurant. They step aside as we approach, and with that, the two of us pass through into the interior of the rift.

When we come out the other side, I have to admit that I'm impressed with what he's done with the place. It's only been a very short time, but already all the rubble from the battle has been cleared away and dozens of tables have been set up across the floor. Waiters walk here and there dressed entirely too elegantly to be delivering greasy burgers and fries and bottles of Pumped! drinks. The people dining there all seem to be quite high-class and don't all seem to understand how to eat a burger without dripping sauce all over their clothes. I have to stifle a laugh. A few people sort of glare at the two of us since we're cutting the line, but they relax as we walk straight through and into the tunnel leading deeper into the dungeon.

"We'll be making the jump from this point here." Mr. Wang points to a small hallway that I don't recognize—then again, I *was* moving through the place pretty fast. I follow him inside the hallway, which leads to a small control room. Techs are still hard at work getting everything in place, but they step aside as Mr. Wang nods to a nearby worker sitting at a computer.

"Alright, contact central."

"Contacting central," the man confirms. There's a sharp beeping noise, and he nods. "We've established a connection with the Rift Crystal."

"Good. Target these coordinates." Mr. Wang hands him a slip of paper. "Now we just have to hope that the dungeon hasn't moved in the last half hour."

"What happens if it did?" I ask, suddenly nervous.

"You'll be shot out into interdimensional space between the dungeons." Mr. Wang shrugs. "Your guess is as good as mine what *that* might look like. I suppose we'll find out!" He pauses, then adds, "If, of course, we're wrong, which we aren't."

I nod slowly. My chat goes wild with speculation, but I mostly ignore it. That's not something I ever want to experience, that's for sure.

"Opening portal now . . . Three . . . Two . . ."

With a flicker, a portal opens at the far end of the room, perfectly filling up a metal frame that I only now notice. Mr. Wang gestures at it, and I slowly pull myself upward.

"You'll do good," he says. "Just get in there, kill whatever you see, and you'll come through alright. You've done it a thousand times."

"I know. I'm not concerned about it." My eyes narrow. "You, on the other hand, seem rather concerned."

"Ah, not at all!" He smiles and waves his hand dismissively. "Not at all, my boy. Now . . . Go get that guy."

[DarkCynic: Yeah, Jason! You can do it! Probably.]

[IceQueen: He beat him once! He'll beat him again.]

[FireStorm: Yeah, but Harold has had time to level up.]

[RazorEdge: So has Jason.]

The chat continues to debate the assorted merits of the upcoming fight, but I ignore it and simply march forward into the portal. Lights swirl around me as I enter, and with that, I'm sucked away.

Now, as I hope I've conveyed, portal travel is always a bit tricky and never pleasant. Ever. Rift portals are worse than your standard dungeon portals, and getting teleported *through* a rift portal is even worse.

This one, a dungeon-to-dungeon portal, is perhaps the worst yet.

Why is that, exactly? Well, this is the first one where I've actually been able to see things inside it. I'm shooting through a long, narrow tube. My body is all distorted, just like it feels, but . . . all around me, out beyond the tube, are masses of light and color and darkness. A *lot* of darkness. I can only assume that these are dungeons and other such things, but I can't tell for sure. Suddenly, I see that I'm shooting straight toward a particularly angry-looking blob of light that looks to be on fire.

That would be my destination.

I brace myself as best I can, though it's hard to do so when your body is all made of goo. Suddenly, I flash out the other side and find myself stumbling into a large antechamber filled with fire and lava.

It's the perfect supervillain lair, that's for sure. I'm standing on one side of a vast pool of lava dotted with small islands of black stone. I can only imagine that I'm supposed to jump across them, which doesn't sound fun in the slightest. On the far side, a couple hundred feet away, the black walls of the cavern have been carved into a great fortress doorway. There are two enormous stone doors that look to me like they slide back and forth, along with panels of buttons attached to the wall just next to them. It's horrid and imposing and looks every inch like it was made for a fallen hero.

[ShadowDancer: Whoa! Jason, I can't wait for you to get inside that thing!]

[DarkCynic: Yeah! Just be careful when you're jumping across the lava. I could probably do it, but I took three years of gymnastics, so . . .]

[FireStorm: Just be careful, Jason!!!]

I nod to the chat, then slowly walk forward to the edge of the pool. I'm pretty sure I can see things moving around underneath the waves, but I'm not positive about it. It would be the perfect place for magma worms, or something.

[LunarEclipse: Jason! Off to your right!!!]

I look in that direction, where a small blob of lava is slowly rising up into the air. It begins to warble about, and I groan.

"No. Not a lava sprite. I hate sprites!"

The lava sprite doesn't react but simply floats there, watching me. I'm fairly certain it'll stay right there until I'm ready to jump. Sprites are tremendously difficult to defeat since they don't have solid bodies and, thus, are immune to just about every sort of damage that I can deal out. I open up my pocket dimension and call inside.

"Bjorn! Are you good yet?"

There's a long pause, and Astrid slowly pads out.

I'm sorry, Master, but my husband is still quite ill. That warrior wounded him very severely. Perhaps I could help? She turns and looks at the lava, then back at me. *I could make a room look like this, but I'm not going to do a great job making it safe for you.*

"That's alright." I smile and pat Astrid on the head. "I'll make it work. Uh . . ." I try to think, then pull out my Rainbow Dagger. Quickly, I switch it over to ice damage, which I hope will prove useful. It'll either be super effective or not effective at all, and I'm not going to know which it is until I give it a whirl. Slowly, I take my stance, then run forward as fast as I can.

The sprite stays still until I reach the edge of the lake of lava and jump into the air. With that, it shoots forward, trying to intercept me before I can land on the first platform. Quite unfortunately, I'm helpless to avoid the thing as it slams into me, knocking me several degrees to the left. Thankfully, though, I prepared for that and jumped several degrees to the *right* of where I wanted to be.

The sprite wraps around my torso and blasts me with fire, even as I come crashing down onto the platform. The stone shakes, and I get the feeling that it's going to sink within just a few seconds, but there's nothing I can do about that. Quickly, I stand up and stab my Rainbow Dagger down into the sprite. It shrieks and pulls back, and before it can attack again, I leap forward and land on the next platform.

The one behind me cracks and sinks down into the lava, and I leap forward once more before the sprite can react or the platform can sink. The sprite seems to recollect itself as I begin to race forward, leaping from pillar to pillar to pillar.

Smack!

The sprite flashes forward and hits me on the shoulder. Only a split-second warning prevents me from getting knocked into the lava, but I do manage to save myself at the last moment. I teeter over the lava, the platform I'm standing on cracks and starts to tip, and the sprite flashes around for another hit. This time I lash out and strike it with the dagger. A long stripe on the sprite turns black and cools. I rock backward to steady myself, and with that, I jump onward.

The sprite comes around again and again, hitting me from both sides as I jump the last few feet to the other side. I keep my dagger turned toward it and manage to keep scoring at least small wounds against it. The other side grows closer, and I throw myself into the air one final time, then come down hard on the stone.

[ShadowDancer: And there we go! Another win for Jason Lee!]

[ViperQueen: YEAH!!! This is going to be great!!]

Splat.

The sprite suddenly wraps itself around me, tightens its grip, and burns me deeply as it pulls me backward toward the pool of lava. I flash backward with my dagger and stab the thing several times, and I manage to get it to let go only a few inches from the edge of the pool. With that, I throw myself forward, rolling several times to try and put out the flames. The sprite, though, goes in for the kill and darts down to envelop me and put an end to my pesky invasion.

"Not a chance!" I stab outward with the knife and hit it right in its center. It wraps down around my hand and upper arm, and I grit my teeth as the pain becomes so intense that I can hardly think.

And then . . . slowly . . . it turns to stone.

I gasp in relief as the burning sensation fades, and I roll over onto my back and just lay there, staring up at the ceiling. The lava rumbles, though, and I slowly force myself to my feet and start walking toward the doors.

That's one room down. Five more to go. At the end is a boss that I know personally, a boss I have to take down once and for all.

If I don't . . . well . . . there's no telling what the consequences might be.

CHAPTER TWENTY-FIVE

As I reach the stone walls, I lift my arm and smash it against the obsidian. It takes several blows before I manage to crack away the remains of the sprite. As the bits and pieces of rubble sprinkle to the ground, a notification appears.

[You have leveled up!]

[Congratulations! You are now Level 45!]

[Please accept from the following rewards:]

[. . .]

"What do you mean?" I blink in surprise. "I've killed like one thing since level forty-four!"

[LunarEclipse: I mean, it *was* a sprite. Probably it just had enough XP to bounce you up a full level?]

[IceQueen: More likely, that shadow lurker you killed had *so* much XP that it got you close to Level 45.]

IceQueen's suggestion sounds reasonable to me, and I give a nod. "Alright, then. Well . . . before I move on, I need to check out this reward. They're only coming every five levels now, which I suppose makes sense as I get higher up, but I've also lost a *lot* of weapons." I open up the interface. "Let's see . . . Should I take a weapon, a monster, or a skill?"

The chat floods with suggestions almost immediately, but I already know what I have to pick. Quickly, I choose the weapon and smile as a box appears in my hands with a flash. With that, I flip it open and a blade appears in my palm. It's another dagger, glowing with a warm, welcoming glow.

[Dagger of Friendship]

[Rank: A]

[Details: Creatures attacked with this weapon have a 10% chance of becoming friendly toward you.]

I'm forced to stare in shock at the weapon and not because I'm thrilled beyond belief with its capabilities. It doesn't have a high base damage. It doesn't have a long reach. And . . . its effect is that it can make creatures friendly? Don't get me wrong; as a Monster Trainer, that's actually a fairly useful skill to have, all things considered. But with only a 10 percent chance of the effect working and a rather low damage to begin with . . . I don't know. Let's say that I'm frantically stabbing something: I'm either going to have to pause between each stroke to see if it's working, *or* I'm going to accidentally wound the creature after it becomes friendly, thus turning it against me once again.

[DarkCynic: Wow. What a lame weapon.]

[ViperQueen: Ah, don't knock it yet! I'm sure Jason will be able to find a good use for it!]

[ChaosRider: I can't wait to see it!]

I tuck the new dagger away and keep a hold on my Rainbow Dagger. "Well . . . Let's go see what we're facing next."

[DarkCynic: Yeah. He hates it too.]

I smile and shake my head, then slowly walk forward to the control panel. I reach out and press several of the buttons. There are no instructions, no markings, so I just sort of have to hope that something happens. There's a long pause, and then, with a rumble, both doors slide sideways, opening up just like in a space opera movie. I quickly walk forward, ready for whatever comes next.

Well, at least I *think* I'm ready for whatever comes next. As I step through, I find a room seemingly made of metal. Now it *really* feels like the inside of a spaceship or a starship base. The room seems to go straight up and has a massive reactor-like *thing* in the middle surrounded by an immense number of computer consoles. A walkway runs around the edge of the room, climbing slowly but surely all the way to the top.

And, of course, walking around checking on everything are a great number of dark knights. They look like they could have stepped straight out of medieval Europe. The only things that separate them from the knights of old are that their armor is jet-black, they have spikes on their helmets, and they seem to be emitting some sort of evil black mist. So, you know, they look just like the villain in most old-time movies of the medieval sort.

The knights don't take any notice of me at first, and I slowly walk forward. Suddenly, the first of them turns to me and seems to grunt with surprise. Slowly, he reaches up behind his head and draws out a massive black sword.

"You shouldn't have come here," he grunts and starts walking forward. At that, the other knights all turn away from their consoles and realize that they're being attacked. Most of them draw swords, though a few of them simply stand back to watch. All of them are going to see how I fare with this first knight, and then they'll make their decision after that.

"Well, your boss should have been a little nicer to all his employees," I answer. "Do you have any *idea* the complaints I've been getting? The dragonbone sword just turning and killing everyone the moment they get their hands on it. I mean . . . that's hardly the sort of thing that's going to get you good internet reviews."

"A joker," the knight grunts. "Kill him!"

With that, he charges forward, his feet clanging across the metal floor quite loudly. I quickly draw out the Dagger of Doom in one hand, though I'm not confident that it'll find a weakness. Most of these sorts of monsters that I've fought have been fairly immune to anything and everything.

The knight swings his sword at me, and I duck under the blow. I know enough not to charge him right away, though, as he immediately attacks again, slashing backward with brute force. Three more strokes follow, and each presses me backward. As I come up against the wall, he comes to a stop, and I run forward as hard as I can while switching the Rainbow Dagger to acid damage.

I crash into the knight with all my might and knock him backward several feet. As I do so, I stab him twice, once with each dagger.

[Dagger of Doom has discovered a [N/A] weakness.]

So, it's like I thought. The acid from the dagger does do a little damage, scoring his black armor plate a bit, but it's a long way from what I'd like to have done. I stab the knight several more times with the Rainbow Dagger, hoping to damage him a bit more as long as I'm so close. Within a few seconds, though, the knight grabs me with his free hand, spins, and slings me to the ground. I flip out of the way as he stomps down at me, trying to crush me underfoot.

As I spring back to my feet, I switch out both of my current daggers for my Phasing Dagger. I don't like the weapon as a rule, but in the case of a creature with an extraordinarily high damage resistance . . . well . . . it certainly seems like the best option.

The knight swings at me, and I duck once more. He charges forward suddenly and backhands me with his free hand. Once more, I'm knocked backward . . . but this time I catch myself.

Bracing my feet against the floor, I come to a stop and lunge forward inside his range of attack. He tries to hit me anyway, but I stab the Phasing Dagger into his chest. This time my dagger sinks in up to the hilt, and he howls with pain. Black mist shoots out of his visor, and he staggers backward. I follow him and stab him several more times. I don't really know what's underneath the suit of armor, whether it's flesh of some sort or just mist, but I don't take any chances. With one final attack, I slash the dagger across his neck. The metal opens up, and black mist comes pouring out.

"*Gaaaaaak!*" The knight drops his sword and puts his hand to his throat, then staggers and falls to his knees. I stab the dagger down through the top of his helmet, and with that, he falls to the ground. The armor stays together, which makes me suspect that there *is* some sort of physical body inside, though I'll be the first to admit that I don't know exactly what it might be. With that, I turn slowly to face the other knights, who are regarding me a bit more warily.

"Throw down your weapons, and I'll think about letting you live," I snarl softly.

[ShadowDancer: Yeah! Go Jason!!!]

[ViperQueen: Lay down the law, why don't you???]

[ChaosRider: Ah, don't give them a chance to surrender! Just kill them all!]

The knights, for whatever reason, don't accept my offer of surrender. Instead, two of them rush forward, feet clanging on the floor, as they raise their swords. I come forward to meet them, more than ready for what comes next.

Both of them attack at the same moment, slashing at my head, and I drop to the ground underneath their blows. As I come back up, I stab one in the upper leg, then spin and slash my dagger across the belly of the other. Both howl and drop, giving me the high ground. I stab the first one in the back and drop him to the ground with a clatter, then kick the other one in the face. His head snaps back up, and I stab him in the back of the skull. That knocks him down for good, and I whistle.

"You're not a bad little dagger, are you?" I whistle softly, then turn to the rest of the knights. There are four of them on the lower level, all standing in front of flickering computer screens. They all brace themselves, and I know I'm not getting out of this without taking them down.

Oh well. So be it.

"Burnie?" I say. "Why don't you head upward and see if you can't soften up the monsters there. I'll deal with these guys and then follow."

Burnie shoots out of my pocket dimension and flashes upward, and I run forward as hard and as fast as I can. One of the knights swings at me and unleashes a rapid series of attacks just like the first one did. I wait for a moment, timing things, then jump clean over the blows and land on the console just to his right. He blinks and spins, but by that point I'm already in motion again, jumping around behind him. Two quick strokes from my dagger are enough to make him stagger and fall, and I turn to the other three.

Their demises come just as quickly, and I almost feel bad. As the last one drops, I look upward, where blasts of fire are intermixing with the angry roars and screams of the knights. If only I didn't have that phasing weapon, this would actually be quite a competitive fight. As it is, well . . . my health stays high throughout the whole thing.

I run up the walkway just as fast as I can. I come across another knight almost immediately, one trying to fix a computer that Burnie has blasted into slag. He stands up, snarls, and slashes out at me with his sword, but I just wait out of reach until he finishes his attack and pauses. With that, I run forward and slash through his neck. Black mist spills out, and I punch him down.

Up I go, around and around. More of the knights come out to try and stop me, those that Burnie hasn't already cut down. I don't have a clue how many I go through, but it's quite a lot. Finally, I come to the top, where a particularly large guard stands in front of a black door.

"*Arrrrrrrrgh!*" he shouts out at Burnie, who's blasting him with an unyielding gout of flame. He staggers a bit under the attack, and the metal of his armor glows brilliantly as it heats up, but he doesn't yield. Suddenly, he sees me and, turning, starts down toward me. The floor shakes under the blows of his feet, and Burnie lets up on the attack, not wanting to hit me as well. His armor still glowing orange, the knight draws a massive black sword, which glows with a dark energy.

"You think you can just march in here, kill us all, and end the work that we're doing?" The knight roars and slashes downward with his sword. The blow cuts through the floor, just like an energy weapon might do. He raises the weapon again and swings across me, and I jump back. It cuts through the guardrail instead, and I set my jaw. This guy isn't going to go down easily, that's for sure. "You'll regret that, boy. You'll regret it a lot."

"Maybe." I draw in a deep breath. "Somehow, though, I imagine that you're going to regret it a whole lot more than me."

The knight merely grunts, and I feint forward. He swings, and I run at him behind the blow. He swings again, but by then I'm inside his reach and attack with as much vigor and speed as I can muster.

My dagger flashes in my hand as I stab him up and down his body, hitting his knees, his chest, his gut. Black mist pours out, but it doesn't seem to bother him in the slightest. Instead, he simply lets his massive sword hang in one hand, grabs me with the other, and lifts me up into the air by my neck.

"You are a foolish boy."

"Maybe," I gasp out. "Still . . . going . . . to win."

With that, I slash upward and cut through his wrist with my dagger. I fall back to the floor, and he screams, looking down at the stump that was once a hand. The hand itself clatters to the ground while black mist pours across the area. I don't hesitate but lunge forward again and stab him in the knee this time. I don't manage to entirely cut through his leg, but I do manage to kneecap him, and he falls with an enormous crash.

Whack!

He punches me with his sword hand and knocks me over to the railing. As I slam into it, it yields slightly and almost goes crashing down. I gasp in horror, and he laughs and rolls in my direction.

It's an odd attack, though I suppose it might have worked in the right circumstances. But these were not the right circumstances—at least not for him. I jump up and over his body as he slams into the railing, and with that, metal folds around him. There's a loud groaning, followed by the pop of several bolts and nuts. With that, he slowly topples over the edge. His sword falls with a clatter, though his remaining hand catches hold of the edge of the walkway.

"Now this is interesting." I kneel down and stare down at him. He flails about, trying to pull himself back up. To be clear, the drop isn't a long one, and I'm sure he would be able to survive it. That said, he doesn't seem to be thinking clearly, and I don't really want to give him the chance to start. Before he can do a thing, I draw out the Phasing Dagger and let it drop. It slams into the top of his helmet and sinks in up to the hilt . . . and with that, his fingers relax, and he falls to the metal below.

[You have leveled up!]

[Congratulations! You are now Level 46!]

Crash!

The blow shakes the entire room, including the reactor. Lightning begins to arc upward from the destroyed computers below, and I groan.

"No, no!" I glance down at my Phasing Dagger, but I know I don't have the time. Quickly, I stand up and leap through the doorway, which opens at my touch. The moment I'm through, it slams shut.

BOOOOOOOOOM!

The blast shakes the stone, and I sigh. Yet *another* dagger gone. Oh well. I do like a challenge, and this is turning the difficulty up to impossible. I'll just have to keep pressing forward and see where it goes from here.

After all, I don't need a special sort of dagger to kill Harold. Any old thing will do the job. And that's just what I'll do, even if I have to pick up stones from the ground to get it done.

CHAPTER TWENTY-SIX

The hallway where I find myself is small and narrow with a handful of flickering lights. As the explosion dies down, they flicker a bit more, then die altogether.

"Great," I mutter. "The reactor is gone now, and with it goes the light."

[ViperQueen: Ah, you'll do great anyway! Surely you can see in the dark, right?]

[ShadowDancer: He's not a bat.]

[DarkCynic: I bet I could see in the dark.]

[ChaosRider: DarkCynic, no one wants to hear what you think you can or can't do.]

I chuckle a bit, though I try not to let the chat hear it. Instead, I simply place my palm on the wall and start walking forward, feeling my way along. From what I could see before the lights went out, the hall is pretty straight and narrow and leads to another door at the end. It's a simple transition area, one that I don't expect will have anything dangerous.

As I walk, though, I assess my weapons. Let's see . . . I have the Rainbow Dagger, the Dagger of Doom, the Dagger of Kings, the Dagger of Friendship, Ascalon, and Beowulf's Dagger. That's it. I haven't had so few weapons since the very beginning of this whole thing! I'd bring out my pets more, but the area is so close and cramped that I'd hate for them to get slain. Almost all of them are better suited for open combat, not this close-quarters stuff.

In any event, I draw out the Dagger of Doom and the Rainbow Dagger as I reach the end of the tunnel. A huge part of me wants to draw out Beowulf's Dagger to give it a try, but something holds me back. I don't really understand it, or Ascalon, and while I'm willing to use it if necessary, I'd rather not play around with forces that I don't comprehend.

Anyway, as I reach the end of the hall, I place my hand against the stone.

[Error: Without power, these doors cannot open. See if power source can be repaired.]

"Yeah, that's not happening without a whole team of goblins," I mutter. Carefully, I feel around until I find the crack in the door. I'm forced to put down both daggers, and with all my might, I start prying the doors open with my bare hands.

To be fair, I don't actually know how much force it takes to pull the doors open, but it certainly *feels* like a lot. I groan as I slowly pull the doors open an inch . . . then two . . . then six . . . and then a foot. It takes every ounce of my effort to push it open enough to slip through, and with that, I step over onto the other side just as quickly as I can.

As the doors slam shut behind me, I almost wish that I had stayed on the other side.

The room is circular with a small hill of stones in the middle. The stones have tiers like a pyramid or something, which lead up to a central stone where the master of the room obviously sits. And filling the area are things that are pure and utter nightmare fuel.

Hellhounds.

They look almost like Frost Wolves but stand a bit taller at the shoulder and have flames rippling about in their fur, sending up wisps of smoke. They are many and the alpha sits on the stone at the very top, staring down at me with fiery eyes. I draw a deep breath. Somehow, I feel like I've stepped out of a scientific facility and into the Sahara. I carefully draw out my daggers once more and brace myself for combat. This time I don't say a word. It's partly because I can't think of anything to say and partly because my mouth has gone completely and utterly dry.

With a snarl, the first of the hellhounds jumps at me, bounding across the ground with great snorts and snarls. Smoke trails behind it, and I run forward to meet it. It springs into the air upon approach, and I drop to the ground, slashing upward with both blades as it passes overhead.

[Dagger of Doom has discovered an [ice] weakness.]

Good enough for me. The blade turns ice cold in my hand, though by that point, the hellhound has already passed by and landed on the ground behind me. It spins around, flashing white-hot teeth. I stand back up, knowing that this is going to be *quite* a battle.

There's a brief pause, and I switch the Rainbow Dagger over to ice damage as well, and then the monster charges forward. There's nothing I can do but charge forward as well, feinting and dodging to the left as it attacks. Faster than lightning, it spins and bites me on the right arm, digging its teeth *deep* into my body. I gasp in pain—there's just no way to comprehend how terrible this pain is—and I stab it with the dagger in my left hand, the Rainbow Dagger, as many times as I can. It doesn't whimper, doesn't react to the pain at all. It just snorts and gives a shake of its head, which knocks me to the ground. With that, it springs upon me, snarling and snapping at my face.

My blades flash in return as I block its teeth while also cutting at its face. The thing still manages to bite me several times, scoring long gashes across my skin, but I also manage to injure it, and it staggers after a moment. Drawing in a deep breath, I grit my teeth and lunge upward, stabbing it in the throat with both my daggers.

"*Ahhhh!*" I shout, even as I rip the daggers through its body and out the other side. The hellhound sways, and I jump to my feet and stab it once more in the side of the neck. This time it's a bit slower to respond, and I shuck it to the ground. I stab it several more times for good measure, just to make sure it's not going to get back up, then let out a long breath and glance around at the others.

My health is pitifully low, almost 30 percent, and I've taken down one of . . . more than I'd like to count. On the bright side, I'm not dead yet, and I'm liable to level up if I can survive. On the less bright side, I don't really know how this fight is going to go. They don't flinch away from pain, and they have a lot of health.

"Alright, Astrid. I could use some help," I murmur. "Balder, too, if you're up for it. No exhausting yourself, but I wouldn't mind a hand."

The portal to my pocket dimension opens, and both of my wolves come out. They look pitifully small compared with the hellhounds, but they stand tall and firm by my side. My health starts to heal, slowly, but I know I don't have time to take any healing items to help it out.

Then the alpha howls, and the fight is on.

Astrid snarls while Bjorn barks, and the hellhounds charge toward us at top speed. A crack opens beneath one of them, dropping it down into the abyss where it belongs. Balder targets another and causes a pile of rubble to drop down from the ceiling upon it. The rubble tightens around it, squeezing tightly, until a loud *crack* tells me that the job is done. That said, there are still a lot more, and it's up to me to do my fair share.

I run at the attacking beasts, feet pounding across the ground. As the first one lunges, I drop under it and stab it several times, then come up and run onward. I know I can't let them hit me. I'll just have to be faster. As the second one attacks, I swing around behind and stab it a handful of times across the shoulder, then race onward. The rest of them snarl and all begin to charge me, their claws tearing into the stone floor as they attack.

One of them leaps at me from the side, and I only narrowly manage to duck underneath the blow in time to stab it in the underbelly. Another comes up from behind, and only the heat of its breath gives me enough warning to spin out of the way in time. Claws rake across my back, and I spin and drive both of my daggers into the monster.

The hellhound spins around on a dime and snaps down on my hand, engulfing the Rainbow Dagger. The pain is *beyond* extraordinary, and I gasp and pull backward. It bites several more times, and I lose my grip on the Rainbow Dagger. Suddenly, I see the weapon in the mouth of the hellhound, and with one chomp, it bites down.

Crack.

Bits and pieces of metal rain down to the floor as it shatters the weapon in a single blow. Drool mixed with blood drips down from its mouth as it slowly begins to stalk toward me, and I take a firmer hold on the Dagger of Doom.

"Alright, then." I draw in a deep breath. "That's just how we'll have to play it."

I run forward, and the hellhound springs forward to meet me. I slam into the beast with all my might, hitting it in the chest, and stab it deep in the brisket. Smoke pours upward from the point of impact, and I stab it a dozen times, just as fast as I can. Thick, blackish blood drips down, and, slowly, the monster relaxes and collapses.

Awooooooooo!

A boulder flashes through the air and strikes the alpha, blasting it clean off its perch. I gulp, and the other hellhounds in the area all begin to bark and howl powerfully. Slowly, the alpha climbs back up, staring at me with an infernal hatred. I take my stance, then glance to my right as another of the monsters charges at me.

Thankfully, Astrid gives a sharp bark and drops the monster into a rift. The alpha springs forward, tearing up the ground like it's dirt instead of obsidian, and lets its tongue dangle from its mouth. I brace myself . . . and then it hits me.

It's like being hit by a mountain. Its body is as hard as stone, and my dagger does almost nothing to it as I stab it over and over. Simply by putting its shoulder into me, it knocks me backward into the wall. The alpha licks its lips and attacks.

I spin out of the way as its jaw snaps down where I was just standing and stab it in the eye. Flames explode out of the eyeball, scorching across me, and the alpha spins and bites at me. Pain flares through my side, but I remain standing and stab it in the other eye as well. Blinded, the monster begins to howl and thrash about, and I start to wonder if I'm actually going to survive this after all.

[ShadowDancer: Yeah, Jason!!! You've got this!!!]

[DarkCynic: You can do it! I hope. Maybe.]

[ChaosRider: Stab it now! Stab it now!]

I leap at the alpha, but it spins and hits me with its tail, knocking me backward across the room. I come down hard. With that, it lifts its head and sniffs, and I realize that dogs don't actually *need* to see the way that we humans do.

[IceQueen: Hmm. Well, Jason may be done for after all.]

[LunarEclipse: Don't count him out just yet!]

[GoldenShield: Yeah! Miracles can always happen!]

The chat sounds overwhelmingly convinced of my prowess in combat, and I groan and force myself back to my feet. The alpha licks its lips, then snarls and charges forward. Suddenly, I see Balder standing there, his legs shaking, drawing in a deep breath. I give him a small nod and quickly step out of the way. Astrid steps up next to her son, and together, both of them let out a howl as the alpha reaches the place where I would have been standing.

Crunch!

A spike of stone shoots up out of the ground and hits the hellhound in the chest. It punches straight through its lower ribcage and up through its back. For that matter, the spike rises up to slam into the ceiling, forming a skewer of sorts that the alpha is now entirely trapped on. The great hound snarls and spins about, clawing at the ground, desperately trying to break free, but nothing happens.

Crack!

Okay, something starts to happen. Spiderweb cracks spread out across the stone spike above and below the creature. Balder, barely able to stand, begins to sway, and I wave my hand at him.

"Astrid! Get him inside."

Both my wolves turn and bound back into the pocket dimension, and I raise my hands. If the alpha breaks through, my only chance will be to try and tame it. I have no idea if I can tame something so powerful, but it's the only chance I see. The stone continues to fracture, and then . . .

With one last *crack*, the column shatters, and the hellhound steps free. It sways, then slowly starts walking toward me. Blinded, skewered, and it's still fighting? Have I met my match?

I suppose there's only one way that I'll find out for sure.

CHAPTER TWENTY-SEVEN

The alpha hellhound takes three more steps toward me, then pauses. It opens its mouth, and a great amount of bloody vomit explodes across the floor. Then . . . slowly . . . it topples to the side, dead before it hits the floor. I let out a sigh of relief, and my chat explodes.

[IceQueen: Congratulations!!! You got it!!!]

[LunarEclipse: YEAH, JASON!!!]

[DarkCynic: I'm just saying, I could have done it faster, but . . . not bad. Not bad, indeed.]

I smile and nod to the chat in thanks, then slowly turn to look around.

[You have leveled up!]

[Congratulations! You are now Level 47!]

"Level forty-seven, eh?" I flash a smile as I open up my inventory and pull out a bottle of Pumped! soda. "Who here thinks I can hit level fifty by the time I leave this dungeon?"

[IceQueen: You can do it!!!]

[ViperQueen: Hmm. Maybe if you're careful, but it's going to be tough.]

[FireStorm: Yeah, sure! Go for it!!!]

I smile and nod at the chat once more, then glance around as my health begins to rise. There's a single crack on the other side of the room, the only opening that I can see, and I quickly walk over and slip inside. It's barely big enough for me to fit through, but I manage well enough. It feels like the little tunnel starts to slope upward, but I can't *really* tell for sure. Ahead, though, I see a sliver of light and feel a bit of hope flash through me. I don't exactly know *why*, since these dungeon rooms have been insanely hard and I've been coming closer and closer to dying, but a bit of excitement trickles through me too.

What will I find next? What will the next step closer to Harold contain?

As I come to the top of the tunnel, I pause and slowly stick my head out to get a feel for things before I enter. It's a particularly large room, still made of stone like the last one. There aren't really any defining features; it's just a large room. There are some cables running along the walls, presumably coming from the reactor room, but they just run from one side to the other without really doing anything. Presumably, they're part of Harold's plan, but I don't have the faintest idea what that plan happens to be. In any case, I slowly step out of the tunnel and start walking forward while keeping an eye out for anything that might be lurking in the shadows. The far side of the room has a well-defined door, much like the one that I went through to get into the reactor room. The only question is what sort of monster might be hiding in the area. It's barren—there are no obstacles or things to hide behind—which leaves me at a bit of a loss. I just don't see anything.

Wham!

A boulder comes crashing down and lands in front of the tunnel entrance, sealing the way out. I spin around and see a new hole has opened up in the ceiling. Two beady eyes peer out at me, and I take my stance.

"Great."

[DarkCynic: Whoa! Is that . . . ?]

[LunarEclipse: Yeah, I think it is!]

[ChaosRider: This is going to be a hard one!]

I let out a long breath as an enormous snake's head slowly pushes its way out of the new hole and comes down to the ground. The thing is probably five feet wide and has an impossibly long body behind it. The scales look as thick as the armor on a tank and seem to be made of steel. This is a basilisk—I'm certain of it. I slowly walk backward as it uncoils and drops down out of the hole in its entirety. It's at least two hundred feet long, I'd say, and as it opens its mouth, I catch a glimpse of fangs as long as my entire arm.

"Welcome, human." The words echo in the air, though I don't see the snake speak at all. "It will be a pleasure eating . . . I mean meeting . . . you."

I chuckle and slowly raise my dagger. "If I get eaten, at least I'll know that I'm being consumed by someone with a sense of humor."

The basilisk hisses and draws itself up until its head towers a good fifteen or twenty feet above me. I feel like I'm facing down a mountain, and it is *not* a pleasant experience.

"Any chance I could convince you to turn against your master?" I ask. "Just a thought."

The snake doesn't answer except to attack. It flashes forward with the speed of a cobra, and I narrowly dive out of the way.

Blam!

Stone and debris explode through the air as it strikes the stone. As it pulls back, I see a brand-new crater there. *Wow*, that thing is strong. I hardly have time to re-collect myself before it strikes again, and I once more dive out of the way.

Blam! Blam! Blam! Blam!

The snake strikes again and again, and I only narrowly manage to escape each strike. Fragments of stone and gravel slice along my cheeks and hands, but the cuts they cause are only cosmetic and don't drain my health at all. I come up from the last roll as the basilisk pauses, and with that, I know it's my turn to strike.

Quickly, I leap up onto the back of the snake and race up toward its head. The thing spins around and flashes its fangs, but I don't hesitate. As it snarls and darts down, I drop to slide along its scales and slide clean underneath it. Fangs pass only a few inches above my head, but I make it through, come back to my feet, and stab my dagger up into the thinner skin underneath its chin.

Acid hisses from the blade as it cuts deeply, and a blackish blood pours forth. I dive out of the way, somehow sensing that the blood will *not* be good to come in contact with, and hit the floor just in front of the thing. I hardly have time to stand back up before it spins around, attacking again, and flashes down to bite at me.

"You really don't give up, do you?" I spring back to my feet and continue to dive out of the way, rolling again and again as I desperately try to evade the thing.

Blam! Blam! Blam! Blam!

Once more, fragments of stone cut all over my body, but I manage to get to my feet and spring away, then backpedal across the room, keeping an eye on the thing, until I'm out of range of its strikes. Immediately around the snake is a ring of craters, deep pockets in the stone that I'm sure would be nothing but pitfalls for me if I were to try to run through that area again. I've managed to land a single cut against the monster, and I have a strong feeling that even a single bite would kill me. This thing has to be two or three entire grades above me, a level seventy or higher.

Which, of course, will only make my victory that much sweeter.

"Alright, everyone." I pause as the snake starts to slither forward, moving its area of attack toward me. "I need a weak spot. Has anyone seen *any* weak points on this thing?"

[DarkCynic: Not a one, except the little bit under its chin.]

[ViperQueen: Usually snakes have a weak spot on their tail, but I don't see one.]

[LunarEclipse: And I checked the scales over its heart. All of them are intact. No weak points there.]

"Great." I try to think. No weak points excepting one that's dangerously close to the fangs. Bjorn, Balder, and Astrid are all out of commission for the time being until they can heal. I doubt Burnie would be able to do much, and Blub would be unable to break through the skin. I'm on my own, and I just don't know what to do.

Well . . . I don't know what to do except to throw myself fully back into combat.

Drawing in a deep breath, I sprint forward. If I had to wager a guess, I'd say this thing isn't supposed to be taken down by someone of my level, which means that there simply *aren't* any weaknesses. That just means that I'll have to make some of my own. As I run forward, the snake hisses, then strikes down. Once more, I dive underneath the blow, and the resulting blast showers me in rubble. This time, as I come up, I race right up to the base of the thing and stab the dagger deep into its underbelly.

It's not quite as soft as under the chin, but it's also definitely a bit weaker. The basilisk hisses and flinches upward, and I stab it several more times just as fast as I can. This is going to be a battle of endurance, not one of quick victory. As it reorients itself and prepares for another attack, I spring up onto the back of the monster, then sneer up at it.

"Come on, worm. If you can't even land a strike against me, are you really even worthy of your post?"

That gets the monster's dander up, and it swings around and opens its mouth wide. With that, it flashes downward, and I dodge once more. This time, though, I jump *backward.* It's more of a risk, but it pays off, and the snake slams into its own back with extraordinary force. Before it can react, I lunge forward and kick it in the head just as hard as I possibly can.

It may sound strange, but there is logic to it. The fangs of the monster slam into its own back and punch through its own scales. As a general rule, the best thing to break through a monster's defenses are its own weapons. The snake howls and pulls back sharply, then waves its head around a little bit. I don't know how powerful the venom is, but I have to imagine that it'll at least debuff the basilisk by a *little* bit. The snake draws itself up, seems to draw in a deep breath, and then attacks once more.

I can tell that the thing is just a little slower than before and quickly fall back into my old pattern.

Blam! Blam! Blam!

The blows come slower and more forcefully, and I smile. I'm getting ahead of it. Quickly, I ready myself, then spring forward. The thing attacks over my head, and I dart right up next to the underbelly and unleash another series of attacks, desperately trying to break through its guard and bring an end to the thing.

And that's when I get just a smidge too confident.

I remain in place just a second too long and don't pay enough attention to the rest of the monster. While the head sways and reorients itself toward me, the tail flashes around and hits me from the side with simply extraordinary force. I go flying across the room and slam into the far wall, sending out a shock wave with my impact. My health drops to a mere 10 percent, and I have to wonder if that's the single greatest decrease in health that something has ever been able to deal out to me.

[Skill: Bearing of a Knight.]

[Peril Detected.]

I draw in a deep breath and stand up as a warm glow fills my body. The basilisk seems to draw itself upward, aware of my sudden change and uncertain exactly how to react. I take a deep breath, knowing that I don't have much time to be able to take advantage of the snake's uncertainty. I take a tight grip on my weapon . . .

No. I realize, it is just a hilt. Slowly, I look down at the broken blade and notice that the rest of it is still stuck in the body of the snake. It must have broken off when the tail of the monster hit me! I drop it to the ground, and the eyes of the basilisk widen slightly.

I open up my inventory and scroll for a moment. I have the Dagger of Kings, but it has a base damage that's pretty bad when compared to most F-Ranked weapons. That leaves me with few options.

I can either use Ascalon, or I can use Beowulf's Dagger. Ascalon is nice, but when fighting something that's *so* high above me in level, I really don't want to risk the unfamiliar feel of the blade. Slowly, almost desperately, I pull out Beowulf's Dagger.

The blade is the color of blood. The hilt seems to be made from either bone or tooth—I can't tell exactly—while strips of leather hold it all together. I can feel the power flowing through it the moment I touch it, and a new strength seems to fill me.

[Skill Acquired!]

[Grendel's Bane (passive): Deal extra damage when doing battle against serpentine creatures.]

[Skill Acquired!]

[Primordial Hero (passive): Stat increase of 200%.]

My eyes open wide as *all* my stats increase by twofold on top of the increase that Bearing of a Knight has already given me. The snake seems to sense that as well, and I slowly look up to meet the eyes of the creature.

"And now you meet your end."

With that, I charge forward, my movements coming so

fast that even I can hardly follow them. The snake doesn't have a chance to move as I hit it in the neck and slash the weapon clear through.

BLAM!

The force of the weapon strike tears clean through the monster, spraying the far wall with a good deal of blood and bone. As I drop back to the ground, the basilisk, now with a rather mortal-looking wound in its neck, sways and starts to spin around back toward its burrow.

"Oh no, you don't."

It makes no plea but also doesn't slow down. I charge forward just as fast as I possibly can, which, as you've seen, is *quite* fast. With that, I throw myself into the air and slash at the back of the basilisk's head with all my might.

A powerful blast of energy erupts off my blade, and I cut clean through the snake in a single blow. The head falls to the ground with a *thud*, and the body begins to twitch about in a grisly sort of death dance. I land on the ground next to the head and watch as the eyes of the monster slowly glaze over.

[You have leveled up!]

[Congratulations! You are now Level 48!]

[You have leveled up!]

[Congratulations! You are now Level 49!]

"Wow. It really *was* a bit of a beast." I smile as my extra buffs for being in peril and fighting a snake wear off. That said, between two extra levels and the Primordial Hero skill . . . well . . . I'm not feeling too bad, all things considered. Slowly, I turn toward the final door, only for a portal to open in front of me.

Quickly, I take my stance. The portal swirls with lights

and colors, and I suddenly pause. It's not the same sort of portal that I usually see. The energy isn't dark. It's actually . . . well . . . it looks like the sort of portal that I actually wouldn't be opposed to walking through.

Before I can even consider it, though, something else walks through. A person flares with light as they emerge, coming to stop on the stone floor of the cavern. With that, the portal closes behind them, and the light fades away.

[DarkCynic: Who's that?]

[ViperQueen: NO WAY!!! That has to be . . .]

[LunarEclipse: IT IS!!!!!!]

CHAPTER TWENTY-EIGHT

As the light fades away, I'm left looking at a person who looks almost like a barbarian warrior. He wears leather armor, the sort that people wore before metal armor became a thing. A cape hangs from his shoulders, made from a lizard-like hide. His right hand is missing and is instead replaced with something that looks like a small knife. He has a bearing of power about him, and I slowly walk toward him.

"Something tells me that you're not here to kill me."

"No, it never entered my mind." The man shakes his head. "Well, some of the decisions you've made have made me want to throttle you, I suppose. But in general, no, I'm not here to kill you."

"Are you here to help me kill Harold?" I nod toward the door.

"No, I'm not," the man says apologetically. "That said, I *am* here to help you. I've been watching you for some time now, and the time has come to step in."

"Then . . . who are you?" I ask quietly.

"You know me in the chat as GrendleH8tr." The man slowly puts his hands—well, one hand and one knife—behind his back. "In real life, I'm known as Beowulf."

My jaw drops to the ground even as everyone in the chat begins to exclaim that they knew it all along.

"Beowulf? You mean the guy that Lancelot was talking about?"

"Indeed." Beowulf gives a small nod of his head. "By the way, don't worry too much about his demise. It was a bit more of a light show and a bit less fatal than it might have looked. His job was to get my dagger to you, and he did it well." Beowulf gives a small chuckle. "I don't think he intended for you to take his sword, but I also know he doesn't begrudge you it, either."

My head begins to spin. "What exactly is going on here?"

"It's really quite simple, and I imagine that you know most of it already," Beowulf answers. "Your world is locked in a celestial battle. Forces of evil, from the portals, are desperately trying to overrun your world and bring your civilization to its knees."

"Yeah, I got that much." I frown.

"Indeed. The dungeon bosses, the whole dark order, are governed by a hierarchy. It doesn't work altogether that well—everyone just fights each other to climb the ladder as fast as possible—but the queen at the top knows how to put everyone in the right places in order to secure a favorable outcome."

That gives me pause. "The queen. I've heard a lot about her. I mean, only bits and pieces, of course. But . . . who is she?"

"I cannot reveal her name. Like you, I have rules that I must follow. That said, if you put much thought into it, I imagine you would be able to figure it out." Beowulf shrugs.

"Now, you need some answers, and I will provide what I can. The portal that you fell into, the one leading to the dragon-bone sword?"

I nod. "Yeah. What do you know of it?"

"The sword is an ancient weapon, one that harvests the powers of both the wielders and the victims, giving all back to a source," Beowulf explains. "When Harold fell into the lava all that time ago, he was contacted by the weapon. He was offered a deal, and he took it. He became the master of the sword in exchange for ensuring that it would travel around the dungeon-verse and be wielded by a variety of other masters, thus having the chance to slay as many warriors as possible. You found it sooner than expected in the Pumped! factory, which was quite fortunate. After the dragonspawn was killed, the sword passed into the hands of the ogre mage." Beowulf pauses. "At that point, I'm afraid that you have me to thank for dumping you into that dungeon. I didn't want the sword to grow too powerful, and I knew that you were the only person who would be able to stop it. After that, the sword was sent to the leader of that cult, *far* away from you."

Understanding starts to dawn on me. "But then . . . *you* sent them back to New York."

"I did. The moment that Harold handed Master Throm the sword, I contacted him and told him to move the portal. I'm sorry to say that he *was* able to kill several warriors with it, but you were able to stop him very soon after. Master Throm never realized that he had received two sets of instructions instead of one, and Harold didn't realize that his plans had been at least slightly thwarted until after Throm was defeated and the sword returned to him once more."

"I see." I frown in thought. "And then Harold took it back?"

"He knew that you were going to track it down again, so he withdrew to his lair to await your presence. Since then, he's been brooding, waiting, preparing." Beowulf gestures at the door. "He's right through there, waiting for you. Too terrified to come through that door, too bold to flee. A perfect recipe for complete and utter defeat."

"I sure hope so," I murmur softly, then turn to him. "I have so many more questions. Why are you helping me defeat Harold?"

"As I said, I have my rules to follow." Beowulf shrugs. "Now that my time is passed, I cannot battle the creatures of darkness directly. That said, I can assist. The queen is . . . I wouldn't call her *wise*, necessarily, but she's extremely intelligent. A loose cannon like Harold, while seemingly destructive even to his own side, can be quite useful if controlled properly. She's been doing just that, using him and his sword to get rid of dungeon masters that she views as problems. Master Throm and that cult were getting far too powerful for their own good. That ogre mage? He was only dragging people down with that dead-end dungeon he'd been running for ages. Neither was useful, so they were dealt with. I don't know this for certain, but I believe that there's a particular dungeon she has been preparing for Harold. It's been empty for a time but has slowly started to fill with some of the most powerful beasts in the dungeon-verse. When Harold came to control the dragon-bone sword, should he have filled it to its full potential . . . he would have been nearly unstoppable."

"Interesting." I nod slowly. "Well, I'll get rid of Harold for you."

"Good." Beowulf smiles at me. "Oh, one more thing I suppose you should know. Your old friend Krak?"

A small flicker of anger passes over my face. "Don't mention that name to me."

"Oh, you can hardly be angry at him for betraying you. He *is* a dungeon boss, after all." Beowulf shrugs. "He's another one that the queen is watching quite closely. His ambition is almost unmatched. Since you last saw him, he's been quite busy, and I have a feeling that there are few dungeon bosses she won't sacrifice to see him rise. If *he* comes into his power, as he wants, he'll be able to lead armies forth on Earth unlike any ever seen, far greater than Harold would be able to do. Once Harold is in the ground, you'll need to turn your attention back to Krak."

"I'll do that," I confirm, then pause. "What of the queen herself? How do I kill *her?*"

"For that, you'll need to either lure her out or gain access to the dungeon where she lives," Beowulf answers. "She, too, is bound by rules. I believe you've already heard about Astral Dungeons, which can't appear until a certain number of warriors reach a certain level. The queen's dungeon will unlock after someone, anyone, passes level ninety-five." He pauses and holds up a finger. "Now, I do want to caution you. If you pass level ninety-five and her dungeon unlocks, she'll be able to march upon Earth with her armies whether or not the rest of the warriors are ready to deal with her. You're a pretty good one-man show, but if you reach that point, you'd better be dead certain you can kill her without the support of an army. If you're not, you'll have to step back into the shadows to let everyone else level up."

"I see." I pause in thought. "I have so many more questions."

"Unfortunately, my time here grows short." Beowulf gives a small bow. "Perhaps a word of consolation: even in this age of science and discovery, there must still be mystery and enigma in the world."

"What does that mean?" I snap.

"Just that I can't possibly give you all the answers to *everything*, and if I did, you'd be bored because you'd know everything." Beowulf slowly steps back toward his portal. "You've got this, kid. Keep your head on straight and Harold won't be able to touch you."

"Got it." I let out a long breath. "I hope."

Beowulf smiles, then turns and vanishes into the portal. As it closes behind him, my head is left spinning, but I draw in a deep breath and take my stance.

[DarkCynic: I'm confused. Did that actually help you or was it just a random infodump?]

[LunarEclipse: I'm going to go with random infodump, but so cool!!! And you have to admit, that dagger is epic!!!]

[ViperQueen: YEAH!!! Alright, Jason! Go forth and knock Harold down to size!!! Please?]

[GoldenShield: Yeah! And then, once he's dead, go get that queen of theirs!]

I give a small nod, then slowly draw in a deep breath and walk forward toward the door. This fight, I'm sure, will be quite a difficult one. Harold was a tough egg to crack even back when he was still fully human.

Oh well. For the safety of Earth, I just have to remove him. If that's my job, I'm going to do it just as well as I possibly can.

CHAPTER TWENTY-NINE

As I approach the door, it begins to rumble and slide away long before I get there. Through it I can see Harold standing in the middle of what looks to be a rather scientifically advanced room. He looks just like before, as if his whole body was made of fire, leaving almost all his humanity behind. Curiosity fills me, but I try to keep it at bay as I slowly and purposefully step through the door. It slides shut behind me, and I glance around, getting a feel for the battlefield.

The center of the room, just behind Harold, looks to me to be a giant portal machine. Take what Mr. Wang had cobbled together in the Pumped! restaurant, and this looks like the same thing on steroids. There are coils and springs and gun-looking things and dozens of computer consoles. I slowly take my stance, holding Beowulf's Dagger firmly in my right hand.

"Jason Lee." Harold speaks slowly and forcefully, his voice echoing throughout the room. It's terribly supervillain-esque, to be sure. "You found me."

"You weren't all that difficult to find." I glance around the room once more, a bit more pointedly. "Now, mind telling me just what exactly all *this* is supposed to be? It looks like something you'd find on a starship."

"It is," Harold answers firmly and simply.

He provides no other explanation, and I slowly hold up my hands.

"Okay? Mind giving me just a *bit* more than that?"

Harold flashes a small smile, barely visible through the flames that flow around his body like clothing. "You'd like to know, wouldn't you?"

"That would be why I'm asking, yes." I raise an eyebrow, then slowly cross my arms. "Let's see. I'm going to wager a guess that when you set up a dungeon, you have to have an entry point where the portals lead to as well as a boss chamber. This would be the boss chamber. You set up the dungeon with the toughest monsters you could get your hands on, slowing down anyone that happened to get inside."

"*Brilliant*," Harold says, mocking me. "That's what any half-baked dungeon boss would do."

"Correct, but this dungeon obviously has a slightly different purpose than most." I gesture at the mechanisms. "I've seen something like this before in another dungeon. You want to open up portals directly from the boss chamber. That's backward from what's supposed to happen. It has to take a *ton* of energy to do that sort of thing. Hence the reactor I suppose, but . . ." I cross my arms again. "The other rooms don't seem to serve a purpose, and you're not the type of a person to do something without a purpose."

"You're getting warmer." Harold holds out his hands and

lets a bit of fire flare up. Apparently, *he* can be a joker as well. "Any guesses?"

"Two. The first is that you're hoping to attack other dungeons," I answer. "This setup isn't designed for opening portals to Earth, because that would be too obvious and would risk letting a warrior *straight* into your office. This is designed to open up portals to other dungeons. The only question is why. Unless . . ." Something strikes my mind. "You're stealing rooms from other dungeons. That's why the hellhounds and the basilisk were so random. You're using this to steal rooms from other dungeons."

Harold gives a bow. "Something that's never been done before, to my knowledge. I've run a few tests, and when I'm through defeating you, I'll be able to build my dungeon out as large as I want. With the help of this sword, I'll be able to populate it with thousands of vanquished souls, creating an army unlike any ever seen before."

"Grandiose, but I suppose it's ambitious." I flash a small smile at him. "And you're not afraid that you might upset someone else, like, I don't know, Krak?"

"That lizard is nothing," Harold snarls. "The dragon that tried to use my body was weak, and he paid the price. Krak merely wants to look important, to climb the ladder and impress the queen. Me? I want only one thing: to get revenge on Earth."

"And what did the Earth ever do to you?" I snort. "You were born on Earth, you were raised on Earth, you got your powers on Earth."

"I was abandoned by people from Earth!" Harold snaps.

"Everyone has been, at one point or another," I retort. "That's hardly a reason to go on a homicidal rampage."

Harold's fire begins to burn even higher and brighter. "Then just consider me a maniac."

"I already do." I slowly take my stance. "Come at me. Let's bring this to an end."

Harold watches me for a moment, then slowly holds out his hand. With a flicker, the dragonbone sword forms in his hand. The runes glow, then begin to burn, casting a deadly glow over the area around us. I watch him closely as he slowly rises up into the air. He's watching me closely too, looking for any opportunity, any opening.

I don't plan to give him one.

Suddenly, the runes flare even brighter, and with a hiss, the dragonspawn leaps out. It looks about, then snarls and runs at me. A short sword appears in its hand, likely the weapon that it was equipped with prior to being handed the dragonbone sword. I look up at Harold and raise an eyebrow.

"I defeated the dragonspawn once. You're going to make me defeat it again?"

Harold doesn't say a word, but his eyes begin to burn just a bit brighter. The dragonspawn picks up speed as it leaps across the ground toward me, and I race at the thing. Beowulf's Dagger glows in my hand, and I feel the weapon reacting to the fact that the dragonspawn is a serpentine creature.

As we come together, the monster lashes out at me. I raise the dagger and block, and with a mighty *crack*, the dragonspawn's blade shatters into a dozen pieces. It has only a moment to blink before I spin and slash the dagger across its chest.

Boom!

A blast of energy erupts off the blade and carves the

monster clean in two. Its top half is blasted off into the distance, and its bottom half is slammed into the ground. That's the end of it, and I look up at Harold once more.

"Impressive. You've grown stronger." Harold still doesn't sound concerned, though his eyes look at least somewhat scared to me. "Let's see how you fare against *this* foe."

With a flicker of energy, the ogre mage appears on the floor in front of Harold. He holds a wooden staff, which he raises to point at me. Dark energy ripples down the length of the weapon, and a mighty torrent of dark lightning explodes across the room.

I step out of the way, and the lightning explodes against the wall, showering me in rubble and slivers of stone. The mage snarls, then prepares another attack. This one flies fast and strong, a ball of black fire. I dodge that one too, which seems to make him angry. Slowly, he swings the staff around his head, gathering energy, and then slams it down.

Cracks explode across the floor, and a torrent of black fire shoots up. I leap nimbly out of the way once more, then charge forward, jumping over the cracks as I leap toward the ogre. The blade glows in my hand, and I prepare to do him in.

The ogre changes attacks as I come closer, and he begins shooting a mixture of fire and lightning at me. I continue to dodge the attacks, my enhanced dexterity giving me a much greater range of motion. As I make my final approach, the mage snarls, and a massive ball of lightning forms on the end of his staff. He fires it with impossible force, and I raise the dagger and catch it firmly on the blade. The lightning ripples down the red metal, and I lunge forward to stab the monster in the gut.

Zzzzzzzzzzzzzzzzzz-booom!

The ogre explodes into a red mist, sending fragments of ogre splattering across the room, across the computer consoles, the portal generator, and just about everything else. I catch the staff on the way down, spin, and throw it straight through one of the larger computers. Sparks explode from the thing, raining down on the area around it, and I nod in satisfaction. An instant later, the staff explodes and destroys everything around it.

"As I said, you've grown to be quite impressive." Harold slowly floats down to land just in front of me. "I'd send that shadow lurker after you too, but you killed it before I could."

I shrug. "That's the price you pay for using subpar help. Besides, it would only delay things anyway. Are we going to fight, or are you going to keep playing around with parlor tricks?"

Harold seems to take offense at that, and he snarls and draws backward, readying the dragonbone sword. With that, he flashes forward and carves through the air with a long glowing stroke. I raise my dagger and parry it, feeling a jar shoot through my arm.

This fight isn't going to be a cakewalk. Enhanced stats or not, he's still a formidable foe.

Harold spins, using the fact that he doesn't actually have to touch the ground to his advantage. The sword becomes a blur as he whirls into me, and I only narrowly manage to block it a few inches from my skin. He snarls and withdraws, then attacks with an overhanded blow. I block once more, and we disengage.

"You don't really know how to use that, do you?" I raise an eyebrow as he snarls down at me.

"I can use it well enough," he answers. With that, he attacks again, and I defend myself as he unleashes a deadly series of blows.

Harold becomes a blur, a fiery blur, as he strikes at me. High, low, he does everything in his power to break through my defenses, but I manage to stop each one—just barely, mind you, but I'm holding him at bay. As he forces me backward toward the door, I take a deep breath, then suddenly lunge forward, breaking the tide of battle.

Faster than he can react, I duck under a blow, lunge forward, and strike up at his face. He forms a shield out of pure fire and just manages to block me, but I get close. I smile, then attack again, making sure to stay close enough that he can't get a proper swing at me. He snarls in frustration as I make strike after strike . . . And then I manage to land one on his arm.

He's just a smidge too slow in forming a shield, and I slam the blade into the burnt flesh. A howl escapes his lips, and he tumbles backward in pain and anger. I follow, only for him to release a concussive blast of flame that hits me in the chest and flings me back to the ground behind. As I climb to my feet, he charges at me, sword extended, and I leap up and swing the dagger with every ounce of force I have.

CRACK!

An earsplitting crack echoes through the air, and a great split erupts down the length of the dragonbone sword. Almost instantly, flame and energies begin to pour out. Ghostly figures form in the air around us, swirling and twisting about, and escape into the ground all around. I watch closely, and Harold wails.

"No! No!"

The sword seems to wrench itself out of his grasp, and it spins around to point straight at his chest. I have a feeling I know what's about to happen, and I leap forward with all my might.

"No!"

The dagger comes crashing down on the exact same point where it had fractured earlier. This time the blow is fatal, and the sword explodes violently. I'm lifted off my feet and slammed into the far wall, almost fifty feet away. It feels like every bone in my body has popped out of place, and I slowly slide to the ground.

[ShadowDancer: Nicely done! That was epic!!!]

[LunarEclipse: Yeah, but . . . what now?]

[FireStorm: Now he offers Harold a chance for forgiveness!]

As I climb to my feet, I find the sword lying on the ground in pieces, clearly broken. Harold stands on the other side of the wreckage, staring down at it in horror. His eyes slowly narrow, and I know that forgiveness isn't something I can offer.

"You fool," Harold whispers. "You . . . I *hate* you!"

With that, Harold rises up into the air, flames swirling all about him, and flashes at me. He flings two fireballs, enormous blasts of flame and energy, and I only narrowly manage to dive out of the way. Before I can even come out of the roll, he swings around behind me and unleashes a torrent of flame after me. Metal melts, computers flare and die, and I run from the blast just as fast as I can. Harold, though, is faster, and I find an impossible level of heat swirling around me. Fire engulfs me, burning me to my core, and I scream in pain. My health drops rapidly, and Harold laughs as he flies around in front of me, not pausing the attack for even the briefest of moments.

"And now, here you are." Harold laughs. "Friendless. Out of tricks. Health dropping. What will you do now?" He sneers at me. "Nothing. You can't do anything. No matter how hard you try, no matter how hard you strain against me, you will fail. You will die, like the dog you are."

I take a deep breath, which only burns the inside of my lungs, and dive to the side. I have a brief moment of respite before Harold readjusts his blast of fire. Gritting my teeth, I race forward at him, but he just shoots up and out of the way, maintaining a constant beam of fire.

[Health: 50%]

[Health: 45%]

[Health: 40%]

The pain becomes almost unbearable, and I fall to my knees.

[Skill: Bearing of a Knight.]

[Peril Detected.]

My stats all rise, and I slowly climb back to my feet. My health is still dropping but slower now, and Ascalon glows brilliantly upon my back.

"Cut out the tricks!" Harold roars. "Fight me fair and square!"

With that final word, he lets loose one more blast of heat, the flame burning almost pure white.

[Health: 30%]

[Health: 28%]

[Health: 26%]

[Health: 24%]

"Plead for your life," Harold says, mocking me. "Beg me to live! Beg me to spare you! Beg me that you might see another day, slay another monster, have a chance to defeat me again! Bow before me and perhaps I shall give you a place in my dungeon! You're not a half-bad warrior. Perhaps the two of us, together, can conquer the world!"

"I . . . wouldn't . . . count on it." I stare up at him, aware that I'm not going to be able to reach him at his height. My arms ache so much that I doubt I could even throw a dagger high enough to reach him. "I'd rather die."

Harold's smile mocks me ever the more. "That can be arranged."

[Health: 15%]

[Health: 12%]

[Health: 9%]

[Health: 10%]

[Health: 12%]

My health suddenly starts to climb back upward, and I pause. The fire is still crackling and roaring around me, but . . . what's happening? It doesn't seem to be affecting me anymore!

[DarkCynic: Aw yeah! That's what I'm talking about!]

[ShadowDancer: He's back!!! HE'S BACK!!!!]

[IceQueen: Most epic comeback ever!!!!!!!!!!!]

Slowly, I turn around to find the portal to my pocket dimension flickering and Bjorn standing in front of it. He still looks worse for wear: his hair is shaggy, his legs are shaking . . . But there he is, tall and strong, defiant eyes staring up at Harold with unbridled hatred.

No one touches my master and gets away with it.

Behind him, the portal flickers, and Astrid steps out as well, followed by Balder. The three of them stare up at

Harold, and in that moment, the flames entirely die away. Harold is left there, hanging in the air, staring down stupidly at the three of us.

"Do you really think you all can prevent me from—"

Bjorn, Astrid, and Balder all snarl at the same time. It's hard to describe exactly what happens next, but it's certainly a spectacle. A shockwave hits Harold and blasts him out of the air and into the back wall, where he's pressed into the stone so hard that the rock begins to crack around him. He screams and starts trying to lift himself away, only to be slammed back once more. Ice forms on the walls around his body, forming a perfect ring, and then grows steadily inward. Closer and closer it creeps until it touches his body. The flames die out and leave him as a simple charred corpse. He continues to twitch, even as a layer of frost grows across his skin.

"Please," he whispers. "Please . . ."

"You want to stand next to me?" I slowly step forward, regaining my strength. My own skin begins to heal, and charred layers of flesh smooth back over. My health is now at 75 percent and rising rapidly. "You want to join me as we defend the Earth? You want to help me save the world from the hordes of monsters trying to lay waste to our civilization?"

"Yes," Harold whispers. "Just . . . give me a chance."

I slowly set my jaw. In truth, I don't know what to do. Maybe he's sincere . . . But a moment ago reducing the entire planet to rubble was his top priority.

"I'm sorry." I shake my head. "I hope you're sincere and that you receive mercy on the other side. That said . . . I have a whole world to think about. Goodbye, Harold."

My three wolves give one sharp howl, and a spire of stone

stabs out through Harold's chest. He gasps and looks down at it, only for the stone around him to crack and squeeze inward. Spikes of ice, dozens of them, stab through him, and a hand of stone closes around his body and crushes downward. Blood seeps through, staining the rock, and with that, my wolves quiet down. There's a *thud* as Harold's mangled corpse falls to the ground, and I let out a long sigh.

[You have leveled up!]

[Congratulations! You are now Level 50!]

[Please accept from the following rewards:]

[. . .]

"Well . . ." I have to admit that I'm a bit shaky. My peril effects turn off, and I give a nod to my pets. "That was . . . Thank you."

None of them answer, but that's likely because they're all so exhausted that they can hardly stand. One by one, they all turn around and walk through the portal into my pocket dimension, vanishing from sight. With that, I'm alone again, and I sigh.

[ChaosRider: Uh . . . Jason? I don't mean to be a wet blanket—that was an epic victory and all—but . . . how exactly are you going to get back to Earth? You sort of wrecked the portal generator.]

I laugh as I look around at the damaged equipment. "You know what?" I answer. "I don't have the faintest idea. I suppose I'll just have to come up with something. At the moment, though, I'm not worried about it in the slightest."

CHAPTER THIRTY

As it turns out, it takes almost two hours before I'm able to get out, but honestly, I don't mind the downtime. It's been a *crazy* amount of time since I entered this dungeon—I don't even know how long at this point—and I'm exhausted. I sit down against a destroyed computer console and wait, and that's really that. I have a Pumped! soda just for the sake of it, not even to heal—just for the joy of enjoying a good bottle of pop.

Through it all, I continue to have a regular exchange with Mr. Wang via the chat.

[Moneybags: Don't worry, Jason! We're going to get you out of there! The dungeon moved when you blew everything up, so it's just taking us a few moments to pinpoint your location.]

"Take your time," I answer. Like I said, I'm enjoying the rest, and, frankly, it's giving me a chance to think about things. What Beowulf told me is a lot to take in, and I'll admit that

I don't know exactly what to do with it all. The queen, Krak . . . There are many, *many* dangers out there, and all of them want to crush the Earth beneath their feet like a cockroach. As a resident of Earth, I'd rather that not happen. It's just a question of figuring out exactly how to do that.

Finally, as I'm finishing up my third Pumped! bottle, a portal swirls and opens.

[Moneybags: And there you go! Pop right on through and you'll be back home!]

I nod and stand up, glance one last time around the room, and then slowly walk forward. With a flicker, I pass through the portal, slurped up just like always. For a long, painful moment, I'm sucked back through the interdimensional void, back through the swirling lights and darkness, and then . . .

With a flash of light, I stumble out the other side of the portal and right into the club. I blink in surprise, then turn around to see the portal generator sitting right next to the bar instead of inside the rift dungeon itself.

"Uh . . ." I pause. "This doesn't look exactly like I remember it, and I didn't leave it all that long ago."

"Indeed!" Mr. Wang beams. "As it turns out . . . Well, the technology is quite complicated, but as long as we use our rift as a sort of sounding board, we can open up portals from the real world just like we did earlier inside the restaurant. It saves a trip, and now we can formally set up our base here, in this club."

"Uh-huh." I slowly cross my arms. There are a lot of things I need to talk over with Mr. Wang and the location of our "base" isn't one of them. "Don't get me wrong, I appreciate it, but I'm not sure that a high-class club is really the right place for a base for warriors."

"Don't worry about a thing!" Mr. Wang waves his hand dismissively. "I'm having the place reformatted to fit your specific needs! There might be the odd guest who pops up from time to time, but I won't be throwing any cocktail parties here, at least while the dungeons are still appearing."

"That's good," I murmur with a nod, then draw in a deep breath. "What sort of reformatting are we talking about?"

In response, I hear the sound of a power drill from off to the side and glance over to find a handful of workers installing what looks like a *massive* weapon rack where a wine bottle display used to be. There's a disassembled pile of metal near the entrance to the helipad that looks to me like an armor station, and there are crates upon crates with warnings about explosives and that sort of thing.

"This is really quite the setup." I raise an eyebrow. "What's going on?"

"Something that happened in the dungeon." Mr. Wang points me toward a set of chairs. "Care to take a seat?"

"Can I join too?" Ali calls down from above. I glance over my shoulder to where she seems to be supervising the construction of a practice range on the upper levels of the club. I wave, and she quickly makes her way down the nearby stairs. Soon, the four of us are sitting in the plush chairs, and Mr. Wang folds his hands.

"Alright, Jason. I know a man who has a plan in mind when I see one, and you fit that bill." He gives a small smile. "What's going through your head?"

"A lot of things." I cross my arms in thought. "Did you hear what Beowulf told me?"

"I did, yes," Mr. Wang confirms. "At this point, just about

everyone on the planet with internet access has heard it. A lot of hunters are really taking it to heart. That's what all of this is, really."

"Good." I flash a small smile at him. "Then here are my thoughts. First, we need to target and take down Krak. If what Beowulf is saying is true, and I have no reason to believe that it isn't, he's the next biggest problem. If this mysterious 'queen' really is setting him up to be her top general or something, we need to make sure we take him out of commission."

"I agree." Mr. Wang nods. "I have some thoughts on that front, actually, but I'll wait until you're done to properly confirm."

"Good." I glance over at Ali. "Then, we come to the matter of the queen herself. A bit further in the future, but not as far as I might like, when someone, *anyone*, hits level ninety-five, she'll be able to emerge. And from what I'm seeing, unless there's a very compelling reason not to, she'll probably attack in full force the moment she has a chance. We need to make sure we're ready for that. I can take on the queen herself, but everyone else will have to be at a point where they can take on her minions."

"Indeed." Ali gives a small nod. "In answer, we've been broadcasting orders. Every hunter who has the desire to survive is increasing their training routines. They're delving into more dungeons, clearing things faster, and trying to level up. We've also established a skill-sharing pool, so to speak. Anyone who gets a skill that lets them level up faster is to do so just as fast as they can, but if they find a *second* skill, they're to give it to someone else, thus making sure that we can level up the entire playing field just as fast as necessary. We're also pooling other skills and weapons that people aren't using. They're to give them to us so that we can then give them to the people who need them most. We'll whip this army into shape in no time."

"Good." I give a small but firm nod. "And who's overseeing this army?"

"I am," Ali says. "I've fought alongside you, I know what the dungeons are like, and I have an eye for organization. I'll be able to keep everyone in line and ensure that they get to the right places at the right time."

"Good. Just make sure you keep an eye out for infiltrators, subversive types, the works," I murmur in thought.

"Don't worry, Jason." Ali smiles and waves her hand. "Look, you just get yourself leveled up as fast as possible so you can knock the crown off that queen the moment she pokes her head out of the portal. Leave the rest to us."

"Good." I let out a long breath. "That covers *most* of my thoughts, then."

"What are your other questions?" Mr. Wang asks. "Anything important? I thought that covered everything, at least based off what I could remember."

"There's one more thought that's been bumping around in my head." I pause and cross my arms. "This time around I met both Lancelot *and* Beowulf."

"Correct." Mr. Wang nods. "Literary fans across the world are suddenly taking a greater interest in this apocalypse than ever before."

"I just have to wonder who *else* is out there." I shake my head, trying to think. "What about the other knights of the round table? Robin Hood?" I pause for a moment, and a cold dread sinks across me. "Or worse."

"Worse?" Mr. Wang raises an eyebrow. "So far, everyone you've spoken about has been someone good, someone helpful. Both Lancelot and Beowulf were quite useful."

"True." I pause. "That said, Beowulf made it sound like I should know who the queen was. What if there are others who *aren't* so nice? What if some of the gods are real? Thor, Odin, Loki, and so on?"

"Well, if they are, I'm sure they'll be helpful to you." Ali smiles and pats my arm. "I mean, there were good ones, and there were bad ones. It'll all shake itself out well enough."

I raise an eyebrow. "I don't know about that. I've read some of those original mythologies, and even the 'good' ones were sort of nasty. I doubt we'd get much help from any of them."

"And I think we're putting the cart before the horse," Mr. Wang says, then slaps his thighs and stands up. "I'll see if I can find a name for the queen. My experts can research similar literary material and see what we can come up with, which should give us a good idea of what you'll be facing. In the meantime, you'd like to track down Krak, and I'd like to see if I can help with that."

"If you could, I'd be really appreciative." I nod and rise as well. "What do you have?"

"Not a lot, but . . ." Mr. Wang waves me toward the portal generator. Next to the generator is a large computer system used for generating coordinates, where a technician is rapidly typing something out. "We managed to isolate the signature of the rift that Krak took control of."

"Really?" I have to admit I'm surprised. "How'd you manage to do that?"

"There were scanners running at the time." Mr. Wang shrugs casually. "Once we contacted the companies running said scans, we just had to upload the data into our own systems. It took a little bit to clear it up since they weren't looking for the things we check for now, but it was enough to allow us to track the rift as Krak has moved it around. We think he's doing something similar to Harold: moving his dungeon about and gathering up monsters and warriors for his army. The only thing is that he seems to be actively attacking and destroying other dungeon bosses in his quest for power."

"Attacking and destroying other dungeon bosses?" My jaw drops. "You're kidding!"

"I wish I was." Mr. Wang shakes his head. "As near as we can tell, it's leveling him up too. He's gaining in power quite rapidly, and his dungeon is expanding as well."

"Then . . ." I pause in thought. "What do we do?"

Mr. Wang shoots a look at me, and I give a nod.

"Alright, folks, I'm going to have to sign off for a moment."

[DarkCynic: What? Why?]

[IceQueen: So that Krak doesn't hear his plans and figure out a way to beat him, obviously.]

[RazorEdge: Do what you need to do, Jason! We'll be right here as soon as you're back!]

With that, I disconnect the livestream and fold my hands behind my back. Mr. Wang disconnects his livestream as well, and Ali does the same. When we're all good and secure, Mr. Wang dismisses the techs and waits until *they've* walked to a safe distance. He's really not taking any chances, that's for sure. Slowly, he reaches up and taps the screen. It looks a lot like when he was targeting Harold's dungeon from the rift: it shows all the dungeons in the New York area as they slowly move about, shifting and connecting and then withdrawing.

"Right now, Krak has withdrawn his rift. We don't know where he is, but we suspect he'll be back." Mr. Wang points at a particularly bright dungeon on the northern side of the map, up near the Jersey area. "This dungeon has been connected to a junkyard for a few days now, steadily growing more and more powerful. Side note: we can't prove it yet, but we believe that the dungeons grow in intensity the longer they remain connected to Earth without being intruded upon. Anyhow, this is the class of dungeon that he's been attacking—this level and higher."

"You want to set a trap for him." A smile spreads across my face.

"We think that if we can discretely insert you into the dungeon—sort of snipe you in, so to speak—you might just be able to catch him," Mr. Wang confirms. "We obviously don't know when he'll be attacking or, technically, even *if* he will, but it's our best guess and the only chance I see of catching him off guard."

"Why can't we just shoot me into *his* dungeon?" I ask. "When he shows up to eat this one, why not just target the other one and launch me in there?"

"Several reasons." Mr. Wang grimaces. "The short answer is that he keeps it moving. Our computers don't have enough time to lock the coordinates properly. We're dealing with fourth-dimensional analytics here. It isn't something that any of us really understand. We just know that when certain numbers line up, you can send a person through in one piece."

"I see." I slowly rub my jaw, then give a nod. "Well, it's

worth a shot. If nothing else, I'll have another dungeon I can clear out."

"Good." Mr. Wang gives me a nod. "Then step back over there, next to the chairs. You can turn your livestream on once you get there, and I'll get the portal fired up."

"Right you are."

I slowly walk over to the chairs, then turn around. Mr. Wang has blocked the computer, and I quickly fire up my livestream once more. As everyone asks me what the plan is and cheers for whatever I have coming, I smile and hold up my hand.

"Not to worry, not to worry! There's plenty of action coming your way." I nod to the portal. "Now, before I go jump through this thing, who wants to see what my reward for killing Harold happens to be?"

[ChaosRider: Me me me!!!]

[IceQueen: Choose a weapon!!! Choose a weapon!!!]

[DarkCynic: Yeah! Do it!]

"Alright." I open up my interface. "Weapon."

With a flash, a box appears in my hand. Slowly, and with a great flourish, I flip it open. There's another flash of light, and . . .

[Incendiary Dagger]

[Rank: A]

[Details: Anything stabbed with this dagger will immediately take internal fire damage equal to half their health.]

"What?" My jaw drops. "That's incredible!"

[DarkCynic: Yeah, but it'll be impossible to kill anything with it. You'll always only be able to drop its health by half, so . . .]

[ViperQueen: Yeah, but can you imagine taking on a BOSS and instantly knocking it down to 50% health?]

[FireStorm: THIS IS GOING TO BE GREAT!!!]

With that, Mr. Wang hits the last few buttons and the portal swirls and opens. I nod to Ali, who gives me a thumbs-up. It's a crazy idea to set a trap for an upstart dungeon boss, but . . . that's just my life these days, I guess. I run forward, daggers in my hands, and dive through the portal.

Energy ripples around me, and I'm sucked away.

Off again, and on to my next adventure.

ABOUT THE AUTHOR

Kaz Hunter is the author of the Apocalypse Reincarnation, System Bound, and Rise of the Strongest Sovereign series. A graduate of Texas A&M University (go, Aggies!), he started writing on Wuxiaworld and Webnovel. He has since moved on.

www.ingramcontent.com/pod-product-compliance
Lightning Source LLC
Chambersburg PA
CBHW020650120726
47906CB00001B/210

* 9 7 8 1 0 3 9 4 5 4 6 1 3 *